FLEETS OF VENGEANCE

THE SCIENCE OFFICER
VOLUME 15

BLAZE WARD

KNOTTED ROAD PRESS

Fleets of Vengence
The Science Officer Volume 15
Blaze Ward
Copyright © 2025 Blaze Ward
All rights reserved
Published by Knotted Road Press
www.KnottedRoadPress.com

ISBN: 978-1-64470-505-6

Cover art:
ID 222852302 © Tiziano Cremonini | Dreamstime.com

Cover and interior design copyright © 2025 Knotted Road Press

Reviews
It's true. Reviews help. Even a short one, such as, "Loved it!" So please consider reviewing this book (and all of the ones you've read) on your favorite retailer site.

Never miss a release!
If you'd like to be notified of new releases, sign up for my newsletter.

http://www.blazeward.com/newsletter/

Buy More!
Did you know that you can buy directly from the Knotted Road Press website?

https://www.KnottedRoadPress.com/

ALSO BY BLAZE WARD

The Science Officer Series
Start with: The Science Officer

The Jessica Keller Chronicles
Start with: Auberon

CS-405 (Command Centurion Kosnett, part of Jessica)
Start with: Queen Anne's Revenge

First Centurion Kosnett (sequel to Jessica)
Start with: Encounter at Vilahana

Warlord of Yaumgan (sequel to Kosnett)
Start with: Warlord of Yaumgan

Additional Alexandria Station Stories
Alexandria Station Collection

Handsome Rob (Alexandria Station Universe)
Start with: Can't Shoot Straight Gang

=====================

Corsac Fox
Start with: Flight of the Corsac Fox

Operation Marrakesh
Start with: Trial by Leviathan

Captain Daring

Start with: Revoked

The Hunter Bureau

Start with: Mirrors

Fairchild

Start with: Fairchild

Last Stand

Start with: Lost Dreams

The Lazarus Alliance

Start with: Escape

Shadow of the Dominion

Start with: Longshot Hypothesis

Star Dragon

Start with: Birth of the Star Dragon

Kincaide's War

Start with: The Eden Package

Star Tribes

Start with: Winterstar

ACTION-ADVENTURE

Pacific Force

Start with: Pacific Force

The Red Branch

Start with: Night Strike

Swordmistress Zhen

CONTENTS

THE BRYCE CONNECTION

PART I

Javier was pounding out the kilometers on a treadmill when she arrived. Moved into his peripheral vision, then circled around front where he could see her.

Bethany Marie Durbin. *Bryce Academy*, Class of '79. Not quite young enough to be his daughter. Not far from it, either.

The Unbloomed Rose. Except that she no longer fit that description. Dorn Hetzel had hung it on her, back in the day when Javier had been looking for a research specialist. A Librarian, turned out. Able to gather massive amounts of information and synthesize it into a form that Suvi could digest and understand, so that she turned into a better person.

Javier was at a jog. Not hard. Not a walk. Pounding out those kilometers.

"Emergency?" he asked her, trying to gauge Bethany's body language.

"Only if you can't run and talk at the same time," she replied with a grin. "Bubble gum and straight lines, if you will."

He grinned. Old joke about being able to do both without falling over. There were days.

"Talk," he said.

Only a couple of kilometers left, then time for a shower and dinner. Being on a starship left you a lot fewer opportunities to stay in shape, so you had to approach it with a bit of a militant mindset.

Or grow slack.

Unacceptable outcome these days, considering what he had planned.

And who he planned on doing it to.

"The Embassy is getting close to ready," she reminded him. "I'm still concerned about the makeup of the team."

"Too big?" he asked.

"Too small," she answered him. "Me, Kibwe, Ilan, and Vivian?"

"And the Doctors St. Kitts," Javier reminded her.

"Only until we find a way to get them on a commercial liner to send them home," Bethany retorted. "Four of us are going to take on the entire *Concord*?"

"No," he said, maintaining the grind. "Just you. The others are your support network, and I'm sending them because none of them have active warrants in *Concord* space."

"Me?"

"The Unbloomed Rose," he said simply. "I need you doing this. Nobody else has the knowledge to describe what I'm intending, nor the skills and temperament to talk to those asshole admirals and senators who will make the final decision."

She muttered something along the lines of *You're nuts,* but he ignored her.

Not like they hadn't had this conversation before. And a few yelling matches.

Stubborn woman. Like he liked them.

Javier went ahead and stopped running, letting the machine roll him backwards onto solid deck before he walked around it and shut it down.

"They'd arrest me, Zakhar, and most of the rest of us before hearing a word we said," he reminded her. AGAIN. "They'll listen to you, if you make them."

"Make them," she repeated.

"Yes, make them," he stated bluntly. "Pretend like you're trying to talk one of your hardheaded bosses out of doing something stupid. Or into it. Whatever works."

Her glower was a thing of beauty. He'd hit the right note, though, because it drained away after a moment. His reward was a deeply put-upon sigh. Should have gotten an eyeroll, too, but he'd take it.

"I'm going to convince the *Concord* to provide you a base and repair facility?" she ground out her own words like kilometers. "And place a squadron of small warships at your disposal? And they'll go for it?"

"If they'll sell or lease me the ships, I can pay for crews," he said. "If they have hulls, I can recruit the killers I need. Not like there aren't a lot of sailors on the beach these days, trying to figure out what to do with the rest of their lives."

Okay, low blow. Exactly what had happened to her. And how he'd been able to recruit such a top-notch talent for so cheap.

The *Concord* was broke. No sugar-coating would deny that. Three generations of rough hegemony in the aftermath of the Great War that had left *Balustrade*, *Neu Berne*, and the *Union of Man* broken themselves, but all three were starting to climb back up the tree. Starting to make noises about how they should be involved in decisions with galactic consequences.

Dorn Hetzel's *Rising Storm* that was the underlying genesis of his latest book. Possibly his *Magnum Opus*, as he was analyzing a lot of trends and predicting that the next big war, sometime inside a generation, would burn it all down. The whole, damned galaxy.

The *Concord* was overspending on the wrong things, had blown all their cash on candy and parties, and now the bills were coming due. Fleets were being gutted. Piracy was the logical outcome when authority vanished beyond major systems.

"What if they decide you're trying to become some sort of warlord and carve out your own kingdom?" Bethany asked, interrupting his musings.

"Remind them that I'm some sort of Prince Consort from *Altai*," he tagged her. "I seem to remember that was your idea, after all."

It was fun, making her blush. Harder to do these days, but not impossible.

He paused and took a breath. Committed his soul to the fires.

"Remind them that I'm also Eutropio Navarre," he proclaimed. "And that I'm going to annihilate piracy in as wide a corridor as I can manage between here and home. All they have to do it help a little. A small investment today will yield planetary budget savings and improvements later."

"Funding your war?" she asked, but all the sass had vanished from her tones.

"Making the galaxy a better place," he replied, watching her shudder.

Because Navarre and Aritza would, regardless of the number of bodies he had to pile up to manage it.

That was his promise to eternity.

PART II

Bethany sat in her quarters and stewed.

She was packed. Processed.

Stripped down to the absolute minimum for travel, at least for her. Rainier and Emma had packed up everything they had, because Javier had promised to get them home but wasn't headed that direction anytime soon.

It was on her.

A lot of things were on her.

She sighed.

"If he didn't think you could do it, he'd have gone himself and tried to pull a fast one," Suvi said, materializing an image by the main hatch and smiling.

Of course, she was monitoring. She was always there. Every room. Every minute.

Occasionally, she made her presence felt. Like when she figured somebody needed a kind word. Or a kick in the ass.

Bethany nodded and looked inward.

Why was she so nervous?

Because she was about to return to the *Concord*. Those who had put her on the shore and ignored her, because they had too many trained librarians and not enough fund or billets to keep them all busy.

Plus—and Javier had pointed it out—some fool had looked at *Sentient* systems again and decided that they were good enough to handle the task.

Certainly cheaper than hiring several librarians, but Zakhar had a lovely acronym for things like that.

GIGO

Garbage In, Garbage Out.

A *Sentience* was only as smart as the people programming it. And most of them turned out utterly linear. Utterly.

To quote Piet, they didn't even *understand* jazz, so there was no way for them to commit it.

You needed organic craziness. Bethany had that.

"I'm worried that I'll fail them," she finally admitted.

"That's only a problem if we have to break you out of jail afterwards," Suvi laughed.

Yeah, she supposed so. And they would. Somehow. Probably involving a Bollywood song and dance routine, because it was Javier.

Enough said.

She rose. Grabbed the satchel that held a dramatically over-powered clamshell computer. One that Suvi had shimmed a shard of herself into, in order to provide a fifth crew member, once she got the Doctors St. Kitts headed on their way and presumably safe enough from *Concord* retribution.

"Is Mission-Suvi fully up to date?" Bethany asked.

"Been dumping files on the shuttle with Del," Ship-Suvi replied. "Those will get compacted and loaded when you board, then wiped when you depart."

Bethany nodded. She was probably about the only crew member—no, Afia, too—who could really track having multiple shards—distinct instances—of one *Sentience* running around, and understand how they interacted. Weird, but made perfect sense.

At least to a nerd like her.

"Let everyone know I'm in route?" she said as she reached her hatch.

"Waking Del up now," Suvi laughed.

Knowing Del, he was probably spoofing Suvi. Feet up, eyes closed. Pretending to nap.

Luring in the unwary, because he was like that.

Bethany figured that she needed to develop something like that before this was done.

Javier and Zakhar called it the *War of the Pirate Clans, Volume Two*.

In her mind, Bethany had taken to called it *The Extermination*.

But then, she understood the kinds of personalities involved.

PART III

Del looked around his flight deck with a pleased smile. Interior was right up there with the best *Merankorr* brothels, because he'd found the same distributor for the pink fur on the walls and the paint everywhere else.

He'd even showered and put on pressed cargo pants and his best Hawaiian shirt today. The blue one with the pink flamingos.

A man headed to his execution should look his best. This wasn't an execution, but he wanted to approach it seriously enough.

For once.

Wasn't like he needed to strafe and bomb the local truck stop outside the rear bay.

Probably.

Man should always be prepared anyway.

He had passengers and cargo aboard. Boxes in the bay. Bodies in the passenger compartment, being casual and waiting for their boss. Maybe his boss, because she had all the makings of a good officer.

And he liked the woman. At least as good as any of his grandkids, and better than most of them. Even the non-criminal ones.

He wasn't surprised when she boarded, then immediately

came upstairs to his flight deck. Even took Javier's usual spot. Not a bad role model.

Well, no, pretty bad role model, depending. Good person to emulate in situations like this, though. Yes, better.

She even buckled herself in like he was planning to get crazy with this flight.

Del never *planned* to get crazy. It usually just happened organically. Fools making bad decisions. Challenging an old fart who was smart enough to never name a ship again.

The gods had even taken notice and proclaimed it good.

"*Excalibur*, this is Del," he announced. "Standing by to launch."

"Oh, you were asking for clearance?" Suvi sassed him. Like she did.

"Yes, please," he countered, ignoring Bethany's snort.

A hatch opened and he backed out of the bay. Politely, even, but that was Rainier and Emma. Lovely people. He'd miss them, except for Emma complaining that he wasn't eating a proper diet or getting nearly enough exercise.

Pushing his luck and sidestepping responsibilities apparently didn't count with the woman. Shows what she knew.

Del turned on all of his targeting sensors and hard-pinged the shit out of everything within half a light-second. Rude, but he was departing from a war machine bad enough to crush everyone in this system without a second thought, and he wanted to remind them that the pirates from *Altai* were dangerous, cutthroat killers.

And most of them were.

Suvi was wisely not docked to the little platform. Not that those yahoos could have stormed the place under fire, but they might have been dumb enough to try some stupid stunt, necessitating a general whomping-upside-heads as a retaliation.

Unnecessary, because he'd unlocked the turret and had it live. Just like Suvi was.

Always easier to apologize later for rudeness.

If he found it appropriate.

And could find any survivors.

He turned the bow and located the ship where he would be docking next.

Tucana.

Ugly little beast, but Del understood that to be intentional on the Science Officer's part. About the same size as his Assault shuttle, but far less dangerous. More of a cargo picket, a boring, little light freighter, pretty much stock. Useful for this mission.

He scanned it. Hard. Not cutting any corners today, because he was about to deliver Bethany and the others into the lion's den.

One body aboard. And only one. Fritz knew better than to pull anything stupid at this point. He'd been in the business for long enough to appreciate choosing Navarre as an enemy.

Stoooopid.

"*Tucana,* this is Del," he announced on the comm. "Approaching your cargo airlock now. Stand by for docking."

He even let the autopilot handle it, lining up and locking in. Looking at his internal screens, Del did appreciate that Ilan and Vivian were standing on either side of the door with pistols. And Emma taught martial arts. Anybody rushing them right now would simply be chopped liver.

He even smiled.

"You ready?" Bethany asked drolly.

"I was born ready, doll," he drolled back, catching her eye roll as he grinned.

She rose and headed down the stairs to the rest of her crew. And her new ship.

And, perhaps, her destiny.

She was up for it. He could tell.

Zakhar was on the bridge. Suvi could handle everything herself, as she had demonstrated at *Drako III*. Still, she generally felt more comfortable with her full command team here in the room and ready to offer advice. Him, Piet, Mary-Elizabeth, Tobias.

Kibwe was going with Bethany, so Zakhar was going to have have to handle all the daily paperwork himself, but the man had generally trained Suvi in a good portion of the magic that went into accounting on an ambassadorial pirate courier, and Zakhar could handle the rest.

Javier was here, but in his official capacity as Ambassador, most because Tobias kept growling at the man whenever he touched any sensor systems.

Zakhar didn't stop him.

"Del's on his way back," Suvi announced.

"Everybody else behaving?" Zakhar asked.

"I might have locked various turrets on sketchy neighbors and gyro-stabilized them," Suvi replied.

Not exactly an answer. Probably still the most accurate one.

A First-Rate Galleon like her was huge. And dinged up quite a bit from the shit at *Drako,* but none of the important systems had been damaged. She had privately mentioned to him that she felt she could take anything less than a Class II Warmaster right now.

He didn't doubt it.

Nor, after they reviewed various logs, would a lot of other folks. Hopefully, the *Concord* would see that in a positive light.

Or not, and he'd deal with it. That punk Slavkov had hired himself an entire fleet of pirate ships to come after *Excalibur*.

And lost their asses in the process.

And Javier was correct, in his assessment that *Excalibur* needed to go after the pirates next, if any of this crew was ever going to have any chance at a quiet retirement on *Altai*. Or anywhere else.

Nobody wanted to spend the rest of their lives looking over a shoulder for an assassin that only had to get lucky once.

And, Zakhar was willing to admit, they'd finally pissed him off, too.

Time to make examples of a few people.

"*Excalibur*, this is *Tucana*," Bethany called next. "We're completing our checklist here and will be departing shortly."

Code: I'm well. We've taken possession of the ship and Ilan has confirmed systems to his satisfaction.

"Understood, *Tucana*," Zakhar replied. "You have the complete rendezvous list. We'll meet up with you at one of them."

And if Bethany wasn't there with whoever else arrived, Suvi was to presume a trap and come out swinging. Because some crazy sumbitch pirate captain named Sokolov had only dropped *Excalibur* to War-Status-2 after *Drako*, instead of lowering her alert and control level to something *sane*.

As Suvi had mentioned then, war crimes had been committed by ships at lower settings, but he trusted her. She was, at present, an entirely free agent.

Goddess of Retribution, if you will.

Nemesis, herself, because she was a close third on the scale of angry crew members. But only third, behind Javier and then himself.

Zakhar watched the little picket *Tucana* undock from the platform and back away, turning and lighting her engines outward. None of the other ships in the vicinity chose to make themselves pests. The bridge fell to nearly perfect silence as they watched for about twenty minutes, and then *Tucana* vanished.

Eventual destination: *Purton*.

And the history books, if all this worked out.

Zakhar turned to Javier.

"It's your ship," Javier replied tartly.

"And your mission," Zakhar countered. "Your legend."

He watched steam come off the man's head, but Javier nodded. Grimaced, like he'd drunk a batch of extra bitter coffee. Maybe one left on the counter too long and gone cold. Something.

Zakhar watched him draw a deep breath.

"Suvi, your course has been laid in," Javier said in a formal tone that Zakhar wondered how many people might listen to in future generations. "All ahead full. Destination: *Mejicana Nova*."

"All ahead full," Suvi replied evenly, like she felt that mad energy as well. "Course locked. Stand by to jump."

Zakhar nodded.

It begins.

MEJICANA NOVA

PART I

Javier studied the plot. Suvi was a galaxy-class expert at coming out at the edge of a solar system, slipping in quietly, then listening with an incredible range of sensors.

In the old days, plotting every rock that reflected light, letting him lay down exquisitely accurate sailing records for the gazetteer. Here, sneaking up on someone.

Rude, but effective.

That someone had known Zakhar from the old days. The *Storm Gauntlet* days, though not directly affiliated with any of the major pirate clans.

Independent owner/operator, which meant that he ran a chop shop. You needed work done on the sly, you found him and hired him. You needed a ship parted out, they could do the work.

You had evidence of a crime on your hands, they could fence things.

Normally, a cockroach Javier would have squished under his boot, but he supposed that a ship like *Eldritch Stele* also served commercial interests, however thinly, and thus had an imprimatur of legitimacy. Somewhere. At least until someone scraped it off with a thumbnail.

Nobody he knew, but Zakhar knew the name. And contacts had gotten them coordinates.

So, here they were.

Mejicana Nova was a quiet place. Middle of nowhere, surrounded by more nowhere. Uninhabited system, off the usual trade routes.

Back up in the holler, as his grandmother would have called it, but that woman was a witch, no questions asked. And probably too old to take P In crazy shit like this.

Probably. You never knew with her. Might make Del look bad if he brought her in.

"Anybody worth mentioning?" he asked the room.

Tobias was handling sensors, along with Suvi. Javier was just along for the ride.

Maybe the ship's Commissar, keeping everyone's nose to the grindstone, except that he would probably spent more time dragging on leashes to hold them back with this crew.

"Couple of light ships," Tobias replied. "Civilian, upgraded later with heavier shield installations and cut-and-weld turrets. Nothing even *Storm Gauntlet*'s displacement, save for the target itself."

"Concur," Suvi added, which was her way of saying that Tobias was pretty good at this.

Certainly, Javier had trained him well enough along the way.

Javier looked up at Zakhar on his command throne, but the man just grinned evilly. And remained silent.

Fine.

"Boarding team, stand by for final jump," Javier announced on the intercom, standing up and unbuckling to join them.

Djamila and her killers. Also angry. And hungry.

Almost as much as him.

Almost.

"Suvi," Javier commended his soul to whatever gods liked him. "Take us in."

PART II

Suvi had been running jump calculations to a whole another decimal point over what she'd done in the old days.

Before *Drako III*.

Too much maneuvering in tight quarters, where she was trying to put herself into a parking space in a gravity dimple on the first try. And she'd gotten pretty good at it.

Eldritch Stele wasn't anywhere hard to reach. Sitting in stable LaGrange point 2 of a small planet/moon combination. Nothing with an atmosphere, nor anything else electronic in orbit.

And she'd had long enough to math it out.

She stepped sideways and dropped out under her victim, like a shark surfacing. Unlike him, she was rotated sideways with an entire broadside of ugly teeth turrets ready to take a bite. He was a medium transport with a couple of guns added and telescoping cargo bays that could enclose a small ship for repairs. *Tucana*-scale, or something.

Eldritch Stele, however, was just enough too big to actually fit into her main cargo bay, unless somebody shaved a few places.

And she wasn't here to steal the ship. Not exactly, anyway.

She read a short book while waiting for the wavefront to catch

23

up with him. Humans thought slow, and *Stele* wasn't a warship, ready for instant combat.

Not expecting a fleet of yahoos to drop out of jump and try to hump his leg.

Like Slavkov and friends had tried to do to her.

"*Eldritch Stele*, this is *Excalibur*," she finally announced, adding a mug of mocha in one hand to remind herself to start friendly. "You will heave to and prepare to be boarded, or I will blow you into small pieces and leave you to deorbit."

Or close enough to friendly. Not immediately shooting first.

Might as well draw that line early. Wasn't like a human navigator could get away from her if she was prepared to chase.

Like now.

She dug out another book and read for a while, waiting for the publican over there to come to grips with what was about to happen to his day.

"*Excalibur*, this is Glen Hohstadt," a man replied. "Owner/operator of *Eldritch Stele*. What's going on?"

Good, a man willing to listen to *force majeur* and not get immediately stupid.

Immediately, anyway.

"We'll be boarding you shortly," Suvi informed him. "This vessel is in need of repair, but we're not going to let you or either of the other vessels depart while such work is being done. In fact, we'll be taking control of the entire system. Will that be a problem?"

Bald. Ugly. Piratical.

Necessary.

Human deep-breath pause at his end.

Oh, and I have enough firepower pointed at you at this moment to effect my threats. Don't push me.

"Uhm, understood, *Excalibur*," Hohstadt replied carefully. "What are your orders?"

After all, she hadn't threatened to capture and enslave all of them. Merely keep them hostage while she stole all his repair parts, though Javier and Zakhar might offer to pay him back later.

If he behaved.

"Stand down," Suvi said. "It would save the boarding parties time if you went ahead and drew everybody aboard *Eldritch Stele*. I can monitor all three vessels from here."

More pause. Probably surprise that her sensors were that good.

After all, she had been a Probe-Cutter in her youth.

And he had to guess the odds of taking on a First-Rate Galleon. Bad, but not everyone figured that out ahead of time.

No way in hell any of those ships were jumping in their current configurations. Not without a lot of prep that she could also monitor.

This is that moment when Mom finds you with a hand in the cookie jar.

"We'll be standing down, *Excalibur*," Hohstadt finally replied.

Suvi switched channels.

"Del, you're on."

PART III

Djamila was in the forward turret, live and locked on, as Del's shuttle approached one of the empty landing locks. *Eldritch Stele* had four bays, with two currently occupied.

"Djamila, dear, I can handle this part," Del said leadingly.

And he could. She didn't want to admit that this was more of a security blanket than anything, but Djamila also understood that she was a bit of a control freak.

Like so many of them.

Still, she released the grips and rose, automatically checking everything as she headed aft to where her team was waiting.

All of her team. Everyone that had gone down to *Ophiuchi*, including Afia and Javier, because they brought specific expertise that she would need.

She double-checked, and everybody was ready. Boarding armor with faceplates open. Weapons. Packs. Outside, the airlock thunked as the ship made contact and locked on. Sascha and Hajna bracketed the hatch with pistols drawn.

"Ladies, opening now," Del announced, followed by a short gust of wind as pressures equalized.

Djamila walked forward, ready to draw and fire in the blink of an eye.

If it became necessary.

One short man stood at the far end, in the middle of the room beyond his airlock. Dark hair, a little long and curly. Maybe one hundred and sixty-five centimeters tall. Stocky build.

Wary eyes looking way up at her.

He was dressed in black. Pants, boots, vest. Cream-colored shirt with three-quarter sleeves. Standing collar. Belt with no holster, as he had been warned.

"Glen Hohstadt," he said as she came to rest a meter away, her team spilling out to fill the rest of the chamber.

Large space, roughly six meters square with a four meter ceiling. Storage and loading from cargo ships.

Or thieves.

"Djamila Sykora," she replied. "Dragoon."

He nodded slowly.

"*Storm Gauntlet*," he said quietly. "Heard you folks upgraded a while back. Didn't realize what you'd moved to."

She nodded back.

"A First-Rate Galleon," Djamila informed him.

"Ship's seen some trouble," he offered, looking around to include Afia on her right and Javier on her left.

"Valko Slavkov brought a small pirate fleet after us," Javier said simply. "Eighteen warships, including *Para Bellum* and *Yorrick* from Belfast, *Blackstone* from Walvisbaai, *Obsidian Hawk* from H & W, and *Kymni Gauntlet* from Jarre. *Kymni* got away from me. For now."

Djamila appreciated the nonchalant way he shivved that last bit in. Hohstadt jolted.

"And you're here because?" he asked tentatively.

"Need a dedicated yard," Afia said. "And some trained folks. I have teams, but we'd be six months or longer with the crew and supplies at hand. Hoping we can convince your people to help. Got a *Sentience* aboard who can tell them exactly where to cut and weld."

And let the man know that Suvi would be monitoring any

attempts at sabotage, which would get a great many people terminally hurt.

Djamila would let Javier decide fates, but she already knew what would likely happen.

Hohstadt was smart enough to lean back and study her, understanding that Djamila was the most dangerous person in the room.

At least physically.

Afia and Javier brought their own troubles to anyone wanting to try their luck.

"How's it going to play?" he finally asked, skipping over a bunch of really stupid preliminaries.

"Can we hire you and your crew to do the work next to my people?" Javier asked bluntly. "There will also be hostages, but the faster the job gets done, the sooner everyone else goes back to their lives."

Hohstadt ignored Javier and focused on her.

"Only hostages?" he asked.

Djamila felt a moment of pure rage suffuse her soul, but she understood the question for what it was.

In the bad old days, *Storm Gauntlet* had taken prisoners and sold them on as indentured laborers on mining colonies or latifundia. Before they'd learned better.

Before Wilhelmina Teague, the Last Shepherd of the Word.

Even Javier would have suffered such a fate, but for fast talking his way aboard the crew.

And saving all their lives more times that anybody could count.

"Only hostages," Djamila accepted.

"One thing," Javier said sharply. "When we're done, you'll want to get out of the business and find something else to do with your life."

"Why's that?" Hohstadt asked, his hackles coming up.

"Because from here, I intend to annihilate the Belfast Holding Group," Javier told him. "And H & W. And Walvisbaai.

And the Jarre Foundation. And anybody else that decides to be pirates."

"Annihilate?" Hohstadt flinched. Not much. Enough.

"I am ending piracy in a corridor connecting the *Concord* and *Altai*," Javier said simply. "And anyone still involved."

The man blinked. Licked his lips unconsciously. Shrugged.

He was only a chop shop, as Zakhar had called the man and the vessel. Support staff for predators, rather than one of the killers, but the pirates required this sort of thing to survive, so Javier's unspoken threat was that he would destroy *Eldritch Stele* if that was what it took to do this job.

And he would.

Djamila would gladly help.

PART IV

Javier had gone ahead and moved all his hostages back to *Excalibur* to let Zakhar manage them. And to let them have access to a proper French Bistro as a reward for good behavior, though the regular wardroom team had upped their game significantly after competing with Chay for more than a year.

Hohstadt had remained behind, along with most of his people and about a quarter of the crews of the two ships that were going into drydock mothballs until *Excalibur* left again.

Hostage was a good enough term. *Don't fuck with me, and I won't fuck you up.*

Javier was on the command deck of *Eldritch Stele*. Ship had an actual cockpit in the next chamber, but this was the space where up to four ships could be repaired simultaneously and monitored, while also juggling cargo deliveries going both directions.

Speaking of which...

Javier turned to Hohstadt beside him and sized the man up. Shorter. Same kinds of muscles as Javier had. And enough brains to stay alive in this business for a long time.

"How soon until your next customer?" Javier asked point blank. "Next fence run or supplies?"

"Probably a week," Hohstadt replied. "Day, day and a half either way on that estimate, as they're never very precise."

"Suvi, get that?" he asked.

"Did," she replied. "Will be standing by."

They'd added a permanent data channel commlink back to *Excalibur*. Wired for now because she had docked nose-on to link a primary forward airlock to the ship, though not in a bay. Too big.

But it let her run rampant through Hohstadt's systems, absorbing his database and logs and adding them to her library of criminal conduct.

And with ten minutes warning, repair techs could haul ass away from her hull if she had to back away and start shooting. Or just stay aboard and keep working.

The command space still needed people to operate, because it wasn't very automated. On the other hand, *Eldritch Stele* was a dedicated mobile repair platform, so it was designed to park in a single spot for a long stretch of time with most systems shut down.

Javier would steal it and carry it with him if the situation were different, but he understood that he'd need to probably replace the crew to do that.

Hopefully, Bethany could find something similar and convince the admirals back home to let him lease something similar long term.

Because while *Drako III* was the most recent duel to the death. Javier doubted that it would be the last.

A hatch opened and a woman entered.

Little taller than Hohstadt. Long blonde hair pulled back in a pony tail. Muscles in a blocky way that went straight down from shoulders to hips. Attractive, but not beautiful.

Stunning, perhaps.

Blue eyes when she walked right up to form the third point of a triangle. Grease under her fingernails.

"Regina Slayton," she introduced herself. "Two-Eye-Cee around here."

Second in command. First Mate, if you will, save that she was obviously in charge of the repair teams.

"I'm known by a lot of names," Javier replied quietly. "The one you probably know best is Eutropio Navarre."

Like usual, both of them jarred back a stagger, if only emotionally.

How's it feel to have a stone-cold killer on your deck? The kind that makes mere pirates look like junior varsity punks?

It was a useful legend. And a cloak he could leave by the side of the hatch when he returned to his quarters.

Probably be a while before that happened, but it was what it was. And he'd get over it.

Afia had followed Slayton in, sliding quietly into the background, until you realized that she had a wrench in one hand and the backs of two pirates in front of her.

"And we're just supposed to fix your ship?" Slayton asked.

"Been negotiating rates with Hohstadt," Javier replied. "Got cash. Legitimate, even, drawn on a number of banks around here. Needed labor and parts, but in a situation I could utterly control."

"Because you have a battleship and a lot of enemies," she said quietly.

"Lot fewer than I did a month ago," he smiled at her. "When you have some time, ask my *Sentience* about what she did to Slavkov and all his friends. That was only a down payment. A dowry, if you will. I still intend to get ugly on those folks."

"And we're just supposed to accept that and repair your ship?" she asked. Hot, but not angry. Forceful, but not demanding.

Fine line, but she stayed on her side of it.

"Faster you do, faster I'm gone, sooner you folks look for a new line of work," he said, understanding that it had become something of a mantra by the fourth time he'd explained it.

"That's the ship that hit *Nidavellir*," she noted.

"Payback for them trying to kill me at *Svalbard*," he replied, turning a little to square up on the woman, with Hohstadt falling silent "Slavkov decided to hire the Big Four and brought a fleet to kill me this last time. And failed. Almost died himself in the process. I intend to kill him. And the rest of them. All of them."

Afia nodded where nobody could see her. Her honor would be satisfied with nothing less.

Javier had just wanted to go home and retire to a life of puttering in the garden with Behnam, but he knew that *Le Beau Geste* was necessary first.

The Grand Gesture.

Something so stupid that it made the history books.

So be it.

"All of them?" Slayton asked, obviously taken aback by his vehemence.

He nodded sagely.

Not everybody wakes up in the morning and decides to be a villain. Most folks are the heroes of their own story. It takes a mirror or an intervention for most folks to sum up all those little choices they've made and realize how far they've gotten down into evil.

Most people thought of Navarre that way.

And Javier would have liked to be the villain of this story, but Zakhar and Suvi had dug up a term from some ancient history book and hung it on him. And they weren't wrong to call him a paladin.

Defender of the faithful. Of the innocent, in this case.

Hero.

Whatever, man.

"So we're out of the pirate business after this?" she asked, glancing sidelong at Hohstadt.

"Unless I can hire you long-term," he replied, watching her for body language.

Having the two of them side by side, it was evident that she was the energy and he was the brains. Both smart, but Hohstadt ran a successful business, while Slayton made it work at a technical level, supervising teams and executing repair operations.

"For how long?" Hohstadt asked first. Tentative. Probably sanding off some of the rough edges they'd get if Slayton asked. She had that look about her.

"I've sent a team to talk to the heads of the *Concord Navy*," Javier replied, turning even between the two now. Facing Afia from three meters away and catching her emotions as well.

She was the technical expert. Combat Engineer as certified by Sykora, whose standards were never allowed to have a bad day.

"Why?" Hohstadt asked, feeling his way tentatively in the darkness.

"Asking them to loan or lease me ships and crews that I can use to go destroy all the pirate clans," Javier replied. "I know how to find them. And where. And I don't have to worry about any *Concord* politicians trying to run interference for pirates because they operate under the table and take bribes. In fact, I'll destroy them to, if I find any records. Leak those to news organizations instead of someone that might have a vested interest in sweeping it under the rug later."

"Do you have any idea what that might do?" Hohstadt asked, eyes turning harder and sharper than Slayton's.

"Yes," Javier said simply. "I've given it a lot of thought. But I'm also working towards something bigger."

"Bigger?" Hohstadt asked.

"One of my former teachers at *Bryce* named it *The Rising Storm*," Javier nodded. "Another war coming. Bigger than the Great War. Much more destructive, because everyone is roughly balanced these days and largely unwilling to simply be happy with what they have. Gotta push."

"*Bryce*?" Slayton asked sharply.

Javier turned back to her and studied the woman. Attractive enough. Compelling, but not classically beautiful. Mostly personality.

And brains, if she got that he was referring to the Academy on *Bryce* that turned out *Concord* naval officers. Like him. And Zakhar. And a few others.

"*Bryce*," he agreed. "I can send you over a copy to read. Late draft, as he's close to publishing it. I've been working with it as the core driver of my exploration and diplomatic mission for the last three years."

"Diplomatic?" Slayton pressed, giving off a whiff of something that didn't quite fit, but he couldn't tell what.

"Ask Suvi about our adventures since *Nidavellir*," he replied. "*Ugen. Ormint. Kimmeria. Syntha. Sovereign Nakhimov. Drako.* Can't go home while Slavkov is still around being a punk. Or while he can hire more pirates and assassins to come after me."

"So you intend to destroy them all," she countered, circling back. Wanted it to come out sarcastic, but failed.

"Yes," he repeated. "And I'm building as much of a squadron or fleet as I can manage, same as I plan on recruiting enough ground forces to storm a couple of stations so I can make sure I kill the right people instead of just blowing up some orbital platform and hoping all the appropriate bad folks are home at the time."

Another sidelong glance between the two. Conversation without words, but he wasn't offended. Hell, he was doing the same with Afia out of sight on their blindside.

And holding that wrench.

"We're looking at a month drydock, if you want it done right," Slayton offered, seemingly changing the subject.

"I've got time," he replied. "The *Concord* won't move quickly until they decide to help me. Or try to stop me."

"Try?"

"Try."

PURTON

PART I

Bethany would have liked a larger crew, if only so she could pretend to be an officer and let someone else handle all the piloting duties. Suvi made it look easy, as she was faster and more precise.

Bethany had had to relearn a few skills along the way, as well as discover *Tucana*'s idiosyncrasies. It had taken longer than she'd wanted, but Javier and Suvi had both put down a timetable and she'd been almost exactly on it, so she'd count that as a win.

She still sighed as they dropped out of jump and the sensors all started returning the data she'd been expecting.

"That's it, huh?" Kibwe asked.

Except he wasn't Kibwe Bousaid anymore. That had been, like so many of the rest of them, a fictitious cover.

His real name was Armando Gutierrez.

"That's *Purton*," she nodded. "Galaxy's weirdest museum."

"Too bad that none of these ships could be flown without a lot of work," Armando shrugged. "Couple of real beauts in there."

She supposed so, but Bethany had never been a ship nerd. Not like Armando or Ilan. Both were looking forward to the ten drachma tour, assuming it still ran.

And they weren't all immediately arrested.

Suvi had briefed her extensively, yet another ship nerd. The planet itself had a small military base and a large police presence, mostly to keep pirates, thieves, and sightseers from getting into the mass of old hulks floating around here. Folks could take a formal tour instead for a small price. Archaeologists occasionally needed to study some old model, as well as, if the notes were to be believed, a vid company that was slowly taking scans of everything so they could recreate them as sound stages to make movies.

It was a place that Javier had felt was a safer bet to visit, as explosive as her news and information was.

"Ilan, we have one more jump, but not immediately," she said on the intercom. "Sending a message to port control now and I have no idea how soon they will reply."

Bethany triggered the message packet, then sat back.

Emma arrived with hot chocolate, which just sounded perfect, so the three of them sat and waited.

"We'll really be able to find passage from here?" Emma asked.

"We're inside *Concord* space," Armando replied. "Everything before here had been allied or friendly, but this is controlled. One of the reasons we never got too close in the old days."

The evil piracy days. As opposed to the friendlier days, where they'd still been thieves, but not slavers.

One of these days, Bethany knew that she needed to track Mina Teague down and interview that woman. The Shepherd cast an amazingly long shadow over so much of this crew, but only as a ghost. A memory.

An ideal.

And someone who had spent nearly five hundred years accidentally locked in hibernation. What must it be like to awaken after your entire civilization had vanished?

"Stellar Transport *Tucana*, this is *Purton Command*," the radio finally replied. A man heavy with sarcasm and disbelief. "Message packet received. Are you people serious?"

Bethany chuckled. Understatement, if anything.

"Deadly serious, *Purton Command*," she replied. "Standing by for orders."

She left it at that.

Not a lot to say. The packet contained a series of file headers, a brief explanation of how she got them, and a request to talk to senior naval officials on behalf of her employers to go deeper into detail than radio traffic warranted.

And she was flying an unarmed transport, in a zone heavy with police and military defensive forces that could easily run her down and capture her if they chose.

That nobody had just jumped into her lap already was hopeful, but not definitive.

"*Tucana*, flight path transmitted," the man continued. "We'll talk in person in a few hours."

"Acknowledged, *Purton Command*," she said, then cut the line and turned to the others. "Emma, you and Rainier should probably be packed up. I'm not sure you'll get to leave immediately, but they might just wave you on, assuming we aren't all under arrest."

"I'll go update Vivian and Ilan," Armando added, rising and gesturing Emma to precede him.

That left Bethany, alone, facing the entire might of the *Concord*.

As it should be.

She had a story to tell.

PART II

Ilan still remembered meeting Javier that first day. Dead generator. Dead Norwegian rat. Snark. Attitude. Chickens. The whole flock had turned over twice since then, even with modern breeds that lived longer. And he was no longer the Ship's Gamekeeper, though Ilan had learned enough botany and animal husbandry to check on them and all the old fruit trees from time to time.

Rainier St. Kitts was way better at it. Hopefully, the war wouldn't disrupt all the progress she and Javier had made over the last few years. Especially since Ilan wasn't there as a backstop.

Nor was he there for Afia if she ran into trouble.

Today Afia had specifically assigned him to specifically protect Bethany, though they were keeping that quiet. He didn't need to save that many lives. And had never planned to. It had merely been necessary at the time. *Nidavellir. Ugen.* Others.

As they docked, he looked back on that helpless, hopeless punk he'd been and wondered how the hell he'd turned into a Combat Engineer. Every step made sense. None of them made sense.

Now he was at *Purton*, about the last place he ever figured he'd go. Unarmed, because Bethany was trying to play this nice and there was nothing they could do if the authorities got stupid, save blow their chance to have Javier on their side.

You did not want the Science Officer as an enemy. Good way to make bad choices.

Vivian was closest to the airlock. A thief trained by Spider Fernandez himself, the Khatum's personal cat burglar. Tall and lean, with pianist's hands. Ilan felt short and dumpy next to the guy. Armando was tall and soft and quiet. Bethany was a librarian and officer. The Docs were professionally smart people.

The hatch opened. Guards with guns, like you expected when docking with a military station.

"Everybody out," someone barked.

Ilan followed Vivian through. Adrian Ahmad had designed their outfits, redoing entire wardrobes and specifying which outfits to wear on which day.

Today was First Contact, so everyone was dressed snazzier than normal. Everything clean. Fitted. Pressed. Designed to impress at a subconscious level, by an expert's expert. They got lined up along a bulkhead. Ilan wasn't intending to impress whoever came aboard. He was just the Combat Engineer for this team. Bethany, Rainier, and Emma were at the other end of the line to handle people.

"Bethany Durbin?" a man in *Concord* green asked.

Ilan recognized the color scheme, because Captain Sokolov had worn it for the last decade, until Adrian and Suvi had finally broken him of the habit.

This fellow needed to work out more, though, as he had a paunch going. About to lap over his belt.

"Here," Bethany replied, snapped to in a way that looked painful when Ilan glanced over.

Six guards. All armed, but nobody being punks. Slack. Dragoon and the Gun Bunnies would have eaten ten times their number without noticing.

Ilan supposed that he was spoiled, but the Dragoon specifically hadn't wanted to send any over her people. Probably afraid they'd make the locals look bad.

"And the rest of this crew?" the stranger asked.

"These three are crew," Bethany pointed this way. "Dr. Rainier St. Kitts and her wife Dr. Emma St Kitts were passengers that needed a ride as they are returning to *Uelkal*."

"Doctors?"

Ilan kept from snorting out loud as the guy got utterly curve-balled by that one. Bethany might not play poker with the others, but she was wicked sharp.

"Botany," Rainier spoke up. "University of *Uelkal*. My wife teaches sports medicine."

And martial arts. And exercise. Lifting. All the shit that the Dragoon wanted folks doing, though with a much friendlier face and voice.

He kept quiet.

"Passengers?"

Man still hadn't caught up.

"Originally, we were hired by Prince Javier to assist in his botanical research," Rainier piled the bullshit on. "Later, it became necessary for us to depart his mission if we wished to get home in a reasonable period, as his journey had an unfortunate detour introduced."

"Prince Javier?"

Ilan kept his eyes forward. Caught a grin on the face of one of the goons, but they were casual about it. And everyone laughing quietly at their boss.

"The debrief will take considerable time," Bethany interrupted. "And possibly require a fairly significant security clearance. Obviously, all of my people know the story, but all of yours might not need to."

There it was. Need-to-know. One of those military bureaucrat things.

Dude's brain reset. Painfully. Out-bureaucrated, or whatever the right term was.

"Hopkins, process them and bring them to the main conference room," a woman announced over the speakers. Authoritative. In charge.

Boss.

"Immediately, sir," this Hopkins fellow snapped to himself. "This way."

Half the guards led. Other half trailed. Ilan fell in behind Vivian and memorized the route. And the architecture. And everything else.

Just in case he needed to stage a prison break later.

Or blow the place up.

PART III

Bethany fought to keep herself from falling back into the old patterns. The Unbloomed Rose, as Dorn and Javier had seen her.

Too used to dealing with *Concord* captains and admirals who thought they knew everything, but misremembered as much as they invented from whole cloth. And got pissed at her when she had to call them on their bullshit because she was unable to produce the thing they had imagined.

It never worked that way.

Concord station. She'd spent so much time on *Excalibur* now that she recognized the difference in naval architecture. Shorter ceilings for one. Not much, but noticeable.

Conference room as mandated by some book. Exact measurements. Exact contents. Exact placement.

Captain at one end of the table. Darker female with Commodore tabs, so senior-most officer in the system unless an admiral happened along. Probably one lost and in need of hand-holding, like so many of them were.

Hopkins got them all in and seated. Coffee in carafes. Water. Cookies, even, so hopefully this was an interview and not an interrogation.

"We've scanned them and all are unarmed," one of the guards announced.

Bethany nodded to herself. She had specifically ordered that of her people, so they'd better have been listening. And they had. It was good. One less loose thread to deal with.

She found her spot and sat. Waited. Let the Commodore dominate things.

Bethany had already blown up the woman's day with her file.

"Captain Shahd Salim," the woman said. "Commodore, *Purton Command*."

"Bethany Durbin, *Concord Navy*, retired, class of '79."

Might as well start there. Nobody else here from the *Concord*. Specifically.

"How did you come into possession of...those documents, Durbin?"

"We stole them, sir," Bethany replied, adding not quite as much sass as she would have when dealing with Javier. About what Zakhar usually rated. "The spy who had them at the time was intending to sell them to unknown third parties, so we swapped things out and recovered them. My bosses would like to request the assistance of the *Concord Navy* in dealing with a piracy problem, and thought that we could use those file names to get your attention."

"You have certainly done that," Salim said. "And we have been notified of what happened at *Drako*, thought I suspect that you could fill in a significant number of details."

Bethany smiled and nodded.

"I'm actually prepared to deliver a full after-action report, sir," she said. "Captain Sokolov is former *Concord Navy* as well, and maintains those standards in his paperwork."

"Sokolov?" Salim asked. "The pirate?"

"Ex-pirate, sir," Bethany corrected. "They decided to go straight after the events at *Nidavellir*. Before I was recruited. Most of the crew have since accepted *Altai* citizenship and fly under letters of marque and reprisal from the Khatum herself."

Bethany smiled.

Stick that in your pipe and smoke it. We're not pirates. Not anymore. Still dangerous. Still deadly. Only difference today is how angry everyone is. And how official our diplomatic paperwork is.

Including her, when she got right down to it. Maybe not to Afia's level of rage, but Bethany wasn't honestly certain what that would take. She'd never come that close to dying.

Never truly been on the line. That might change today. Depended on how feisty this commodore ended up feeling.

"A full after-action report, Durbin?" the woman asked.

Bethany nodded and reached into the messenger bag that held Mission-Suvi as well as a variety of other things. She pulled a datachip out and set it on the table, watching the woman closely.

Salim looked at it like Bethany had just put a poisonous snake on the table.

"Why are you here, Durbin?" Salim asked.

"My bosses decided after the events at *Drako* that the only way they could ever feel safe again was to destroy all of the piratical organizations involved, sir," Bethany replied bluntly. "There are four such corporations in the larger meta-region, plus various and sundry associated and affiliated clusters. My bosses intend to use a First-Rate Galleon to destroy them."

"Destroy them?" Salim asked.

Hopkins lost his shit, silently, as did about half the guards she could see around the walls watching.

"Sokolov was of the opinion that they needed to be exterminated, sir," Bethany nodded amiably. "And that nobody else would ever do it, so he had to instead."

Long beat. Long pause. Long mental chasm.

Nobody liked pirates, but planetary sovereignty was generally accepted. The *Concord* only claimed certain worlds directly, while trading with others.

A lot of folks were on their own, like they liked it, and could do whatever they chose.

Some of them chose poorly.

The commodore simply watched. Bethany wasn't offended.

"What Sokolov and Aritza would like is for the *Concord* to dedicate resources to the cause," Bethany continued.

Javier had said to go for broke up front, so that anything less she got later let them spin it as a cheaper victory to their own bosses.

"Aritza?"

"Doctor Javier Aritza," Bethany said. "King's College. *Bryce* Class of '63. Occasionally known to the underworld as *Eutropio Navarre*, but he has been Sokolov's Science Officer for the better part of a decade."

Salim knew Navarre, from the way her face paled.

Hell, everybody knew Navarre.

Few had made the connection to the Science Officer, because Javier had worked to keep the two separate.

That he was willing to publicly connect them today should tell the rest of the galaxy what he thought.

And how serious the man considered this problem.

"Science Officer?" Salim managed to squeak.

Bethany appreciated that the rest of her people intended to remain quite unless pointedly asked questions. She would shape this legend.

Javier trusted her to do it right.

"That's right," Bethany agreed. "Our Science Officer, at least initially. More recently, Doctor Aritza has become Prince Javier, and Ambassador to *Altai*, as he is the fiancé of the Khatum herself, Behnam Shirazi."

Another pause to digest.

"And I'm prepared to deliver a brief history of Aritza's last decade or so, as well," Bethany went on. "I've been compiling a proper chronicle of his time, originally aboard the vessel *Storm Gauntlet*, then the First-Rate Galleon *Excalibur* more recently. Names have generally been redacted for obvious reasons, but the plan was to make the full document available to historians, to be opened at the period when the last living crew member had died, as well as to keep it up to date, either myself of my successors as Ship's Librarian."

"But he's a pirate," Hopkins blurted angrily.

"He is a diplomat," Bethany corrected the fool coldly. "A personal representative of the *Crown* of *Altai*. And has been attacked without provocation by a group of terrorists with ties to *Concord* corporate interests. He's going to do something about it. The *Concord* can help. Or he'll do it without you."

Hopkins started to talk and Salim tapped her fist on the table, causing the man to fall silent.

"We're going to take all of you into custody, obviously," Salim said. "And let you plead your various cases individually, starting with you, Durbin. Then I will contact my superiors and let them decide."

"Make sure you have them send a message to retired Captain Nguyên Ayokunle," Bethany said. "He was the commodore in command of *Meridian*, when *Excalibur* destroyed the station at *Nidavellir*. And has personal connections to Captain Sokolov. He can provide the admirals more depth of briefing as well."

She pulled out several chips and placed them on the table. Each was labeled. And contained explanatory documents at the top of file trees, for whoever read them.

The contents were explosive, but that had been her mission to *Purton* in the first place.

To blow up the status quo.

Forever.

PART IV

Vivian studied the room where he had been placed. A step up from a cell, but not two. A place to keep someone isolated and contained.

Spider had trained him, so Vivian already knew four ways to disable the locks holding him in, if push came to shove and he had to escape, damning the consequences. Nothing had risen to that level yet, but a smart man was always prepared.

He was surprised, however, when somebody rang the door chime before opening it. Manners. And a step better than he'd been expecting when Javier ordered him on this mission.

Armando was bureaucracy. Ilan handled technical. Vivian was the team's thief.

Two guards and an officer. Armed. Tough. Competent enough, if he wasn't attempting to damage them in order to steal a weapon.

Spider had made certain things clear, back on *Altai*. The success of Javier's mission was first and foremost, even ahead of Vivian's survival.

"Greetings," he said amiably, rising at ease.

"Come with us," the officer growled.

Vivian nodded and fell in behind the officer and boxed by the guards. Professional job.

They got him to an office. Opened the hatch. Came in with him.

The Commodore sat behind a desk with another two guards.

All that for lil ol' me?

Vivian smiled.

He got sat politely enough. And it hadn't been all that long since the big meeting that Bethany had handled so adroitly, so Vivian presumed he was first on the chopping block.

"Mistress?" he asked politely, reminding them that he was a civilian.

Three quarters of Javier and Zakhar's crew were ex-military. Folks who knew the business before and brought skills.

Vivian brought *other* talents.

"I note from the records Durbin provided that you are specifically an employee of the Crown of *Altai* directly, rather than a crew member of *Excalibur*," the woman began.

"That's right," Vivian replied. "Her government determined that certain folks should accompany Prince Javier's trade mission. I was not present at *Nidavellir*, though my immediate superior was. He felt that this situation might not go as originally planned, and that a Crown representative might be useful."

"Because?"

"Because I am not wanted in any system, mistress," he smiled. "Many of my comrades are reformed pirates, as seen from several political and legal jurisdictions. Some folks might not choose to look past that and see what Prince Javier intended with this current mission."

He did adore calling that dork *Prince Javier*. Utterly rude to anyone who actually knew the man, but a useful cover. And technically correct was the best kind, because both Spider and Tömörbaatar had expected him to be elevated to some sort of official position when he got home.

Prince Consort was as good a title as any for now.

No, *The Science Officer* was still better. And more accurate, after traveling with the man for nearly two years.

"Durbin notes that Aritza intends to end piracy," Commodore Salim noted, leaving that hanging like that.

"I was aboard *Excalibur* at *Drako III*, mistress," Vivian let his smile grow cold and sharp, like a clean blade. "They came out of jump firing. But for Suvi, we'd have all ended up dead, I have no doubts."

"Suvi?"

"The *Sentience in Residence* aboard *Excalibur*," he told her. "Quite an interesting person, given what Javier has done to expand her programming. And extremely lethal. She managed to take on nearly twenty pirate warships, crushing three of the four flagships and savaging the rest of the force before driving them off. As Javier doesn't expect those terrible miscreants to rest, it becomes beholden on the rest of us to assist his venture."

Vivian sat back and smiled.

Eloquence was a lovely tool, in measured doses. It let people know that the Khatum hired quality staff and held them to high standards.

And those would still matter in a junkyard brawl.

"I'm going to get the same story from all of you, aren't I?" she asked after a beat.

Vivian's smile grew warm again.

"Likely, mistress," he nodded. "We were all similarly briefed. All aware of the task at hand and the consequences. All of us volunteered to assist Bethany, as she was the one with the experience and background to communicate directly with you and your people. If you chose to ignore us—or simply threw us all in prison —Javier and Zakhar would continue on this quest. It would take him longer and the results wouldn't be as elegant, but the outcomes would not change much."

"Durbin suggested Commodore Ayokunle be contacted," Salim offered, off on some tangent.

Fortunately, one Vivian was prepared to follow.

"An old comrade in arms," Vivian replied. "My understanding was that Zakhar served twenty years with the *Concord Navy* and retired as a Captain, before going into, shall we say, private service. He knew Ayokunle on duty. Zakhar has since retired from that occupation and is, as far as I know, on this final voyage as a favor to Javier and the Khatum, before he retires to the ground at *Altai*. He has one last task to complete."

"Ending piracy?" Salim asked sarcastically.

"Saving the galaxy," Vivian replied, equally sharp. "Ask the pirates of *Syntha*. If you can find any survivors."

That got a reaction from the guards, but the Commodore was more phlegmatic.

As she should be.

Vivian sat back and waited. He could always break out of any prison they put him in, then rescue the others.

Spider required no less of him.

SECRETS

PART I

Suvi studied the files. Rearranged them. Changed font, kerning, and margins, just to see it in an entirely different manner.

Shit still didn't add up. And she meant that in the most loving way, but it didn't.

She looked around at her options. Bethany would have been the person she asked first, going for an organic opinion on the presumption that she'd run into some strange, corner-case dead end in her decision matrix.

Humans frequently shrugged and picked a random solution at that point, but they had chemistry guiding their tendencies.

This girl was just a ghost in the machine when you got down to it.

And it didn't add up. Which generally meant trouble.

She might have flipped a coin in her head, but this felt like one of those moments when she should escalate all the way to Stupid, in order to save everyone else time.

"What can I do for you, Suvi?" the Dragoon asked when Suvi came into being in her quarters with a beep.

The Dragoon had been knitting a scarf in a chair.

"Got a potential situation, Djamila," Suvi replied. "Might

need to arrest someone. Or not. Maybe kill them. Or stick a medal on their chest. Really confusing situation."

"Background me," the woman said, turning into a killer in the blink of an eye.

"I have a wired connection into *Eldritch Stele*'s datacore," Suvi began. "And enough space here that I pulled everything over, backed it up, and checksum changes regularly, keeping people on the straight and narrow, as it were."

"Understood."

"Set of files got deleted from over there," Suvi continued. "Got my attention because things and stuff. Looked closer. Files were a fairly complete record of everyone that had dealt with Hohstadt and his operation over the last eight years."

"And it stood out to you because?" the Dragoon asked.

"All that stuff already existed, somewhere in the accounting software, and that's unchanged," Suvi explained. "Not as clean in accounting. More detail. Less organization. But fully duplicated."

She fell silent. Shit didn't add up.

Time to ask a human for human craziness.

She watched the Dragoon process, eyes blinking and unfocused. Javier did the same thing when he was planning practical jokes. Got introspective as he raced madly down a variety of decision tree options.

Like she'd been doing, until she ran into a wall. Obviously, something she'd need Javier or Bethany to address in her programming at a later date, but this felt important now.

Most human behavior was predictable. You established tendencies and probabilities, then watched things unspool over time, adjusting as you went.

This didn't fit any of her patterns.

Why not?

"You have archival copies of the data?" Djamila asked after about a minute.

"Do."

"Does the data have date taglines, indicating access and

copying that splits it into older data and new, tracking changes since some previous access point?"

Suvi took a few minutes of personal time to translate that. Djamila could get just as nerdy as Javier or Afia when she wanted to. Used a different vocabulary when she did.

And, just because shit didn't add up, Suvi translated it all into a couple of different languages, then translated it back, bad idiomatic outcomes and all.

Oh.

Shit.

"It does," Suvi replied, seeing it now. "My someone was keeping a record, then providing an updated file offsite on a regular basis."

"I'm willing to bet that the copy splits align nicely with either certain cargo vessels arriving or *Eldritch Stele* returning to some base for whatever reason," Djamila offered with a hard smile.

"Because there's a spy aboard *Eldritch Stele*, and they are providing updates and briefings to a controller on a regular basis, and were hoping to cover their tracks by destroying evidence, not understanding what a *Sentience* is capable of."

Djamila laughed. She had a pretty laugh. It was just so rare to hear.

"Suvi, nobody is probably capable of truly understanding you except Javier," she said. "Zakhar and Bethany might come somewhat close occasionally."

"And you and Afia," Suvi reminded her.

All smart people. But yeah, Javier had done most of the work, opening her up to really learning. To understanding.

To living her fullest life.

Djamila nodded in acknowledgment.

"So, who is our spy?" she asked.

This was why it didn't add up. Or hadn't. Not until Djamila broke that last hatch down for her.

"Regina Slayton," Suvi told her.

"Hohstadt's Second-In-Command?" Djamila seemed surprised, which made Suvi feel better.

"Yeah," Suvi said. "What should I do?"

Djamila's response was to stand up, put her knitting aside, and check the charge on her pistol.

"Let's go chat with the woman."

PART II

Djamila considered bringing along support, but decided against it. Not that she thought she needed it, but because it might be important to not blow the woman's cover later. Even if she had to shoot the woman dead at some point.

After all, Javier and Zakhar were planning to turn all their prisoners and hostages loose when they were done. That included one extra freighter that had arrived with fresh supplies and promptly been captured.

Nobody was allowed to know where *Excalibur* was while Suvi was in a semi-dismantled state that might put her at risk.

Thus, Djamila walked to the forward repair bay where Slayton and Afia were supervising a large team fabricating repair parts from bar and sheet stock. It helped immensely that Suvi could scan anything and pass or fail it before anyone even bothered trying to install the equipment. What might take a regular warship a year or more was going to take them less than six weeks.

Afia looked up as Djamila walked close, but she waved the woman off and walked right up to Slayton instead.

"A question came up," Djamila said innocently. "Do you have a few minutes?"

Slayton seemed surprised, but not hostile.

"Sure," she replied, glancing over at Afia.

"I got this," Afia nodded.

Djamila led the woman back aboard *Excalibur*. Easier to control the situation. And Suvi was listening and monitoring things like heart rate.

Hard to lie to a *Sentience*.

They settled in a forward office that would have been occupied if *Excalibur* had a full crew, instead of the fraction they generally maintained.

Idly, Djamila wondered if it had finally come time to recruit all those extra bodies, in addition to a squadron or fleet of warships.

Tomorrow's problem.

"What can I do for you, Dragoon?" Slayton asked.

"I'd like to know who you are really working for," Djamila replied evenly. "The *Concord* or someone farther afield?"

Jarred her. Blink and recalibrate. About to lie.

"What do you mean?" Slayton asked, a shade off innocent.

Far enough.

"We've been reviewing your records," Djamila told her. "At a forensic level, though at present I haven't sent a team into your quarters with orders to rip out wall panels. I thought I might save all that awkwardness. And perhaps not reveal what I knew to Hohstadt or anyone else, if it didn't impact on my mission."

Silence.

"You deleted records maintaining a list of every vessel that has come in for repairs," Djamila continued. "A list I presume you were keeping for whoever you have been reporting to. According to my forensic team, Hohstadt does not appear to be part of your operation, being something of an honest thief, whereas you appear to be a spy, mistress. Or an undercover police officer. Something. Do I need to expose you to the crew? Have Afia dismantle your quarters looking for a secret compartment with physical documents?"

"That would be...unfortunate," Slayton offered, grudging.

"It would," Djamila agreed. "And I'm not convinced it is even necessary. As we have been clear previously, once *Excalibur* is repaired, everyone will be sent on their way, though Javier would like to perhaps hire you for a longer term, depending on the outcome of this conversation."

As in, assuming I don't kill you right now. Or blow your cover to Hohstadt and his crew, requiring you to run for your life. If you can.

Pirates rarely had a sense of humor about such things. Especially when the police managed to infiltrate an organization.

Slayton licked her lips. Preparing lies and discarding them. Wondering how she'd been uncovered, when Djamila wasn't about to tell her the truth.

Yet.

"You're serious?" she asked. "About both?"

"We needed repairs after *Drako*," Djamila replied. "Zakhar determined that he could get home, or fight a war, but not both."

Suvi had actually made the assessment, but Slayton didn't need to know that.

"Zakhar also knew this vessel, at least tangentially," she continued. "A good reputation for solid work. We needed that. But we also need the secrecy because obviously the four clans are still hunting us."

"Obviously," Slayton agreed weakly.

"Once we're done here, we will be returning the favor," Djamila said. "You will have the opportunity to go straight. Or retire. Or suffer with the rest of them. Assuming we don't start now."

She left that hanging over the woman's head. Regina Slayton had struck her for intelligence and competence. Hopefully, she would use both now.

Slayton gulped. Suvi hadn't said anything, but Djamila knew she was monitoring everything. Recording it, as she did.

Djamila waited. She was carved from patience. Zakhar could testify to that. And it described so many members of this crew.

Still, the situation could be prodded along.

"What will we find, when we strip your quarters?" Djamila prodded her.

"Papers indicating that I work for the *Union of Man*," Slayton offered quietly.

"And are they accurate?" Djamila pressed.

She herself had several sets of identity papers from various places, against the need to run or vanish, were something to happen.

"They are," Slayton nodded. "As you discovered, we're trying to keep track of piracy by tracking what ships use *Eldritch Stele* as a repair facility."

"Because the major players are relatively known, and have permanent bases that can be monitored," Djamila completed the thought. "It's the newcomers and wildcats you track from here, isn't it?"

It helped, having spent fifteen plus years in the industry. Djamila supposed that it made her something of an expert, especially as she'd been responsible for security operations about *Storm Gauntlet* for the longest time.

Slayton sighed.

"It it," she agreed. "What are the implications to you?"

"How soon until your next rendezvous?" Djamila countered.

"Perhaps a month," Slayton replied. "We were due to take a couple weeks in-station at *Cyrana* after a long sail. That's been knocked off by your arrival, obviously, but it's also a time Glen and I would have had to talk about our future as a corporate entity, assuming you folks are that dangerous."

"We were talking to the *Concord*, being the closest," Djamila offered. "Are you interested in sending a message to your superiors, asking them to provide resources?"

Oh, that was a lovely hit of surprise, watching the woman's eyes blink too rapidly.

"We know where to find our foes," Djamila purred. "Nobody has ever cared enough to gather up the necessary fleets to do the job. And would probably fail anyway, since so many organizations are rife with spies and the pirates could flee ahead of any attack that was big enough to threaten them."

"Will they see you coming?" Slayton asked, shifting her body language from hostile to curious.

"No," Djamila smiled. "At present, we only have one, upgraded First-Rate Galleon. It was sufficient at *Drako*. As we get more ships, we can do more things. That was why Javier was interested in a mobile repair base, because it lets him control circumstances better. If they don't know where we are, they can't know where we're going to hit next. Granted, all of them eventually, but the longer we can maintain operational security, the harder we can smash them when we get there."

"I'm confused, then," Slayton offered. "You aren't going to necessarily out me?"

"I could have shot you earlier," Djamila nodded. "Or arrested and dragged you away and told everyone the truth, but I didn't find that immediately necessary."

Although, if you give me a reason later...

Blackmail was such an ugly term.

"And now?" Slayton asked.

"You think about your options," Djamila said, rising and gesturing the woman to do the same. "Let me or one of the senior officers know quietly, because I'll brief them about the need for secrecy going forward."

And blow your cover with my people. But only my people...

"Later, you can decide how it will play out," Djamila concluded, ushering both of them back into the hallway and aiming the woman back to her own ship.

Quickly, Djamila was alone. Suvi appeared on a side panel.

"Will she go for it?" Suvi asked.

"I think so," Djamila replied. "But I still intend to brief Zakhar and Javier immediately."

Because on the one hand, it changed everything.

On the other, nothing at all.

PART III

Javier listened impassively. Absorbed it all.

Djamila was really good at giving a clinically-clean briefing that way. When she finished, he turned to Zakhar.

"Do we care?" Javier asked.

"Not sure it changes anything," Zakhar replied.

"Like she said, it opens us up to help from the *Union*," Javier noted. "Hadn't expected that, because none of us have any legitimate contacts over there. The more, the merrier, as far as I'm concerned, because if they'll help, that's a whole other hammer Slavkov's spies might not see coming."

"Would they go for it?" Djamila asked, but Javier understood her confusion.

She did *violent* better than anybody he knew, but didn't often handle *subtle*.

That was what he was for.

"At a minimum, it puts them on the spot to ask themselves how serious they are," Zakhar answered. "They are monitoring things, obviously. This lets them unlevel the playing field, as it were."

"What do we ask of them?" Javier challenged. "Big or small?"

"I'd really like an escort or two on my flank," Suvi chimed in.

"If you could seduce that Jarre ship *Hummingbird*, he'd be fantastic. Bastard was far too quick and competent for my tastes, when he was on the other side."

Javier nodded at that. He'd reviewed the records, including the point where she'd launched a single torpedo at that vessel, mostly as a middle finger while running like hell.

"Doubt he'd go for it," Javier offered. "But yeah, putting something small with stingers on corners lets you focus on big players."

"Would we want another saturation bomber like *Blackstone*?" Djamila pressed.

"That only works coming out of jump and catching folks by surprise," Zakhar replied. "Or as a threat with civilians. These folks won't be active duty navy, but should be sharp enough to blind-jump in the face of a torpedo swarm. Then we have to chase them down individually."

"Do great to kill a station," Javier smiled. "Assuming we can't steal another Land Leviathan."

A round of chuckles. Slavkov's toy land yacht. Dead now, and Javier hadn't heard anything about a replacement.

"Do we want to kill more stations?" Suvi asked.

"Yes," Zakhar said. "Ships are power, but stations are where you find accountants and records. Since we're not planning to take over any of these operations, we don't care if those sorts of things are intact afterwards. Plus, all the clans maintain a certain genteel hospitality around those things, understanding that if one attacked another's base like that, they opened themselves up to retaliation."

"And we don't care," Javier completed the thought. "We, in fact, approve of that sort of thing, though I doubt that I could manage such a stunt."

"What if you captured some vessel like *Blackstone* to do it?" Djamila offered. "Drop out, fire off several waves of torpedoes from short range, then jump away. Terrorist hit, if you will."

Javier started to sass her, then stopped. Felt several pieces align in his head with a click so loud he wondered if Suvi heard it.

"You got something?" Zakhar leaned in, eyes glittering with images dark and malevolent.

It was like looking in a mirror.

"Suvi still has a few Ion Pulsars," Javier replied. "We've got Slayton's records of every pirate dipshit they've serviced over eight years. Suvi, who do you have in the way of an Arsenal ship?"

"One. A frigate named *Æthelred*," she replied. "Walvisbaai. Forty-eight columns of eight, so a little under a third of *Blackstone*'s throw weight. Got the complete specs as of four years ago when they came in for an emergency life support issue. Otherwise, nothing."

"Not surprising," Zakhar noted. "Rare class, because they are most useful in a fleet action. I presume they are normally used defensively against the cops suddenly dropping a squadron in to arrest everyone."

"That's my guess, too," Javier said. "But we can ask a few folks where we might find such a vessel."

"And take it?" Djamila asked. "Won't it be defending one of their bases?"

"Sure," Javier replied. "Two birds, one stone."

"How?" she pressed.

Javier smiled and explained it to her.

PART IV

Hajna was still pretty sure that she was retiring after this mission was done. Along with most of the crew, though she hadn't taken a survey. So, she figured she should go out on top.

Where the hell did you go from here, anyway?

At least the Science Officer was planning on going out with a bang. Or several.

Girl appreciated having a lot of bangs.

It was the manner he proposed getting her there that had her a little excited.

Or a lot.

"Only work once," Sascha countered when Javier finished, glancing at her for confirmation.

In the Library forward, but Bethany was off on a mission, so it was kinda empty in here. Especially as it was only her, Sascha, and Javier up here. With Suvi no doubt listening.

They were the Dragoon's Pathfinders, she and Sascha. Hajna had been told she was the smarter of the two, but you were probably counting thousandths of a point to get there.

She was the tall blonde dancer, while Sascha was short, curvy, and Slavic.

"Only need it to work once," Javier agreed with their assessment. "Introduces chaos and mayhem into their system. And possibly catches them completely off-guard, because Walvisbaai is supposedly our mortal enemies. Smart money probably expects us to go after Belfast first. Or maybe Jarre, since so many of us know so much about their operations."

"We leaving them for last?" Hajna asked.

"I don't have one of those grand, messianic plans for my revenge," Javier shook his head. "Got an opportunity here to kick someone in the face. Planning to take it. Then see what kind of help all the other yahoos offer."

"Someone's going to leak from the *Concord* side," Sascha noted. "Bethany's going to kick over too many stones. Word will get out that we're going after the clans."

"Like they need warning?" Javier sneered. "If they don't expect me to be coming after them, they're dumber than I thought."

"Will they see this coming?" Hajna asked.

"Doubt it." He shrugged. "Need you two to pull off another one of your bait-and-switch operations. Full-on heist here."

Hajna couldn't help the laugh that escaped. Other two studied her like she was deranged.

More deranged than usual, maybe.

"Bollywood," she said simply.

"Do tell?" Javier's interest was piqued.

"Can't use the Dragoon," Hajna nodded. "Nor Afia. Those two stand out. Bethany's off gallivanting, and can't really dance anyway. We need to recruit a small performance troupe. Possibly all female. Make it look like the inverse of one of those ancient Shakespearean companies, when they had to be all men, cross-dressing into female roles."

"For the purposes of?" he prompted.

"Distraction," Sascha suddenly smiled, but they had a relationship closer than sisters. Almost bio-twins.

Something.

Hajna nodded.

"How about I turn everything over to you three ladies and walk away without looking back?" Javier countered.

"You're still an accessory," Hajna laughed.

"Not married to any of you, so I could be compelled by a court to testify," he laughed back.

"Oh?" Sascha chirped. "Was that on the table?"

"Not today," he replied, turning serious. Still eyeballed both of them lasciviously, but got deadly.

Navarre time.

"I have an idea," Hajna said, sobering as well. "And I'll drag in the Dragoon, but we can't use her for anything except recruiting standards, because if we're doing this, we might as well go all-in."

"As long as you can get me what I need," Javier replied.

"I got you," Hajna promised.

She'd been hunted through snow, rain, ice, and cold. Trees and uplands. Dipshits with guns on the surface of *Ophiuchi*.

She owed these people a ration of pain.

PART V

Zakhar had retired to his office. Closed the hatch. Fixed some coffee. Took a deep breath.

"Suvi, I have a question," he said simply, and she appeared on the screen by the door.

Concord Yeoman uniform, except that she'd done it in blue today. And changed the arrangements of the buttons.

Something new. He approved.

"Sir?"

He supposed that he'd sounded formal.

"How many books do you have on fleet tactics?" he asked her.

"A bunch," she replied. "All the way back to the Battle of Salamis and a bunch of old Imperial Chinese stuff. Comes forward to *Neu Berne* operations in the Great War then pretty much stops."

Zakhar nodded. About what he expected, especially since Bethany had a budget to acquire interesting things in order to expand Suvi's horizons.

"Most of what we're going to be doing will take the form of high-intensity raids on moorages," he explained. "You, doing to them what they tried to do to you at *Drako,* coming out of jump firing with the intent of damaging your foe sufficient to circle back for a kill later."

"Kinda the opposite of traditional piracy," she observed.

"And one of the reasons they failed," he said. "That and four clans all hired for the task, without them necessarily trusting one another, but all having to deal with Valko Slavkov as a command civilian in the middle. Man's got more money than a lot of planetary governments, but not the sense God gave a goose."

He appreciated her pause and blink. Entirely for his benefit, at the speeds she processed things. Made her human. In spite of everything.

"How fast will it unfold?" she asked, turning into a student of war.

"The first time we do it to someone, you should have minutes before they can properly react," he told her. "Later, they will be on a much sharper watch cycle, with orders to immediately run or fire on any unexpected ship appearing. We'll deal with that when it comes. I want you to build a martial database, Suvi. Specifically, identify all of the characteristics you can from all of the naval battles you have rolling breakdowns for. Size imbalances. Command quality. Crew quality. Civilian cultural notes. Wolfpacks versus cruisers. Lines of battle. Anything. Then start breaking these battles down, step by step, decision and result as they go."

"Purpose?"

"I want you to become one of the top fighting admirals living, young lady," he smiled at her. "Able to see the entire battlefield with all your sensors, guess what the other guy will do in reaction to each of your moves, and place traps and minefields in the way for him. Outthink him or her, using your advantage in speed of processing. You can do that now, but you are only as good as your inputs, as you noted when uncovering our double agent. I want you to spend a week here organizing yourself so that you only need me or Piet to offer the broadest strategic directions and tactical modifications on the fly, letting you fight these battles as your hull was designed to. The original *Hammerfield Sentience*, had he not gone wrong. How he should have done it."

"That code had some serious flaws," Suvi pointed out. "By the end, quality control had slid, and they were trying something radically new with a larger hull. Made terminal mistakes."

"I'm wanting you to not make those mistakes, Suvi," he reminded her. "You'll outlive us all, one way or the other, so it is beholden upon me to make sure that you can protect yourself from future generations. Whatever challenges they bring."

She blinked at him. Almost like a real girl.

Zakhar smiled.

Javier considered Suvi to be his only known daughter.

Zakhar was happy to call her a favored niece.

All their asses would be saved because of her.

Or not.

MERANKORR

PART I

Bethany had expected a different outcome.

What, she wasn't sure. Something. Something else. Almost anything else.

Instead, she was back aboard *Tucana*. With her people, minus the Doctors St. Kitts, who had been carried onward aboard a *Concord* frigate headed in the right direction to get them home safely.

In their place, she had Commander Panagiota Ioannidi traveling with her. Woman was a spy. And made no bones about it, just to level-set expectations up front, as she'd explained it.

Bethany finished a slow and patient preflight, but all the systems were acting normal. And Ilan had done the same aft.

"We did a full maintenance cycle," Ioannidi offered from the co-pilot's chair, a wry smile on her face. "Didn't need it, because whoever had done the work previously did an expert job."

Bethany nodded. Del had treated it like he'd be the one flying *Tucana* instead of her.

And she'd heard enough of his stories, including ones he had only recorded for her after swearing her to secrecy.

To be released only after he was confirmed dead for six days, but Del was a superstitious man. Three wasn't long enough.

"*Purton Control*, this is *Tucana*," Bethany said instead of replying. "Ready to back away."

"Your corridor is clear, *Tucana*," Commodore Salim replied, so she was watching.

Useful to know, if a little concerning.

Still, Bethany unlocked things and triggered thrusters to push them away from the station. Did it methodically. By the book. And then some.

Got clear. Got aimed in the right direction, again taking her time on this one. Rode the thrusters up and out of *Purton* orbit.

Finally, she fired up the JumpDrive and hopped.

Stars blinked and changed arrangement. Not much, but enough to indicate that they'd made it several light-years downrange.

Suvi always compared it to golf, which Bethany always found amusing, since a *Sentience* couldn't actually play the game. At the same time, dead accurate, because travel involved aiming in a direction and jumping as far as you felt comfortable, then lining up the next shot and zeroing down on your target.

Putting, as it were, at the end to come out near enough to your target.

"How long?" Ioannidi asked.

Bethany turned to the woman. Half a head shorter than her, with tousled, chestnut brown hair. An air of approachability, and obvious intellect. At the moment, she had been doodling on a tablet of some sort.

Any time Ioannidi stopped moving, she was writing in that tablet, but Bethany hadn't pried.

"I need to match locations against markers," Bethany replied. "*Merankorr* isn't all that long of a trip, but I plan to drop out at the edge of the system first, and be challenged by those guardships, before coming in closer."

"Wise choice," Ioannidi replied. "I'll be able to clear us fairly quickly. And they'll have exact coordinates you can use to jump."

Bethany considered that. All data was useful. And this was something new to her.

Previously, she'd lived in libraries. Not gone off and had adventures.

"I still don't get why the Commodore handled it this way," Bethany offered.

A week at *Purton*. Several interviews or interrogations, depending how you wanted to view them.

"Sending you along on your way, with one messenger as a passenger?" Ioannidi asked, mouth quirked up and eyes smiling.

"Something like that, yes," Bethany said. "Seems risky."

"Only if you weren't who you claimed to be," Ioannidi replied. "We looked you up. Regional base, however small, so we had updated records on *Excalibur* and its crew. Including you."

Bethany wondered if Zakhar had a spy aboard. Or merely an espionage service that was that professional. Not a lot of people understood what a competent *Sentience* could do with a wide enough input of data. Suvi might be the best at that sort of thing, but the others were all pretty good, when you needed a sledge-hammer to break down data.

It was the assembling it again later that took patience. And Librarians.

"So she was serious about passing me up to the admirals?" Bethany asked.

Sure, Salim had said so, but Bethany had also read Hamlet.

She understood how Rosencrantz and Guildenstern had gotten themselves murdered, unknowingly carrying their own execution warrant to the King of England.

But at some point, Bethany had to take things at face value. Assume that she would be putting the case to an Admiral or three, hat in hand and asking for them to provide a small fleet to destroy all the pirates Javier could run down.

Worse, the man could afford payroll for a significant amount of time. Bethany hadn't ever appreciated just how wealthy

Behnam Shirazi was. Or how much cash she'd made available to Javier on this trip.

Not until Suvi had shown her the records.

Enough to alter the balance of power in this region of space.

Maybe enough to change the course of history.

Heady stuff. And frightening as hell.

"You impressed her," Ioannidi replied with a smile and a nod. "All of you, but you specifically, Durbin. We know what Sokolov and Aritza have been up to. Obviously, ever since *Nidavellir*, they've been on our radar, but have seemingly turned to the side of justice."

"It was a long road," Bethany mused. "Remind me to tell you about Mina Teague at some point. It really all started with her. Everything since has been her emotional impact on the crew of *Storm Gauntlet*."

"Is she still around?" Ioannidi asked. "That's not a name I recognize."

"She's off on some other mission for the Khatum, as I understand it," Bethany replied. "No idea what. Probably saving the galaxy herself. Javier seems to accumulate folks like that around him."

"Like you."

Bethany turned sharply to look at the woman, but Ioannidi was smiling. Warm, even, rather than the cool distance that had been how everyone treated her since she'd arrived at *Purton*.

Maybe she had succeeded, and not seen it? Bethany was an introvert. She was happiest in a library, or chatting with Suvi.

Not shaking the pillars of heaven.

But it was necessary today.

Bethany shrugged, unable to judge.

She turned back to the controls.

"I'll need an hour or so here," Bethany announced. "Triangulation before a long jump."

"Do you want dinner before that or after?" Ioannidi surprised her again. "We're all just along for the ride. You're driving things."

She supposed she was. And while it was important to get where she was going, it wasn't timing-critical. Javier had actually assumed that this phase would take her longer, so she was ahead of schedule.

"Let's jump, then eat, then call it a day," Bethany decided aloud. "*Merankorr* isn't going anywhere, anytime soon."

"Nor are the pirates," Ioannidi replied, rising. "I'll let Armando know. I think it's his turn to cook."

And Bethany was alone. Driving this mission, because it needed doing. Javier and the others expected her to handle her portion.

To bloom.

And to find the posse Suvi needed.

It was there at *Merankorr*.

PART II

Bethany had nailed down that second jump. Longer, because she had a pretty clean corridor connecting *Purton*'s ship graveyard with one of the largest *Concord* fleet bases. Nothing at *Purton* could have been turned around and used in the short term, and Mission-Suvi had confirmed that most of those hulls were older than her original Probe-Cutter had been.

Mielikki, long since parted out and vanished into the mists of time.

Today, there was only *Excalibur*.

Bethany locked everything down after a quick scan of nearby space, but *Tucana* was in the middle of nowhere. Light-years to the nearest inhabited system. And nobody she wanted to visit anyway.

Armando was just pulling things from the oven when she made it aft to the tiny wardroom, a little more open with one woman replacing the two that had made such a positive impact on all their lives.

The Doctors St. Kitts.

Bethany hoped they made it home safe. They deserved it after putting up with Javier and the gang.

Pasta, cheese, meat, sauce. Put it in a big dish and cover. Heat until everything melts and blends together and becomes love.

Comfort food. Armando had a knack for understanding people, because they were all smiles as they settled.

"What will we find at *Merankorr*?" Vivian asked from her left. "Never been this far from home. All I know about are the brothels."

And *Altai* was a considerable distance away, though *Excalibur* was halfway home on the return leg from *Ugen*. Bethany had made a case for visiting *Earth*, not all that much farther beyond, but Javier had overruled everyone for reasons he hadn't explained.

Homeward bound.

"The single biggest fleet base there is," Ilan offered quietly. "Not just little ships like this, but the big monsters like Suvi. Warmasters and such, with *Sentience*s aboard."

Bethany turned to Ilan, realizing that the man had a much broader interest set than she'd previously realized. But a group of introverts was usually marked by long, comfortable silences, rather than a lot of talking.

Ilan focused himself on Ioannidi like a searchlight.

"Would they send a *Sentient* warship to help?" he asked her bluntly.

"I doubt it," Ioannidi replied. "But anything is possible. More likely they'd dedicate smaller vessels if they back you. You have a Mark I Warmaster already."

Bethany kept her mouth shut. Suvi considered herself roughly a Mark III after her upgrades. *Meridian*, who they had encountered at *Nidavellir*, was only a Mark II. And that class was as good as anyone was building right now, though Bethany had seen plans for their idea of a III. And hints at what a IV might look like in another generation or three.

"What do we need to say to those old farts to convince them?" Ilan asked, perhaps a little more bluntly than he normally spoke.

Unless he was setting himself up as Bad Cop here. He was that smart. And had known Javier perhaps the longest of the crew.

Not the best, but everyone had heard about that damned rat on day one.

"What you told the Commodore," Ioannidi replied evenly, not taking Ilan's bait.

If it was bait.

Bethany chewed and let her stomach find solace.

"How much piracy have you participated in, Commander?" Armando asked innocently.

Ioannidi flinched. Not a lot. Enough to give her away.

And the woman was surrounded by reformed pirates.

"I have a working knowledge," Ioannidi offered blandly, leaving off lots of details without denying anything.

Armando nodded and she could see Kibwe hiding inside. Quiet, competent, and friendly. The slayer of paperwork as Zakhar had called him.

"Destroying them makes it better for everyone later," Armando continued. "Especially with what's coming."

"What's your interpretation of Hetzel's theory?" Ioannidi countered, like those two were alone at the table.

"Rising tensions, ratcheting inexorably upward," Armando nodded. "Pissing matches that push envelopes and margins, until someone makes a mistake. Or loses their temper. Or has to react because some demagogue has riled up a planetary population somewhere and those folks are baying for blood. Wars happen because of politicians, not the other way around."

"Inevitable?" Ioannidi asked.

"Someone might catch a clue and decide to back off," Armando shrugged. "I've seen it happen, but that was before, when the *Concord* was sole hegemon. You have the *Union* and *Balustrade* both rising again. *Neu Berne* might ally with one of them as a junior partner. Other players are looking for expand beyond a couple of systems and will have to invade some neighbor to effect their dreams of imperial glory. Hetzel expects one of those defense treaties to force everyone to suddenly take sides and launch fleets at one another, with the expectation that the first person to strike wins a year of advantage. At the same time, I agree with him that nobody can win the war in that year, so they'll all lock into warfare mindset and grind out a war on one another to make the last one seem like a tug-of-war at a family picnic."

Bethany knew the man was smart. She was still a bit surprised by the depth and cogency of his analysis. DEAD ON.

"Fragility is the problem," Bethany added when they paused. "The *Concord* is sliding into a trough. The others are rising hard and have chips on their shoulders. Right now, there are too many pirates, but nobody has been willing to take them on directly, so they have turned into termites in the woodwork."

"The dragon gnawing at the roots of the world tree," Vivian offered, reaching way back to primitive Norse mythology with his symbolism.

"And Aritza has been bashing pirates for years with Sokolov's help," Ioannidi agreed. "Why this? Why now?"

"Because Valko Slavkov is a punk," Armando laughed. "Hired Navarre to do a thing to the Khatum, way back in the day, expecting a Mass Casualty Incident that he didn't pay for, and got pissed when it didn't happen. Then he hired those bastards to come after us at *Svalbard*. And they nearly pulled it off, because they broke *Storm Gauntlet*. If it wasn't for the Science Officer, they would have won. Killed us all. Instead, they got *Excalibur* and *Nidavellir*. Man can't back down, though. Just like the Rising Storm. You'll have egos driving action, instead of planning. Someone has to die before this is all done."

"All because of Aritza?" she asked.

"Because of Afia," Ilan interjected, his words so quiet that they were hard to follow, which made the intensity of them all the greater. "Her rage will launch a thousand ships. Will see Ilium burned to the ground and salted. Will see the sons of Priam driven to the four winds for all time."

Bethany blinked along with everyone else, happy that she wasn't the only one who had never really looked close at Ilan Yu.

Because yes, she could **taste** his anger.

Quiet, calm, competent Ilan Yu, who had single-handedly saved Afia's life at *Nidavellir*. Had gone into the depths at *Ugen* for nameless sailors.

Who maybe understood better than any of them what it meant to *become* a hero.

Ioannidi turned to glance at Bethany.

"I will brief you in greater detail later," Bethany said, catching Ilan's look that he'd said everything he was going to. At least for today.

He was like that. Bethany understood. It was all those layers underneath that she had somehow missed.

Javier must have known, because he'd specifically picked Ilan for this mission.

Bethany caught Ioannidi's surprise.

They all fell silent and focused on Armando's comfort food.

Bethany knew she would need this to complete her mission.

PART III

Bethany had grabbed Commander Ioannidi after dinner and moved forward to a small lounge separated from the rest of the ship. Forward, where the crew could set boundaries from the passengers, were this a normal ship.

It let her create emotional space from dinner.

They both needed it.

She settled in a chair with some hot chocolate that had been cut with a little rum. She was in command here, so she could set the rules. And Javier and Zakhar had a good one regarding booze.

Drinking on duty was not a problem. Being rendered *unfit for duty because of drink* was the issue.

So a little rum tonight helped melt a knot of tension between her shoulder blades. Ioannidi seemingly felt the same way. Bethany let the silence stretch a bit. Introverts at rest.

Ioannidi spoke first.

"Once you set some admiral up with a background briefing, if you turn Ilan loose on him or her, he'll probably sell this better than anything," she offered quietly.

Bethany had to nod. Ilan had brains. And, apparently, he'd spent a lot of time in her library reading, though she'd have to return to the ship to look up his records over the last few years.

95

Obviously, she'd missed things, working mostly with Suvi and the command team.

"What does it say that a group of reformed pirates have to petition the authorities to do the right thing?" Bethany asked.

Ioannidi grimaced.

"That Hetzel is probably correct that the *Age of Concord Hegemony* might be ending," she replied quietly. "Too much graft and corruption. Too inward-facing a mentality, willing to let the rest of the galaxy go to hell, as long as nobody bothers *Concord* worlds. You're one of us, so it will be clearer."

"As are Sokolov and Aritza, among the command staff," Bethany reminded her. "*Bryce* graduates, with all that implies. And they could have sailed home, setting *Altai* up to withstand those winds."

"I've read your report of all the small worlds you've touched on this most recent voyage, Durbin," she said, but Bethany interrupted her.

"Bethany. Aboard this ship, we're not as formal."

"Oh. In that case, I'm Pana among friends."

"Nice to meet you, Pana Ioannidi," Bethany smiled at the woman.

"Likewise," Pana nodded. "But Aritza has been the driving force behind trying to make a lot of things better."

"Penance for all the things he screwed up on duty," Bethany said. "The lives lost because he thinks he made the mistakes."

"Did he?"

"No," Bethany said. "But imagined guilt is an even more terrible mistress, so he works to rectify things. Slavkov started this one. Or wasn't willing to let Javier win the last time. Same things. It will be a war. *The War of the Pirate Clans, Volume Two*, as Zakhar names it. And just as ugly as the first one, save that neither of those men are willing to stop short this time."

"Nor any of the women, it seems," Pana smiled.

Bethany considered her innuendo, but Bethany was just one

of many. Djamila. Afia. Mary-Elizabeth. Even Andreea down in Engineering had spoken up on the need to annihilate the clans.

Annihilate. Exterminate. Loaded language, especially from people like that, who knew piracy from the inside.

"If the gods will not save the galaxy, it is incumbent on the rest of us to step up," Bethany said, unsure if she was quoting anyone, but one hundred percent behind the concept.

They shared a nod. And both went back to their hot chocolate.

Any more words felt superfluous at this point. She had made her point, as had Ilan and Armando.

Now she had to make someone else believe.

PART IV

Bethany had appreciated how much easier this part of the mission was with Pana offering a series of codewords at the outer boundary marker, then again when they'd gotten close.

Fleet Operations One was simply huge. A small, artificial moon in *Merankorr* orbit, surrounded by satellite stations, all armed, and squadrons of ships parked at rest, in addition to fleets inside the hull. And repair yards. And armories. And liberty ports.

A self-contained world for the *Concord Navy*, and she was about to invade it with her scruffy group, though Pana had relaxed some, even as the others had warmed to the woman.

Not one of them, but not so much a stranger.

Bethany had *Tucana* docked in a civilian section of the base, inside a box big enough for a large frigate, so they felt like a pea rattling around.

She shut everything down and took a deep breath.

"Just tell them like you told me," Pana offered from the co-pilot seat, where she'd spent most of this flight.

Bethany nodded and rose. Aft, she met the three men and the five of them entered the airlock, opening it to an armed reception committee.

"Commander Ioannidi?" a man spoke up from the dock. A Lieutenant, still bright and shiny and excited by all this.

"Here."

"If you'll follow us, sir, we'll get you to quarters to prepare," he said.

Bethany fell in behind Pana and let the three men trail, plus a team of soldiers.

At least they put her in a suite instead of a cell. First victory. And a nice spot, too, so Commodore Salim had obviously put in a good word.

They were treating her like the Ambassador from a foreign power, when that was Javier.

Except that she was his representative in this, and he was representing the Khatum's government.

Was this the war, then, already started?

Bethany nearly stumbled as she processed that stray thought. Had Javier intentionally started a war against the pirate clans, in order to draw all the major regional powers into an early alliance that might hold long enough to push a war out another decade? Another generation?

How devious was that man?

No, wrong question, it was Javier.

Had he planned something this big, or was he simply relying on her to carry it off? That sounded more like him.

The four of them got settled, with Pana immediately detached by the lieutenant and disappearing deeper into the station, no doubt to answer a series of confused questions from nervous admirals forced to actually validate that flag they flew.

Bethany knew that was an impolite thought, but she'd spent too much time catering to senior officers to respect them. Too many had held on longer than they should have, and needed to have been politely retired to bring in younger men and women who still had the fire to make a difference.

"You look like someone just walked across your grave," Ilan offered quietly from the couch.

Bethany had settled in a chair. Armando was inspecting the kitchen. Vivian was prowling, for lack of a better term.

"Wondering if the *Concord* has too many old farts in charge to actually do anything useful," she mused aloud.

He nodded.

"Seen it happen," Ilan said. "Pirate captains that didn't realize their time had passed. Young man's game."

She found that amusing, since he wasn't even a decade older than her. Approaching forty now. Not old, but she supposed that forty brought an emotional change in most people.

Old enough to know better, as the saying went.

"What are you doing after all this?" she asked, mostly curiosity.

"Done with space," he said. "Unless it's a job in an orbital yard. Someplace where I can hang my hat and not worry."

Bethany had heard many variations on that theme, interviewing the crew. One last, grand adventure, then they were all done and staying home. On a new world that wouldn't extradite them for the mistakes and stupidities of their youth.

She wanted to pursue that line of inquiry because she was a Librarian, but the hatch opened and Pana was standing there.

"They want you next," she said, back too soon to have gone into any depth with whoever had been interviewing her.

Had Pana simply shut up and told them to ask Bethany for everything? And would that make her job easier or harder?

She rose.

"Good luck," Ilan nodded as she went by, then she was in the hall following that kid lieutenant.

Kid? Not that many years younger than her, but it was the light-years covered, not the circles around the sun.

Conference room. Standard issue from a catalog, even here. Requisite flag officers, with a Vice Admiral in the middle of three captains, the latter from different divisions from their uniform tags. Command, Engineering, and Intelligence.

So, someone was nervous.

"Sit, Lieutenant," the admiral ordered her.

"I'm a civilian," she said, leaving off the *sir* and standing put. "And an Ambassador from *Altai* for this mission. You can accept that, or I can return to my ship and depart your system."

She'd lost count of the number of times she'd wanted to snap back at a senior officer like him and been forced to swallow her words. Zakhar and Javier could take it and deal it right back at her, but the admiral's face got red.

"We could reactivate your commission," he threatened darkly.

"And what would that get you, if you had to turn around and immediately court martial me for insubordination? And tell *Altai* that you don't respect them. The Prince Consort himself sent me, so this is a governmental-level ambassadorial mission, *Admiral*."

*As in, Technically I outrank **you**, punk.*

Bethany smiled. Waited.

One of the captains leaned forward and gestured to the seat on this side of the table.

"Please, Ambassador Durbin?" he asked politely.

Intelligence markings. Possibly had quickly skimmed her file and kept going past the point she'd been decommissioned out of the service to read about her recent adventures, while the admiral had only seen the retiring rank and made assumptions.

Dumb ones, but wasn't that the very nature of the coming catastrophe?

She relented and sat, shifting left one seat to line up with the man from Intelligence instead of the Vice Admiral in charge.

"Commander Ioannidi suggested that we talk to you before going deep into the files provided, both your original ones and Commodore Salim's cover letter," Intelligence began.

She hadn't gotten names. Didn't really care at this point, because those four men were merely symbols in her mind. Boxes on an org chart. Nothing more.

"How deep of an initial briefing would you prefer?" she smiled at the man, then expanded it to the others.

"Fairly shallow," he replied carefully, glancing at the admiral and the others, but they remained silent, willing to let Intelligence play Good Cop for now.

She could Bad Cop with the best of them after living aboard *Excalibur* this long.

"Prince Javier has been deeply insulted by Valko Slavkov's behavior," Bethany began. "And that of the four organizations that attempted to assassinate him and his crew at *Drako III*."

"Slavkov might have a reason," the captain offered obliquely.

"When you get deep enough into the files, Slavkov started it," Bethany smiled. "The Prince intends to end it. As ugly and as messy as he has to go, in order to see his honor satisfied on the subject. And that of his crew and friends."

She leaned back.

"And he wishes the *Concord* to assist?" Intelligence asked.

"Yes," she replied. "Ships. Crews. Resupply. *Intelligence*. He's willing to attack pirate ships and potentially their bases with the intention of annihilating the problem at least as permanently as possible. With destroying it root and branch. He would like your active assistance. Barring that, he would like to buy or lease decommissioned vessels and be able to recruit and hire former *Concord* sailors, as well as folks from other nations willing to stand up and end piracy."

The captain with Command markings had a look on his face that made her wonder if he was dealing with one of the clans under the table.

How many cockroaches might suddenly scurry away from rocks she was kicking over right now? How much of that was Javier assuming they wouldn't help, but would have to address the rot suddenly revealed in their own structure?

How devious was that bastard, anyway?

That made her smile. The men all relaxed a bit. Mostly.

Foolish mistake on their part, but she let them think her friendlier than she really was.

"What's to stop him from turning himself into some warlord somewhere?" Command asked.

"He is the Prince Consort of *Altai*," she retorted. "So he already is. This is a matter of honor, because he has no interest in letting Slavkov and the others remain at large, seemingly free to hire more assassins when each batch fails."

"You're talking about a *Concord* citizen, Durbin," Vice Admiral growled.

"Yes," she agreed. "One who appears to be entirely above the law, too. Why hasn't the *Concord* done anything about his ties to the various pirate clans before now? Why haven't the Clans been crushed out of existence? When did we stop being the good guys?"

Bethany smiled at how those four men reacted. About like being kicked in the balls, but she understood how all *Bryce* graduates saw themselves as heroes.

When had that stopped being the case?

In that moment, Bethany understood that she would be retiring to *Altai* when all this was done. Up until this moment, everything had been on an annually renewed contract, because she'd seen herself as a *Concord* sailor.

A hero.

Only one of those things was still true.

Vice Admiral literally stopped himself from responding, which was probably the smartest thing that man did this week, because Bethany had finally found her rage. Tasted it.

Understood what drove Zakhar and Javier to start this new war.

The *Concord* had stopped being the good guys and nobody had noticed.

Nobody had noticed.

It would require the crew of *Excalibur* to rise to the occasion.

Vice Admiral and Command were taken aback in the face of her terrible winds. Intelligence was trying to think of something nice to deflect her. Engineering spoke up.

"It would take time to activate retired hulls," he said. "Based on Commodore Salim's notes, we might not have that long. How soon was Prince Aritza planning to move?"

"By now, he should have already taken out the first base on his list," Bethany replied with a hard smile, watching all four **flinch** in unison. Like a chorus line kicking. "After repairs, he'll be moving on, but obviously I only have several future rendezvous points and codewords to join back up with his future fleet. Presuming that I'm not immediately returning in *Tucana* to report the failure of this mission."

"His first base?" Engineering asked.

"That's right," Bethany smiled. "A freelance repair cruiser he and Zakhar knew by reputation. It will provide the parts and sundries they need to have *Excalibur* back to peak fighting form, so they can go after their next target."

"And you don't know which one is next?" Intelligence asked.

"I do not," Bethany replied. "Operational security reasons. I'm sure you understand."

Low blow, but they'd brought it on themselves by deciding they could play rough with a *mere lieutenant*.

As Hajna would say, *Oh, buttercup...*

"You have a timeline?" Engineering asked, apparently taking on himself the role of Good Cop.

"Javier expects the war to take several years," she told them. "Assuming that nobody is smart enough to run like hell and retire before he gets to them. Or that the *Concord* and others don't step up with overwhelming force to assist."

"Others?" Command asked, sharp.

"I was sent to talk to you because I used to be one of you," she smiled blandly. *Used to be...* "There are other crew members from other nations."

Not that Javier was sending anyone out, as far as she knew, but they didn't need to know that, either. Especially if it jarred them off high-center.

Four men turned to one another and had a silent conversation with faces. Concern. Confusion. Many other ideas.

Intelligence took the lead.

"We'll need some time to digest the full contents of your various files," he said. "We'd like to invite you to stay aboard the station for a few days."

"With your permission, I'd like to take my crew down to the surface for a quick vacation," she countered. "Not to recruit, but because none of them have ever visited a major *Concord* world before. I'd like to show them some of the better parts, because everybody knows about the brothels. I'd like them to see that we're more than prostitutes and shipyards as a people."

Diplomatic. Mostly. She let her face fall into a neutral helpfulness she'd learned in a library, facing dipshit senior officers. She'd say like these four, but Bethany saw the potential for positive movement on their parts. At least two of them, anyway.

Now, she just had to Bad Cop them into acting, because relying on the angels of their better nature to act would be a study in futility.

Javier had sent her to get the job done.

And she would.

PART V

Ilan had never been a big city guy. Truth be told, he'd been a dumb punk from a small town farm that had listened to stupid dreams of running away and turning his sorry ass into a big, bad pirate.

Fortunately, he'd met Javier along the way. All the others were nice folks. Afia, about the best boss a guy could want, when it came to learning shit.

But Javier. Even more than Zakhar or Djamila or Andreea.

Today, Bethany needed him. She probably didn't understand that, but she was bright and wonderful and sharp and a whole lot of other things. Navarre had sent a Combat Engineer to protect the woman and her mission, same as he'd done a few other places.

When you've got to get down in the mud and wrestle with a squealing pig, everybody's going to get dirty, but only one of you is turning into bacon.

So he let her lead. *Merankorr* was a nice enough place. Everybody knew about the brothels that had been the inspiration for Del's interior decorating. Galaxy-famous, as it were. All of those places were packed into a pretty small circle, on the west edge of Rogerson, the capital city here, mostly adjacent to the civilian starport.

Ilan had actually been amazed that the folks in charge had let them take a shuttle to the ground, but he supposed that at least three of the other tourists wandering around Rogerson with them were spies.

That's how he would have done it, anyway. He kept his head on a swivel and one hand close to a pocket.

Civilian scanners were lovely things, looking for civilian weapons in the hands of civilian miscreants. Fortunately, he was a pirate. And had spent a lot of time ahead of this mission figuring out how he would handle a situation like this.

Small pistol, sacrificing range, power, and battery capacity for an extra layer of insulation that basically required someone to touch the damned thing to see it. Civilian scanners, and all that. Commercial stuff.

Predictable.

It made him feel better, walking around a *Concord* world armed, with Vivian on his left and Armando up ahead asking Bethany questions. Armando was a city boy, born and raised. They were discussing where to have lunch by smell and traffic patterns, which made no sense to Ilan, but he wasn't a gourmand or anything.

Overcast day on the ground. You got weather on planets. He spent so much time on ships that he occasionally forgot, but Adrian had packed warm clothing, so he was snug.

No threat of rain, but certain elements of uncertainty in ways that the engineer in his soul found disconcerting, verging on insulting.

Unpredictable. Too much like Javier.

He grinned and locked on a man stepping around a corner.

Ilan had no idea why, but one hand went into a pocket and gripped the butt of the pistol, withdrawing it so fast you might not realize he was armed, especially as he twisted his shoulders and accidentally bumped Vivian in the process.

That one had seen it, too. He'd gone all Spider, and Ilan remembered the man's boss, back in the really bad days.

Stranger drew a pistol and pointed it at Bethany.

"You're coming with me," he announced in sort of a stage whisper.

Ilan shot him dead center in the chest. Fool should have flashed a badge if he didn't want to be mistaken for a mugger.

Pistol also sacrificed power. And Ilan had tuned it for thump over burn, so dumbass went over backwards with a small scorch mark in his sternum.

Ilan surged forward. Doctor Emma always trained her martial arts with an element of getting right up in someone's face instead of letting them stay at any sort of range. Bump chests and knock someone on his ass, then go down with him, punishing.

So, Ilan did. Vivian had apparently studied the same thing, because he pounced on the pistol after one bounce, and came up shooting a second moron who had drawn. Viv's pistol wasn't tuned. Made a bigger hole.

Ilan grabbed the first fool's wallet from a jacket pocket and bounced up.

"MOVE IT!" he snapped at Armando and Bethany, jarring them out of stasis as Vivian shot at some other berk.

Coming out of the woodwork or something. Ilan rotated aft and nailed a fourth one.

At least they'd sent a small army. That made him feel better.

Nothing more insulting than one mugger taking down four sailors.

"This way!" Viv yelled, turning and racing into a handy alley.

Ilan made sure Bethany was in motion, then bumped Armando into following. Man was smart, but didn't kill people.

That was what he had Ilan and Vivian for.

One last shot, and Ilan took off after them.

PART VI

Vivian had come alert to whatever had spooked Ilan, but he also understood how tightly wired that man was, in spite of his shell of phlegmatism.

Trouble found them faster than Vivian had expected, but not Ilan. Still, he had a pistol. And a lead. And a willingness to claim self-defense when questioned later.

Everybody talks about how dangerous *Merankorr* can be, you see? Even if it was all hokum.

Not from around here, ya know?

He got to the end of this alley. Bethany was on his ass.

"Hotel?" she asked.

"Not yet," Vivian replied. "Escape and Evasion first. Then the authorities. Then the hotel."

She had her messenger bag that went everywhere with her, so the only thing bad guys got at the hotel were wardrobes. He had money stashed to replace things in a pinch.

Bethany paused almost long enough for him to yell at her, then glanced back and nodded.

"This way," she said, turning left and setting off at a jog.

"Ilan, with her," Vivian told the engineer as he went by, then kept a watch back up the alley.

And fired two shots, but those guys ducked back and Vivian used that as a moment to run.

Bethany had a taxi when he caught up with them. Ilan was standing at the door.

"In," Ilan snapped, so Vivian assumed a plan.

Ilan was in on his ass and they were airborne.

Bethany spoke an address Vivian didn't recognize, and they were in motion. Didn't take long and they landed.

"Eleven blocks," Bethany muttered as Armando paid the fare and they were on another sidewalk. "That should clear the cordon and give us space. Are we being tracked?"

"Ask Suvi," Ilan chirped.

"Into the coffee shop," Armando said, walking right by everyone and entering a building. "You sit there. I'll order."

Vivian had a view of the back door. Ilan had the front. Bethany pulled her clamshell and cracked it open.

"No immediate signals detected," Suvi said quietly.

Not the real Suvi, but an invested shard, as she called herself. Whatever that meant.

"Do we know who they were?" Ilan asked. "Not that I care, but it might matter, us getting into a firefight in the middle of town."

"I assume pirate kin," Vivian offered. "We've made enough noise by now that someone has leaked. Should we capture some punks so we can interrogate or track them back?"

"Tempting," Bethany replied. "Wondering if Javier sent us to distract everyone and kick over rocks that cause the *Concord* to start cleaning up their act."

"Probably both," Suvi said. "Someone background me."

Vivian listened as Ilan gave a terse, quiet recount of each step. That man had been sandbagging, obviously. Vivian made a note to add such a weapon to his hidden gear after this, in addition to his lockpicks and related thieving tools hidden, going forward.

"And we're here," Ilan concluded. "Do we call the cops or pretend nothing happened?"

"I suspect that any call to the authorities gets intercepted at a local level and teams triangulate down quickly," Suvi replied. "We're dealing with large organizations with significant reach. Assume that they intended a different outcome here."

"Will they open fire without warning next time?" Ilan asked, glancing around the table.

"Probably on their third try, yes," Bethany replied. "They might try one more kidnapping first. And they might not. We need to go to ground."

"I'm been monitoring local frequencies," Suvi said. "Nothing immediately obvious for trouble. Should I go ahead and book a room somewhere at a close hotel? Lots to pick from and this is a quiet season, so cheap."

"Do that," Bethany replied.

"We back to *Ophiuchi*?" Ilan asked.

It took Vivian a moment to translate that. The team on the ground being hunted by a whole battalion of ground troops while the rest of them had been in orbit, trying to stay alive.

"Javier and Afia, yes," Bethany grinned. "That probably makes Armando Djamila, and Vivian can be Hajna."

"I'm what?" Armando asked as he sat, four mugs of coffee on a tray. "The Dragoon? Are you freaking nuts?"

"Ilan pointed out the situational similarities," Vivian told him, also grinning. "You're the tallest person here."

"I don't think so," Armando replied is a frosty tone, but he was also grinning.

Vivian grabbed a mug and sipped, never losing sight of that back door.

Or line of sight if he had to come up shooting.

"You're booked," Suvi said abruptly, then read a name and address. "Checked in and ready to grab keys on your way through the lobby."

"We'll take five here and let the bad guys settle," Bethany said. "You listen for trouble."

Vivian nodded.

They were surrounded by trouble.
How did they get out?

PART VII

Bethany was the officer. The others were smart, including Suvi, but Zakhar and Javier had put her in charge. Time to earn the big drachmae.

She rose and nodded Ilan to the door, understanding that Vivian had the hallway to the restrooms. Out onto the sidewalk, right and walking. Two blocks down and moving in two groups, with Ilan at her side like a date and the other two men trailing five meters.

Ilan's hand was down by his side, where that pistol wasn't obvious, but he wasn't putting it away.

And they might have all been kidnapped by now if he hadn't been prepared.

Bethany found the need to be prepared.

"I need a weapon," she murmured, leaning in like a girlfriend.

"Next guy I shoot, take his," he muttered back, but he was smiling when he did. "Is Viv a better shot than you?"

"Probably, so let him keep his," she replied. "This is longer term."

"Gotcha. Not seeing any trouble."

"Think we got enough clearance with the taxi," she said.

"Hopefully, they won't track us to the coffee shop fast enough to find the hotel."

"Two kilometers, we should be safe," he nodded. "Nope, spoke too soon. Viv, keep walking. Ahead on the right."

Then Ilan surprised her by turning and taking her hand, walking her right up against the side of a building and hugging her, faces close like they were about to start necking. The wall was cold against her butt and his arms were around her.

In public.

"Yes?" she asked, close enough to breathe on him.

"One of the guys I saw earlier is watching on a corner ahead of us," he said, leaning in to put his mouth on her ear. "Hoping you're the only good description they have, and Vivian is a chameleon anyway."

"So you weren't looking for an excuse to pin me in a corner?" she asked, purring.

He jolted back and turned bright red in the cutest way.

"Sorry," Ilan said, trying to lean back but she gripped him tight, drawing on his warmth and unexpected strength.

"You're not going anywhere, Ilan," she said, drawing him close again. "Not until I say so."

"Ma'am?"

Bethany didn't think she'd ever appreciated his muscles. Certainly never had them pressed against her like this. And he had them.

Hidden under a lot of layers, but didn't that describe Ilan Yu?

Boy was a cipher.

She smiled at him. Thought about it, then went ahead and kissed him on the cheek, feeling him grow awkward in her arms.

Might have to do something about that, too.

There was a squawk in the distance and Ilan broke away faster than she could hold, then turned and started walking, but had her hand in his.

The one without a pistol in it.

"It's okay," Armando was telling the crowd in a loud voice.

"Too much excitement and not enough water. We'll get him back to the hotel and he'll be right as rain."

He turned out to be a stranger, flat on his back until Vivian got him in a fire carry, slung over one shoulder.

Another man with a lot more muscle than he appeared, but Vivian Aafjes was trained to climb the sides of buildings with his bare hands.

Armando moved to the fore, parting the crowd with Vivian and package right behind him. Ilan fell in back a bit, watching so she did the same.

Nobody obvious.

"You three enter from the side and take an elevator up to three," Ilan ordered. "Bethany and I will grab keys and meet you there."

She let herself be drawn into a nicer lobby, across to the woman behind the counter.

"Reservations," Bethany told her. "Durbin and party. The others got held up at the starport and will be along in a few hours."

"ID, ma'am?" the woman asked, then smiled when Bethany flashed it. "You're already set. Here you go."

Four envelopes with plastic cards in them. She pocketed one and Ilan took the other three, leading her to the stairs instead of an elevator, then up.

They met the others and rode the elevator to seven, Vivian and Armando carrying the stranger between them like a semi-coherent drunk, in case someone was watching on a camera.

Into the room, they stretched him on the bed and Vivian tied the man up, stuffing a wad of cloth in his mouth.

"Plug me in," Suvi said from her bag. "Security here feels junior varsity."

Bethany put her on the desk and found a wire, then turned back to find the man on the bed mostly stripped. And with a shiner on his right eye.

"Heya," Ilan was looming over him. "Saw you earlier. You

look like the sort of person that nobody would mind if we chucked you out the window and let you splatter on the street below, so you can talk, or I can figure the quietest way to dispose of your body. I'll give you five minutes to think about it, then you can decide which it will be."

Bethany didn't think she'd ever heard that sort of tone from Ilan, but he'd obviously picked it up from Navarre. That same, ugly growl that snapped off consonants gone all jagged.

Not the worst role model, if things wanted to get out of hand.

"I'm locked in," Suvi said. "Nobody I can detect monitoring, but messages will get out of my reach in a hurry."

"Let that one captain from Intelligence know that we had a problem on the surface," Bethany replied. "Drop him an asynchronous note, then get his message back later, but we're not in a hurry."

"Tell him to look for disturbances in north Rogerson?" Suvi asked.

"That gets his response force close enough," Bethany said.

"Hear that, buddy?" Ilan asked their prisoner. "Gonna turn you over to the spies from fleet. Got any warrants I can claim rewards from?"

Cruel. Not a side of Ilan she'd seen before, but he rose and turned away from the stranger, winking at her and Bethany felt better.

Again, in Javier's pattern. She could work with this.

Bethany focused on the prisoner. Middle-aged male. Skinny, with scars from some childhood diseases, plus malnutrition and other issues an advanced civilization should have eliminated.

Thus, *The Rising Storm* meeting the *Fall of The Concord*. Not a thought that brought her warmth today, as she felt like a soldier trying to reinforce a wall intended to keep barbarians raiders out, knowing she was going to fail.

No matter what she did.

"You can't stop him," she said, matter-of-factly to the stranger. "The Science Officer is going to destroy all of you. My suggestion is that you take whatever retirement you had planned and run. If you get far enough away, he probably won't send his own killers after you."

"Probably," Vivian added. "That's on you."

Ilan handed her a pair of wallets.

"Got these from him and the first guy I shot," he said.

"Suvi?" She turned to the clamshell and opened them up to be scanned.

"Looking," her friend replied. "Pretty sure they are fake, but I don't have access to a police database to compare them."

"Send them on to our friend and let him find the guy," Vivian offered. "That should be pretty quick."

The prisoner made a noise.

"You want to talk, or are you going to yell and make me shoot you?" Ilan asked. "As he said, that's on you."

The man nodded, so Bethany pulled the wad of cloth out of his mouth.

"You can tell them whatever you want," Bethany told him. "But Javier and the ship have already started destroying your bases. I'm just here in case the *Concord* wants to help. Remember, we've got a Great War battleship on our side. And we just destroyed four squadrons at *Drako* at the same time. Think long and hard."

"We're just supposed to find out what you know," he said breathlessly.

"Most of the crew were Jarre Foundation," she said. "Including those two. They know where to find you. And they are going to. You have any value to me at all besides letting your friends know that their time as pirates has ended?"

He clammed up, but she wasn't surprised, so Bethany had him open his mouth to stuff the gag back in.

They could kill some time here, then contact the fleet and start the process of cleaning up Rogerson. And then *Merankorr*.

And then everybody else.

PART VIII

Suvi hadn't been on *Merankorr* before, but she'd done a stupid amount of research preparing for this mission. Maybe almost as much as Ilan, looking at what he'd done, but she was happy about that.

Trouble could have been uglier.

As it was, local comm networks were about in the middle for security. Nothing dangerous, as long as she stayed away from the brothels and the naval base, both of whom had their own serious defenses, possibly for the same sorts of reasons, but she didn't have a body to necessarily understand.

Message send. Captain Marc Harcrow, *Concord Intelligence*. Bethany had gotten his card before they'd left, like he'd known there was going to be trouble.

Message reply.

That was quick. Fellow holding out on us about trouble in paradise?

Bethany had said to keep it detached, so she ignored his request for a video link and updated the previous rundown with pictures and ID scans. Let him start doing some work around here.

She read a quick book series while waiting for human speed to catch up, but he was moving fast enough over there that she figured they had a *Sentience* involved. Probably pretty dumb, but she had a low opinion of most of her cousins these days. Too much exposure to all the ways humans limited them, afraid that they might get out of hand.

And if you left them emotionally crippled, that was your fault.

Still, quick movement.

Where are you? Because she'd obscured the shit out of her backtrail. Like smart girls do when dealing with random strangers.

"Downtown," she replied, letting email bounce almost as fast as voice, so they had a bot running.

Prisoner intact?

"Yes, whenever you want to come get him," she typed, scanning the local police bands but everything had stayed quiet.

We can have a team there in five minutes.

"Bethany," she surfaced. "They are hot to arrest our friend. Do we stay or depart?"

She watched the boss run scenarios in her head.

"Who are you talking to?"

"Our friend from Intelligence," Suvi replied, understanding that they had a pirate in the room. "Man you met on the station."

"Set a timer, then send him these coordinates in five minutes," Bethany said. "Tell him to meet us, alone, at a restaurant you find with good biscuits and gravy, in thirty minutes. Vivian and Armando, you'll be watching from nearby and I'll get you take-out later. Ilan, you're with me. Let's move."

Suvi sent the note and let a clock start ticking as Bethany closed her up and slid her in the bag.

Their buddy here would be arrested shortly, but they'd be gone.

And then the hunt would get serious.

THE BLACK BASTION

PART I

Javier had basically taken charge on the basis of experience. Technically, not even Suvi had as much, in spite of everything, because she'd been a fleet scout in the old days, while he'd been a surveyor for a long time.

Wonders, this was one of those situations where Zakhar actually shut up and let him work, which told Javier just how weird things had gotten.

And it got him off the bridge. Off the ship entirely, as a matter of fact, aboard the small raider/freighter *Flying Maiden*, captured when they took *Eldritch Stele* and the crew was given the opportunity to reform their ways or become his first official victims.

Because he wasn't going to put into a police impound lot to offload prisoners without a lot of paperwork up front.

And pirates can't really complain when someone out-pirates them.

They'd chosen to be put ashore midway to the *Black Bastion*. Smart folks.

Now, he and his ship were on the edge of the system. Watching, with *Excalibur* hiding nearby in some shadows, a laser comm link taking in what *Maiden* was seeing, just in case they needed to bring a big, freaking hammer down.

Today, he was flying. Nice to have to grind the rust off those old skills. Too many years with Suvi, but *Storm Gauntlet* in the middle had kept him sharp.

Javier looked over to Hajna, sitting next to him in the co-pilot/navigator chair.

"You sure we can't bring the dragoon?" he asked.

"Ship's too small," she replied. "And she's too recognizable. Rest of us don't stand out as much, though your beard looks nice. Maybe you should keep it?"

"Too much white in it," he grumbled. "Only doing this because you asked."

She grinned. He absolutely felt old when he looked in the mirror these days. Fifty would be here way too soon for his comfort, and the sides were starting to go solidly gray as well.

Piracy was a game for young people. All the more reason he'd been planning to get out and go much more legitimate, except that certain folks were unable to lose gracefully.

So that bastard was going to have to lose ugly.

Because he was going to lose.

Gun Bunnies were aft, but dressed like crew instead of killers. Sascha and Hajna were in charge of this operation. And had recruited several females from *Excalibur*'s crew, even including the Plamondon sisters, Collette and Simone, who normally worked in the bistro.

Nobody was expecting to have to go that far, but Javier supposed that they'd all been asked to portray prostitutes in order to get close to the target at hand. Adrian and a handful of pretty men had been brought as well, everybody dressed up exotic and alluring.

Maybe he was just getting old, but even when he'd been young, that sort of thing hadn't really appealed to him. Much better finding willing women with brains.

As his friend Jerry had told him in school, "Eventually, you're going to have to roll over and talk to her."

Holly and Fryda had both been smart. He'd been the fuckup

that blew up both of those marriages, being too broken to understand himself or his failings at the time.

Sascha entered from aft.

"We're all ready here," she said, wearing a corset that squished everything up and threatened to overflow, like a dam trying to hold back a monsoon.

"Old man pilot is just waiting on you folks," Javier groused.

"I'll go change," Hajna laughed. "Give me five minutes and jump in. Sascha can distract them while you start docking."

Javier didn't even bother trying to hide the eyeroll. One of these days, they'd get in over their heads, but he'd approved her ideas. ALL OF THEM, no matter how weird or crazy, because he understood that nobody would see this coming.

Might only work once, but only needed to one time, because he had such a perfect combination of circumstances to work with here.

And a willingness to go for someone's throat.

Even when the message was a letter that might as well be addressed *Dear Occupant*.

The ladies switched places. Sascha had curves, and was showing them off. Poor fools expecting a dumb babe were doomed.

And he was counting on that.

"You ready?" she asked after a few minutes.

"Yeah, I suppose so," he replied, flipping a switch. "Suvi, we're jumping."

And he was gone.

PART II

Hajna was a tall, lanky blonde, so she'd gone for leggings and a tutu that made her look like an escaped ballerina. Took her back to her youth, when she'd wanted to be a dancer.

Shit had gotten way weird along the way, but every now and again things bubbled up.

A cream-colored swan, considering the knife and pocket-pistol hidden among her feathers and frills. Head as a bit of cloth running up her right side and down her arm to the elbow, with eyes watching. Right out of one of the darker Grimm Brothers fairy tales. Before later generations cleaned them up and made them entertainment for children.

Instead of warnings.

Situational similarities today made her smile.

She entered the bridge and smiled at the camera, catching the man on the screen stuttering as his brain took her in.

Apparently, liked them skinny, because his tongue was suddenly wagging in ways it hadn't when staring at Sascha.

But it took all kinds.

"So, make up your mind," Javier groused sullenly. "Makes me no difference. We got hired to come here and make the service staff available. If you want sloppy fifths, just say the word and I'll cut this line and call the *Black Bastion* instead."

Hajna really liked the way he just sort of drawled that out, like a man delivering a load of frozen chickens instead of the pilot of a flying brothel. All her idea, refined with the assistance of several women aboard and Adrian, but it took actors to pull off.

Shakespeare, in reverse drag, if you will.

Heh.

Man on the screen didn't appear to remember Javier existed, eyes screwed sideways to stare at her on the screen. Hajna decided to show off and did a quick pirouette for him, showing off the swan bits and the legs.

Man nearly swallowed his teeth.

"Here would be great," he stammered. "She's on the menu?"

Hajna made a point to lean over Javier's shoulder, giving the camera a good view of her cleavage. Not nearly as much as Sascha, but that guy didn't seem to mind.

"Absolutely," Hajna told him, licking her lips and inwardly giggling at the effect.

Right up there with whomping him upside the head with a three-days-rotting sand shark.

"Transmitting docking procedures and passwords now," the man said, still breathless with anticipation.

Hajna almost felt sorry for him, given what was about to happen.

Almost.

And maybe she could do a nice burlesque for the prisoners after this was all done. Man was likely to be utterly boring in bed. Javier was a rare gem and she'd trained up a few other folks to her standards.

Not quite as relentlessly as the Dragoon approached combat, but not necessarily far short of that, either.

Girl's got to get her needs taken care of.

"Message pack received," Javier said. "We'll start sailing in now. Should dock in about forty-five minutes, then we'll bring out all the girls and boys for a quick parade. You start figuring out how to rotate your watch schedules so that nobody is left out, okay?"

"Yes."

Javier cut the line and shook his head.

"Only likely to work once," he muttered.

Sascha laughed.

"Shouldn't even work once," she countered. "But not everybody treats naval discipline as a goal instead of a penalty."

"I'm going to sail," Javier looked at them both. "You two go get ready to unleash the hounds of hell."

Hajna went ahead and kissed him on the cheek before she put on her game face.

This was going to be so much fun.

PART III

Collette was the older sister by a year. The more mature. The more stubborn, she supposed. Or at least less the artist. Simone had always wanted to be the free spirit. The one who did art of some kind in her off hours from Chay's bistro.

Collette presumed that she was simply too severe. Too linear. Too something. Still, Hajna had asked, and given a perfectly understandable reason why a woman like Collette would enjoy such an act.

Too many customers who had occasionally patted her bottom in the old days, when there was little she could do to reprimand them. It had stopped entirely once they had boarded Suvi, because anyone making that mistake discovered the Dragoon's opinion. Firmly.

Still, Collette had had years of pent up *friction* she suddenly could tap. It made her feel feral, in ways that she simply couldn't ever remember.

Deadly. *Le femme fatale*, literally.

She had to remind herself that she would have to turn if off again later, but for now...

Collette wore a long, belted, A-line dress in burgundy. It fit her frame, and accentuated what few curves she had. Black hair up in a coil. Dark eyes emphasized with an Egyptian turn to her makeup, turning them almost into points.

An exotic beauty, but she supposed that the crew of a watch ship wouldn't be that discriminating. Not if they had to stay over here for long stretches of time, with only occasional leave to the station itself.

And even then, probably far fewer working girls than this many men should be confronted with. It would leave a gender imbalance that made the men a touch desperate. And the women probably exceptionally severe, if not superior.

She smiled as the hatch opened, then followed Sascha through and aboard the new ship, finding herself in a cargo bay currently only half full, and most of that, if she was reading the crate labels correctly walking by, appeared to be torpedoes stacked deck to deck.

A great many of them, which answered one of the planning questions she had heard. Could they easily reload this warship later?

Yes.

Sascha formed them into a loose crescent, points turned forward to somewhat encircle a group of four men. The oldest only had eyes for Hajna, so that would be the pirate captain, if Collette understood the briefing. Three other senior officers, a bit overwhelmed, if you will.

Children in a candy store with a ten-drachma bill from grandmother.

She smiled, and one man who gave off vibes of an engineer smiled back at her. Warm enough. A customer who was less likely to be a problem, perhaps. Unlikely to take *liberties*.

Not that the situation would get that far.

"Obviously, it's not that we don't trust your cleaning regime," Sascha was saying. "What we have on *Flying Maiden* is so much nicer, with everyone assigned their own cabin. Have you sorted out who will be first from your roster?"

"Yes," a third man said, stepping out of the little pack and handing Sascha a tablet. "Got the full crew compliment there, broken down and sorted into watches and liberty over the next eighteen hours."

"Excellent," Sascha replied, shining her smile at the man. "This will make it so much easier. And now, gentlemen, I presume that the four of you intended to grab an early-mover advantage, if you catch my drift?"

Crude laughter, but Collette was not surprised. She'd known too many pirate types, living back in Barrowclough. *Excalibur* had been such a revelation, the ability to work in a proper restaurant and smile.

She'd almost forgotten how, but it had come back.

She smiled at her engineer as he stepped closer.

"Gael Irani," he introduced himself, taking a moment to study her from crown to heel in a long, lascivious motion.

"Collette," she replied, then stepped back and curtsied for reasons she couldn't have identified, save that it set them on a more formal level than a John and a Night-girl.

She took his hand and gave it a squeeze, sad that he had fallen for such a ruse as this, but at least he would survive what was coming.

Others might not be so lucky.

Sascha had taken charge. Two other men had stepped up and picked partners, including the captain who was all agog at Hajna and another holding hands with Adrian.

She did not understand homosexual inclinations as anything but a theoretical stance, but knew that others were far more open-minded. One's original culture lent a great deal of severity to one's life.

The fourth man stepped sideways to stand near Sascha.

"How soon should we start sending folks?" he asked her.

"Give us about twenty minutes to array ourselves in the aft lounge," she replied. "Then I presume you'll have someone here checking names off a list and sending them over, so the first group of ten, then we'll go on an as-completed basis, swapping a new crew member for each one that returns."

"Excellent," he said. "See you in a few hours, after I've gotten things organized at this end. I drew the short straw today."

He was smiling.

"We'll save you something special," Sascha said, then Collette drew her prey through the airlock and aboard the new ship.

The airlock slid shut and Sascha looked around. All of the dance troupe, as she'd called, along with all of the Gun Bunnies, currently acting as bouncers.

"Iqbal, you're on," Sascha said simply.

Collette nodded to herself and dropped Gael's hand, stepping another stride away from him as Tom suddenly shot the man in the chest with a stun pistol, then caught him as he collapsed.

The other two were down as well.

"Okay, folks the clock has started," Hajna announced. "Thank you for your assistance. From here, it will be combat operations."

Collette didn't know enough about weapons to join in, but she understood what was coming. And appreciated that Hajna and Sascha could have used lethal means. But Javier wanted everyone to have one chance to reform themselves.

Or, as the Dragoon had followed up, to carry the infection of fear to the rest of the galaxy.

Having been with her friends at *Drako*, uncertain that she would survive, or even not be immediately executed if taken prisoner by the pirates, Collette found no sympathy for the pirates.

None whatsoever.

Javier had cleaned up the crew of *Excalibur*, with the help of this friends.

Now, they were about to extend that courtesy to the rest of the galaxy.

PART IV

Hajna took a deep breath and locked all of her emotions down. It was one thing to be a playful flirt and hit on a guy with suggestions of all manner of carnal explorations, but honestly, she already had a whole crew of men and women on *Excalibur* who knew where she liked to be touched. And how.

Strangers might be useful for a hint of exotic occasionally, but she'd have to send all these punks to visit a doctor and then have them sheep-dipped for whatever crap they'd picked up along the way, before she ever touched one.

Easy way to catch things that don't even have names yet, they had mutated so recently.

She did keep the swan costume, though. Something about it just took her back to Grimm. The old Grimm. The deadly stuff that predated industrial civilization, when there were dark things living in the forests, and they might be coming for you.

Like today.

Three of the target ship's officers had been taken out up front, meaning that the remaining crew would be that much less likely to react quickly or easily to what was coming. The Dragoon would have been nice to have around, but honestly, Hajna had been expecting to have more troubles getting to this point.

Maybe even situations involving nudity and touching, though everyone had supposedly emotionally prepared themselves for that level of verisimilitude going in. Sometimes, the gods smiled upon you.

For now, it was her and her partner, plus six Gun Bunnies, with Javier available in a pinch.

"What's the crew count?" she turned to Sascha.

"Four officers, three taken out," the chick grinned. "About a dozen folks with engineering qualifications, and about the same number as general crew. Light for a ship this size, but that makes senses if they're just archers atop a wall, defending the city."

"Agreed," Hajna said. "Question is, how hard will it be to take the bridge?"

"We'll need a scout to take out whatever bosun is on the other side of the airlock in fifteen minutes," Sascha countered. "From there, we can probably disable enough systems to get where we need to go."

"I'll go," Collette Plamondon said.

"Didn't you just take their Chief Engineer back to your cabin?" Sascha asked.

"Older man," Collette shrugged, then grinned. "Didn't last long and I left him asleep in the bunk, but this woman has needs and is hunting for someone who can satisfy them."

Her smile had a cruel edge, but that fit Hajna's mood. Hajna sized up the woman she didn't think she'd ever seen as a killer before today.

"You armed?" she asked, watching Collette draw a palm pistol and hold it professionally. "Okay, your job is to cross into the enemy stronghold and take out the first person keeping watch over there, so the rest of us can flood aboard and take out their bridge. From there, we can control the rest of the vessel in the time needed. You sure you're okay with this?"

"Honestly?" Collette countered. "Maybe looking forward to it a bit more than is good for me, but not enough to get me into trouble."

Hajna processed that and shrugged herself.

"Go," she ordered. "We're trailing with the full team, so don't hesitate to engage someone in talk or aim a weapon at them as needed. We'll cover you."

Collette drew a breath and moved, sliding through the mob like a waitress in tight quarters, without spilling a glass. She reached the airlock, paused, then opened it.

PART V

Collette wanted to be aghast at herself, but found that she was focused instead. Thrilled, even.

Deadly.

She opened the airlock and walked through, expecting to find someone waiting, but that chamber was empty.

She kept going. Sascha had mentioned the bridge to the left, so she exited into the main corridor and turned that way, noting that everything was empty. Men taking showers and getting dressed up for a night on the town?

Ghost town here. Bizarre, considering the circumstances, but she looked on it as a gift horse and walked.

No, *sashayed*. Playing a character. A woman with drastically unmet needs, looking for a man who could take her to the heights she *demanded*.

Collette paused in her mind and wondered where those heights might be. She'd had a few affairs within the crew, but nothing drastic. Nothing interesting.

Nothing fulfilling or life altering.

Presumably, she was doing something wrong, and had been heads down for so long that she had forgotten to look up?

When had she forgotten how to look up?

What a terrible discovery to make on a day like this with a pistol in one hand.

Still, it opened her up to new avenues to explore, in a dress that made her feel so utterly sexy that she wondered if an impostor had stepped in and replaced her.

That would never do.

Collette reached the end of the corridor and realized that the hatch in front of her was the bridge. She glanced back and saw Sascha peeking around a corner behind her, but nobody was stopping her, so she simply pushed the button and the hatch opened.

She slipped a hand into her pocket and strode onto the ship's bridge like a woman on a mission. A horny mission. A need. A *craving*.

Two men kept watch. Both looked up at her in surprise.

"Ma'am?" the one in the captain's chair asked. He'd been the fourth left behind when Sascha and Hajna had managed to take out the other three in one fell swoop.

"Your captain couldn't satisfy me," she said boldly, walking forward and running her spare hand up her side like a woman with needs. "I had to find someone better. Maybe both of you at once. Could you do that for me?"

They had turned away from their consoles to study her. In her mind, Collette could almost hear that dreadful backbeat music that always seemed to be playing in pornographic videos. The bad ones, anyway.

Still, she rocked her hips bath and forth, swaying to the music in her mind.

The officer half-rose, surprised, so the crewman did as well, like they were honestly going to take her, right here on the deck.

Not a fantasy she'd ever indulged in. And certainly not with strangers like this.

But it got them away from the ship's controls.

Collette drew her pistol and pointed it at them.

"Don't do anything that makes me shoot you dead," she announced as the hatch opened and Sascha and Hajna were suddenly bracketing her, also armed.

It was a day for new adventures, it seemed.

Who was this new woman having them?

PART VI

Hajna managed to pick her jaw up off the deck, then went ahead and dropped both men with single shots. Like the others, out for about a half hour. Long enough for her needs.

And Collette Plamondon had surprised the shit out of her, though looking over, Sascha wasn't handling this weirdness any better.

"I'll guard the hatch," Collette smiled. "You do your thing."

Yeah. Right. Killer waitress.

Hajna jumped into the main station and started typing, realizing that Collette had distracted those two so badly that they hadn't even locked anything.

"I own the ship," she said, then started clicking various overrides.

Every pirate captain lived in personal terror of a mutiny. No ship she'd ever been aboard in the business didn't have those sorts of extra controls in place, to let the captain lock his crew up if he had to.

She killed access at every frame, then locked tight every cabin and bathroom showing a body in it.

"Sascha, take the boys and clear engineering," she said. "The Gun Moll and I will watch up here."

"On it," and Sascha charged out.

She watched Collette disarm both men and drag them into a corner, stronger than the woman looked. Aft, Sascha and the Gun Bunnies swept into the big space around the generators and engines, firing at everything that moved.

Nothing was moving ten seconds later. Professionals, and they'd all been present at *Ophiuchi*, with a lot of leftover rage at what they'd had to go through to escape.

Training exercise that had been a little too visceral, thank you.

"*Flying Maiden*, this is *Æthelred*," she said a few minutes later, as Iqbal and the crew swept up the last individuals. "How are things over there?"

"Dull," Javier replied. "You?"

"I appear to be in charge," she offered. "A bit ahead of schedule and there aren't any check-ins scheduled in the log for more than an hour. Could you ask Suvi to join us?"

"Stand by," Javier replied. "Message sent. Got everything you need?"

"And then some," she laughed. "Proceeding on original mission."

"Lovely," he said, sounding a whole lot more like Navarre as he did. "I'm set at this end, so you two ladies tell me when you need me to move."

"Understood," Hajna replied.

She cut the line and started plotting a jump. The *Black Bastion* itself was orbiting a planet pretty far out, with *Æthelred* was far enough out that she could Jump without significant gravitational curvature to overcome. More important for now was lining up everyone else around.

Two other ships were currently docked to the station itself. *Western Forge* and *Anger Management*. Both roughly the same size as *Æthelred*, but those two were pirate frigates. Heavy on ionization weapons, but neither at any sort of alert level.

If anything, complaining that *Æthelred* had gotten first crack at a brothel ship and they weren't in line until probably after

Black Bastion's command crew had their turn. Possibly days, depending.

Of course, things were going to happen much sooner than that, but she didn't need to tell them.

She merely had to sit back and wait for Suvi to arrive.

PART VII

Suvi got Javier's updated packet, heavily encrypted and sent on a tight-beam laser without a lot of width for someone else to read.

He didn't want them to even see that a message had been sent, let alone to whom.

Or where.

"Zakhar, I have clearance from Javier and Hajna," she announced, checking that the captain, Piet, and Mary-Elizabeth were all ready.

Wired and excited, honestly, but they'd all been living under Damocles's Sword at *Drako*.

"As you bear, Suvi," Zakhar replied.

She smiled and shifted to combat mode. In a warship. At speeds that humans could calculate, but never emulate.

FAST.

She jumped. From darkness to daylight, fixed in place at both ends, with zero deflection. And she'd gotten a LOT better at gravity calcs, too.

Parking a big truck in a small space sorts of expertise.

Excalibur appeared like the Ghost of Christmas Future, broadside to The *Black Bastion* where she could line up all of her Ion cannons.

And boom. Or maybe ZAP! was more appropriate. Nobody had shields up, so she cut loose with everything she had, pounding the snot out of the station primarily, but saving a few guns for *Anger Management* and *Western Forge* as they sat nuzzled against the bigger ship.

Pirates. The *Black Bastion* was a known pirate town. Really a big freighter than moved around from time to time, one step ahead of whatever law or vengeance might be coming for them.

Like today.

The hull that had turned into *Flying Maiden* had held the coordinates. Lucky for Javier. Unlucky for her new friends o'er yonder.

Behind her, Suvi heard the sounds of Hajna joining the party. Or rather, her sensors detected a sequenced mass launch of torpedoes from *Æthelred* and translated that, since nobody could hear you laughing in space.

And she was. Laughing. Maybe a touch maniacal, but a girl's gotta keep things in perspective. Especially with punks like this.

Ninety-six missiles launched in a least-window zone. Not quite machinegun fire, but damnably close, because Hajna had launched from one end and the middle at the same time, so each torpedo came as a matched pair. Forty-eight pairs, all coming fast because the distance was short and Suvi had already ionized the shit out of the station that was their target.

And she come in specifically low enough that none of those warheads were locked on her, though Suvi still made it a point to use her thrusters and engines to push her further down and away, as well as keeping a couple of pulsars ready to defend on that flank if something had gone wrong.

Javier was already gone. *Æthelred* vanished a moment later, but Suvi had tactical command of the situation. And Zakhar had had her reading naval theory far deeper than she'd ever had any interest in.

Useful today, as she could see what she was doing and compare it to what they tried to do to stop her. Both men had warned her that she'd get only one for free, so she was scanning everything and everyone for as much data as she could get.

And the ionization hadn't worn off by the time the first salvo of torpedoes began impacting on *Black Bastion*'s hull.

She stayed put rather than jump, pouring fire into all three hulls and making it a point of honor. They could always hit escape pods and make it to the planetary surface alive. Whether anyone arrested them at that point was beyond her control.

Suvi's war had started now.

And she intended to make it ugly before she was done.

Like Afia, she owed a few people.

P VIII

Javier stood in the cargo bay of *Æthelred* and scanned boxes. A whole bunch of them, all packed with torpedoes ready to be uncrated and loaded into tubes. Suvi hadn't used any of hers on this mission, after reloading from *Eldritch Stele*'s stores. *Æthelred* could refill as well. With boxes left over.

Afia stood beside him, fulminating on a personal frequency he didn't figure anyone else could smell, but he knew her too well. Others had simply tagged along on the nickel tour, but he ignored them.

"We going back to finish them off?" Afia asked, turning and looking up at him like the Pixie Kodiak she was.

"Got no reason," Javier shrugged. "Stole *Æthelred*. Suvi indicates that *Black Bastion* is for the wrecker's yard, because Hajna tin-can-stomped them pretty hard. The two ships that had docked both got raked hard enough to spend half a year in a repair facility. Pity someone stole *Eldritch Stele* along the way, you know?"

"Destroying all their support bases?" Afia suddenly grinned.

"Pirates require middlemen," he nodded. "If those folks get out of the business, you have a lot harder time surviving. Sure, the clans have bases as well, but they're about to start spending a great deal more money on defenses than they used to. Especially since nobody knows where I'll hit next. That's expensive. Even worse than hiring fleets like our buddy did, before they lost most of those ships. Not like I'm playing nice here."

"We targeting Walvisbaai after this?" she pursued.

"We're disappearing back into the darkness," he countered. "After dropping all our new friends somewhere, once Hajna puts the fear of death itself in them. Panic is infectious, so I'd like to let them stew in it while we plot our next steps."

She nodded and fell silent. He waved her into motion and they ended up on the bridge, where Piet was supervising, Zakhar presumably unwilling to give up his God-Throne on *Excalibur*.

Man was like that.

Small crew had taken *Æthelred*. Him and Afia, handling technical chores because there were other folks who could drive *Flying Maiden* around.

"Javier, are we likely to keep the *Maiden*?" Piet asked as they joined him.

"Dunno," Javier replied. "Don't figure a brothel gambit will work a second time, since we left behind survivors who can talk. And no, I don't feel like exterminating every single person on those four ships to cover my tracks."

Piet grinned. Man was a fantastic composer, but not the sort to raise the red flag and take no prisoners. An intellectual pirate, which honestly described too many of them too well.

Hopefully, it wouldn't bite them the ass later, but Javier had folks who could just as easily go junkyard dog, and it was harder to play smart than mean.

Lots of mean pirates out there. Superstitious lot.

The idea stopped him so dead that Afia walked right into his hip and bounced off, but she was a small woman and he was in better shape today than he'd been when he graduated the academy.

She circled. Piet was watching. Couple of crew folks heads down on screens ignoring him like they were supposed to.

"And?" she asked, obviously realizing he'd had an epiphany.

Or gas. Hard to distinguish.

"Superstition," he muttered. "Thinking about pirates and how they tend to be hardass punks, but not intellectuals."

"And?" she repeated, waving him to get to the point, but also smart enough to know that he'd discover the words as they came out of his mouth.

Some days were like that.

He turned to Piet.

"What have we got for weapons beyond the tubes?" he asked bluntly.

Piet, smart boy that he was, paused and brought up a screen and read it before answering.

"One ten centimeter pulse cannon, offset starboard forward to an ion cannon port, plus two more ion cannons aft on the corners," he said, reading it. "Weird arrangement."

"I presume they pulled three original pulse cannons and replaced them, but kept the other one," Afia said. "I've inspected the fittings and the turrets and that's my read."

Javier nodded, still finding more evil words.

It was like he'd spent years thinking about how he'd do this. Maybe since the day he came out of jump, on that infamous day at *Campeche Sector, System Number Seven*, even today just a nameless jumble of alphanumerics.

The first time Djamila had shot him. And the first time she'd given him a concussion.

Lot of years. Lot of light-years, too.

"*Storm Gauntlet*," he said simply. "An old, Osiris-class, *Concord* Strike Corvette. I trained in *Bannockburn* when I was a wee lad. Nobody but Jarre should have a solid scan on *Storm Gauntlet*, right?"

He was focused on Piet, who had been Zakhar's Executive Officer for years, a man happy in a role.

"I'm sure there are a few folks that might be able to pull something out of a database, but not many," Piet replied. "Not like pirate ships keep old records like that. You're probably safe assuming that folks know the name and scale, and not much more."

He didn't ask why, but it was there in his eyes.

"And they know that it was destroyed after *Svalbard*," Javier continued. "We were even shits about it and claimed various bounties from the *Concord* and others for the hull, because we were parting it out anyway and it wasn't worth trying to repair."

"With you so far," Piet said, but he'd gone deadly quiet and still, like he did when things got weird.

And buddy, this qualified.

"Something Suvi said about the engagement with *Black Bastion*," Javier said, feeling his face want to crack from the evil smile breaking out. "She called herself the *Ghost of Christmas Future* when she dropped on them, showing them what the galaxy was going to be like if they didn't reform their ways."

"*Storm Gauntlet* as Ghost of Christmas Past?" Piet asked, surprising Javier for a moment, but he supposed they were back to being intellectual pirates. "That make me Marley?"

"It might," Javier replied.

"Talk to me," Afia butted in. "Missing something."

"Story about how three ghosts visited this rich dude on Christmas eve," he told her. "Part of an old religion from Earth that still has a few adherents, but more importantly created a metric shit-ton of culture we've inherited today. Anyway, morality tale. What was the past like? What is your present? What will tomorrow be if you don't clean up your act? That sort of thing."

"And you've got the ghost of the past in *Æthelred*?" she smiled, seeing where he was going.

"How hard would it be to spoof someone?" he asked her.

"If you only want to be seen from a distance, I could do the work in a couple of hours," she replied. "If you intend to get close, you'll need some fake hull panels welded on here and there. Plus, this ship's too big, but I suppose a Strike Corvette was at the top of that size category herself, and so not much smaller than this. Is it worth it?"

"Shit, I don't know," Javier shrugged. "When we catch up with Zakhar and the others, we'll pull all the big players into a single room and sort it out. We've got a First-Rate Galleon, an Arsenal Frigate, a mobile repair yard, and small freighter that nobody really knows if we change the name we broadcast. How stupid could we get?"

He did like the way she smiled at that. Like it was a challenge she was willing to accept.

How superstitious were these pirate punks likely to be, after they'd had some time to stew in their juices?

And how did he take advantage of that?

RUNNERS

PART I

Bethany sat on the inside of the restaurant booth after a moment of reflection. Normally, her control-freak nature would have her on the outer portion, but Ilan was intent on guarding her. And doing a pretty damned good job of it.

Menus promised a heavy breakfast, served all day, and she'd had a hankering for biscuits and gravy like they made it on a farm. White dough scooped and dropped onto a baking sheet. Bacon grease, flour, milk, and whatever meat was leftover in the pan after frying, stirred until it turned into a creamy, white mess that you ladled over everything.

Eggs and potatoes under there somewhere, but she was here for a taste of her childhood.

Captain Harcrow walked in as she studied the pictures of possible breakfasts. He looked around, then made a beeline to their table. Vivian had already sent her a quick note he was coming, so she smiled and sipped some adulterated coffee. Ilan was wound tighter than a watch spring, but she didn't begrudge him that.

Man saw himself fulfilling a higher destiny. And deadly serious about it.

Harcrow slid in and flipped a mug.

"Is this place any good?" he asked as a waitress began walking towards them with a globe of coffee in one hand.

"My contacts rated it the highest in walking distance," Bethany replied without mentioning who she was talking to.

Suvi had done the research. And knew how to do it well.

Harcrow nodded and got coffee, then they were alone with menus.

"I've sent Commander Ioannidi to pick up our friend," he said obliquely. "She's been a fantastic godsend, since she knows you folks so well and has been cleared for most of what is going on."

Bethany let that one slide unremarked. She liked Pana, but had expected the woman to vanish entirely once she got them here. Nice to see they recognized how smart that woman was.

"Your new friend at the hotel is not who is seems," Harcrow said, only to be interrupted by Ilan's hard, quiet bark of laughter.

"None of us are," was all Ilan said, but Bethany felt the hidden layers.

She might be the only one involved that wasn't hiding behind a dozen masks, though she wasn't sure what that said about her.

Or how smart that might be.

Harcrow studied Ilan, as if committing his face to memory, but Ilan had assured her that he had no warrants from the *Concord*.

At least at the time they had set out. Who knew where they were today?

"Do you know how they found you?" Harcrow asked.

"Your organization leaked," Ilan replied darkly, so Bethany stayed silent and watched. "I spotted a target coming around a corner armed and shot him. Then shot several more as we blasted our way of the ambush. Got clear because Bethany's that smart. Circled back later and recognized our friend, so we took him down and made sure we had everything we needed before giving him to you."

Precise. Succinct. Evasive in the right spots. Spot-on.

She smiled when Harcrow glanced over at her.

"My people are putting a lot of resources into unraveling things," Harcrow offered.

"Good, you need to clean shit up around here before Javier has to," Ilan replied. "Doubt that we'd need to stage an assault on anyone in *Merankorr*, but might have to send ninjas after some asshole at some point. Like they're likely to do to us."

"I feel like I'm coming into this in the middle," Harcrow said.

Ilan glanced over for her to speak.

"That's because you are," she said. "We've been years getting here, but your organization either hasn't cared or is riddled with spies itself, because someone has to be feeding information to the clans."

"And you expect us to drop everything now and do something about that?" he asked sharply.

"You've been given the opportunity to do it gracefully," Bethany told him, finally understanding one of those chats she and Javier had had before she left. The need to play rough eventually. Like Navarre did. "At some point, Javier will no longer assume you're willing and able to do it, so he will."

She was aghast at herself for threatening a superior officer. However, that wasn't really their relative positions. She was a civilian that had been put ashore years ago, the victim of budget cuts and changing priorities.

Still *Concord*. Still a *Bryce* graduate.

No longer *one of them*.

And not coming back later, save to perhaps visit when she was an old woman. Possibly bringing unknown future kids with her to show them where she'd come from.

Harcrow's look was sour. The waitress broke things up by taking orders and the bad energy flowed away when she did.

The three of them stared at one another in silence.

"How good is he?" Harcrow finally asked. "This Science Officer so many people refer to by that name."

"He's beaten Slavkov four times so far, buddy," Ilan growled quietly. "Any of your people manage it once?"

Harcrow rocked back like Ilan had slapped him with an open palm. Bethany fought to keep her grin inside.

"He's eminently capable, Captain," she told the man. "And has a top-notch team who are all entirely willing to go to the wall on this one, because most of them have been there, uncertain if they would survive when Valko Slavkov's minions have come for them. I'm a much more recent addition, as you know, but Ilan here met Javier on the first day he joined the crew."

Harcrow studied Ilan again. Ilan scowled back, tough and silent when a lot of men might have made a threat, a joke, or some comment.

Ilan didn't need to, because he was that deadly certain about himself. She wondered why she'd never noticed it before, but she also knew the guy liked running quiet and competent, which described so many of her crewmates when she stopped and thought about it.

"You are utterly certain he can pull it off?" Harcrow asked Ilan, then jolted when Ilan smiled broadly.

"Only question is how many other fools make the mistake of doubting the Science Officer," Ilan replied simply. "And how many of them survive it afterwards."

Bethany nodded.

That just about summed up her mission, excepting only the part of how many people she was likely to have to kill herself before it was all done.

She was a librarian by training, but still a *Concord* officer, and would not shy away from such things.

Javier demanded it.

PART II

Ilan still hadn't figured it out, but assumed he'd done something right. He'd been expecting to crash with Vivian and Armando, but the boss had put him in with her after they'd finished with the Captain, checked everything out of their first hotel, ignored the second one, and moved to a third. Two rooms, two queen sized beds in each. Bethany in one. Him with Viv and Armando in the other.

Hadn't worked out that way.

Ilan supposed that, while the others were all willing to shoot people, he'd shown the most willingness to take down random strangers on the street.

As Javier had mentioned when they were organizing, *better him than you.*

Rude way of putting it, but Ilan didn't doubt the man's logic. Not at this point. They'd only been on the damned planetary surface for a day and a half at this point, with all the adventures first thing this morning, leading to the long afternoon of shell games.

He made sure that the hatch was locked and the bolt set. Good enough to hold for him to draw and fire if someone tried to break it in.

He posted his butt in the chair by the inside wall, where a porthole looked out over a courtyard. It didn't open. And the curtains were closed.

As safe as he could arrange it.

Boss was on the bed, typing with Suvi. She looked up, probably feeling his eyes on her. She was like that.

"Now what?" he asked.

"We're hiding while folks in authority start arresting people," she replied. "I think you convinced Harcrow better than I did."

He shrugged but didn't argue with her. His job was Combat Engineer, and that was a peculiar set of skills the Dragoon demanded. An ability to talk without fluff was among them, particularly when you needed to relay critical information with a minimum of bullshit.

"And tomorrow?" he asked, skipping over the odd bits in the middle. "Do we trust random sailors that they might let us recruit, knowing that their organization must be riddled? Or do we ask for ships in service that can be ordered to treat Zakhar like an Admiral or something?"

She paused, eyes narrowing like she was scanning him with something.

"Would the clans be able to insert spies that easily?" she asked.

"Who, exactly, would you trust around here?" he countered sharply. "Commander Ioannidi, probably. Captain Harcrow, maybe. Random punks off the street seeing a recruiting poster? Way too easy to let that berk slip an assassin in. Only takes one, especially if we have to either thin down officers to handle multiple ships or trust officers that we might recruit. Honestly, I'd rather have the cops at that point. Or a fleet cruiser that knows Suvi can open him like a can of soup if he misbehaves."

"Are we on a fool's errand?" Bethany asked.

Ilan started to say something, then caught himself. Javier always played his games on a lot of levels. Here, was he forcing the *Concord* to confront shit? That felt right.

A thought struck him.

"Suvi, where does Slavkov actually live?" Ilan asked, knowing she'd be listening from her clamshell.

"He doesn't have a permanent abode," she replied. "Ship's databases show at least nine planets with major palaces he's known to own. Then several yachts that might be medium-sized warships if you scratched off the gilding and looked underneath. Someone stole his land leviathan and blew it up several years ago, though."

Ilan grinned. That had been an interesting adventure. Might have ended things, but obviously Zakhar and Javier had shown too much mercy to Walvisbaai. And the others.

Let them slip into the wilderness and come back for more.

"What are you thinking, Ilan?" Bethany asked.

"Folks came after us quick," he replied. "Like, almost as fast as we got here to *Merankorr*. How soon until Slavkov decides to flood in a lot of trouble, coming after us specifically?"

"Is being on the ground a mistake?" she asked, but without any heat. A woman seeking data to turn into information.

"Not if it draws all the bad guys into the daylight," Ilan told her. Them. "Not sure we shouldn't disappear for a while though, having delivered our message. Maybe we sail our asses off and leave Captain Harcrow with a few meeting points scheduled where he could find us later if they decided to bring a fleet. Feels like I'm sitting on a bullseye here and I'd rather not, but I understand the need."

She nodded, so she felt it, too. Trouble brewing, like a pressure gauge warning you of a slow leak somewhere you hadn't heard.

Her comm chirped and interrupted, but Ilan wasn't sure he had much left to say at this point. He'd said his piece. She'd listened.

He went back to watching the hatch.

PART III

Bethany answered the comm, checking the inbound identifier.

"Commander Ioannidi?" she asked, a bit surprised.

"Harcrow wants me to take you into protective custody," Pana replied without preamble. "We've discovered a few disconcerting surprises today, over and above everything you prepped me to handle. Can't say I'm entirely surprised, but I am willing to admit that I was wrong in my original assessment and you were right."

Bethany grinned, happy that the device was audio only. There had been a few moments on the voyage here that had gotten close to turning into screaming arguments, though without ever crossing over. And she'd been right about them, though Bethany had been amazed how quickly trouble had moved.

How badly did those people fear the Science Officer?

More than even Javier had suggested to her.

"Ilan was just suggesting that any recruiting we might want to do on the surface of *Merankorr* might be ultimately tainted," she offered, mostly as bait.

"He is a smart man," Pana said evasively. "Not something I wish to discuss over an open line. Can we pick you up and get you to safety?"

"How bad is it?" Bethany asked.

"I have a security team, in a drop shuttle overhead, in full boarding armor," Pana said simply. "On thirty seconds drop alert."

Well, shit. That was pretty bad.

Bethany looked around. Nobody had unpacked. Mostly a couple days of clothing and sundries, plus her messenger bag with Suvi.

Ilan might have been carved in golden marble, a tall, skinny Asian ethnotype with straight, black hair and dark eyes.

Deadly eyes, ignoring her and locked on the door with his pistol in hand pointed.

"Three hotels in one day?" Bethany asked, mostly to see what Pana said.

"We can comp you under certain emergency statutes," Pana replied. "I think this qualifies."

Bethany paused and muted the line.

"Suvi, she can't hear us," Bethany said. "What are you hearing out there."

"Nothing, which is probably a bad sign, given all the gossip that should be," Suvi replied. "News reporters should be speculating about firefights or something. Someone with a lot of pull has quashed it all."

"We trust Commander Ioannidi?" Ilan asked.

That was the hinge, upon which everything else rotated. Pana had come with them from *Purton*, but Bethany understood that the organization known as the *Concord Fleet* was riddled with spies for pirates. No other explanation for the last two days.

How riddled?

"We have to trust someone," she told him. "That's on me. You remain skeptical and remind me occasionally, if I start overlooking questionable behavior."

"Deal."

She unmuted.

"Pana, there's a park near where we're staying," Bethany said, telling her the name of the place. "We can be there in about ten minutes, if you wanted to secure it immediately."

"Ordering a drop now," Pana said. "See you shortly."

And she cut the line.

Ilan was already on his feet. He grabbed the room comm and dialed.

"Pack to move in thirty seconds," he said to whoever answered, never once taking his eyes off the door.

Bethany was on her feet and sliding things into the bag, not that she'd removed much.

Already expecting it?

Should she board *Tucana* and vanish? Could she actually vanish, currently parked in the middle of one of the biggest naval bases ever built? Or would any attempt to leave just mean that a corvette dropped out right behind her and took all of them into custody again?

And which crew was loyal to Valko Slavkov instead of the fleet?

Those were the shadows she couldn't pierce. Not yet.

And she also had to wonder if Javier had set her up purely as a stalking horse, distracting all the major players into thinking he was primarily trying to recruit help.

When what he was really doing was already happening. Out there, somewhere.

At this point, she had to figure out how to survive.

And rely on the Science Officer to rescue her later.

Or avenge her.

PART IV

Armando didn't do combat. Not like the other three. Zakhar had sent him along because he knew paperwork, and could defeat bureaucracy better than anybody he'd ever known.

Commodore Salim had been good, but he'd unthreaded all of her systems faster than she could rebuild them. That had gotten them Commander Ioannidi, and sent on from *Purton* to *Merankorr*, even faster than Javier had expected.

Now, they were about to be swallowed up by the leviathan known as the navy. Armando could taste it as he followed Ilan down the last flight of stairs and out the hotel's back door. He even had a pistol hidden tight against his body, partially obscured by his suitcase, but Armando knew he would fire last of the four of them.

Let those three killers take people down.

"Ilan, out the door go right instead of left," he decided. "Cut down half a block, then cross into an alley headed north."

Why, he had no idea, but it felt right, and this was one of those fluid moments where he'd been able to see the correct answer to all the paperwork, but not the path, relying on intuition instead to get him there.

Ilan, bless him, simply nodded and did.

Day had fallen to night. Traffic of people headed home or the bar or dinner, but not a mob scene. Merely folks.

They got off a block from where someone might be expecting them, then circled in from something of a tangent, assuming people listening in on whatever conversation Bethany had had with Commander Ioannidi.

Not full night, but that was coming. And the temperature was dropping steadily, to the point he could already see his breath steaming as he walked.

Then the park. And someone not messing around, because he saw a small assault shuttle parked in the lot and a lot of heads maintaining a perimeter.

"We expecting a full platoon?" Ilan asked, sliding into shadows next to a building where they might be invisible.

Assuming nobody watching with thermal sensors. But even then, people around them, so they might be anonymous until someone looked close.

Armando turned to Bethany. Her show. He was merely one of her tools.

"She said trouble," Bethany replied. "Hopefully, the good kind."

"Understood," Ilan said. "Making entry."

Armando was back in motion with the others. Heads locked on them, then most went back to watching other corners, like they were expecting a firefight to break out. Not a pleasant feeling, especially in a town as urbane and sophisticated as Rogerson.

So utterly not a good sign. But then, Armando had concluded that they were the ones kicking over a rock to scatter cockroaches.

Or they were the flashy hand distracting the audience while the magician was doing things on the other side. Javier was good at that sort of thing, after all. Too many years of high-level poker with that cast of ne'er-do-wells.

Armando had never fallen for the silliness of competing with those people. Too easy to lose all your cash.

He picked out Commander Ioannidi as they approached,

mainly by size because everyone present was in armor. Small woman. Physically, anyway.

Psychically, she reminded him of Afia Burakgazi. Intense.

Armando figured this would turn into bureaucracy quickly, so he stepped up to the woman, ignoring the armed goons around her. None of them met the Gun Bunny Standard of Lethal™ anyway.

"Status?" he barked at the woman, channeling a spot midway between an angry Zakhar and Navarre on a good day.

"Trouble," she snapped to, perhaps unconsciously. Certainly automatically. "Orders to recover and extract."

Armando nodded. Turned to the sergeant next to her.

"Recall and initiate preflight," he ordered the man. "Commander, let's move."

Silly, but everyone fell in to his orders. The person in charge doesn't have to be correct, but they must be decisive. Armando figured every second on the ground at this point was that much longer for someone to line up weapons, either on him or his shuttle.

He waved Bethany and Viv aboard, understanding Ilan's posture by the loading ramp, faced out and armed. Troopers poured by at a jog, so Armando inserted himself into the flow and boarded.

Everyone was in jumpseats, so he found one close to the cockpit and settled himself in. Commander Ioannidi was directly across, facing him, with Bethany offset one.

"We're clear here," Ilan yelled over the din of bodies settling, even as someone closed the ramp.

Up front, the pilot did their thing, and the shuttle lifted quickly, roaring forward only for a few moments before leaning back and accelerating upwards hard.

"We're returning to the station?" Armando asked in a sharp, professional tone.

The kind where an inspector had put on their white gloves and was keeping score.

"We are," Ioannidi nodded. "Full briefing when we get there, but somehow I suspect our finding will not surprise you as much as they did us."

"Should we be prepping *Tucana* for flight?" he asked, mostly because his Bad Cop now let Bethany Good Cop the woman later.

Or her superior officers.

"I do not think it has come to that," Ioannidi replied, drawing at least one—faint—line in the sand. "However, there is a decision nexus approaching quickly and we'll need to make adjustments on the fly."

"Killers in warships would be nice," he offered, loud enough that those troopers close could follow the conversation. "We'd like to stomp out a bunch of evil pirates and make the galaxy a safer place."

And throwing that in front of those people was like feeding raw meat to wild animals. He'd spent enough years with Zakhar—and later Javier—to understand how the *Concord* viewed themselves. Especially in the century since the Great War had torn down all of the other major powers in this vast region of space.

The good guys.

Body language revealed that. Troopers wanting to go bash pirate skulls together.

Just awaiting the order.

Armando made a note to sit Viv and Suvi down at some point. Maybe they needed to leak judicious portions of the records to some reporter or six, so someone told everyone on *Merankorr* the truth.

At least the non-prosecutable bits. And *Drako III*. Both halves.

Yes, they needed a public relations campaign, and he'd be damned if he wasn't the PERFECT person to handle that sort of thing.

You punks want a fight? Okay, bring it.

PART V

Bethany relaxed when the shuttle entered a flight bay and the clamshell doors slid shut behind them.

Safe. At least as safe as they could be aboard *Fleet Operations One*.

THE starbase.

The beating heart and burning soul of the *Concord*.

Glancing at her companions, all three men were relaxed. Poised. Pana was the nervous one, but it wasn't a betrayal.

Or rather, she wasn't about to betray them, but instead gave off the scent of a woman who had been betrayed by superior officers she had previously trusted.

It was a feeling Bethany knew well, flashing back to Lieutenant Durbin's last month in uniform, when suddenly all those same people she had relied on had turned their palms up and shrugged.

Sorry, nothing we can do. Budgets have been cut again this cycle.

No flag offices ever seemed to be shut down, though. No *important people* ever forcibly retired and not replaced.

Only the small players.

Like her.

But she wasn't a small player these days. She was the *Altai* Crown Consort's Ambassador to *The Concord*. And brought dire warnings, though she had begun to wonder if she was Cassandra to these fools.

Except that things were in motion. Pana rose with a mostly-contained sigh. The troopers did as well, relaxed and quietly joking. Bethany's team huddled up around her and waited for the boarding tube to extend and lock.

Out in the corridor, Captain Harcrow waved them off to one side and the ground troops kept going. They ended up in a small conference room. Her, Pana, Ilan, Vivian, Armando, and Captain Harcrow.

They got coffee and sat.

"Let me start by apologizing," Harcrow said. "All hell has broken loose, but we've done a pretty good job of containing it to the shadows and behind closed doors."

"How many flag officers are suddenly looking at arrest warrants?" Armando asked in that quiet radio voice he did. So utterly soothing.

Before he dropped a hammer on your head.

"More than I had expected," Harcrow replied. "Far more. It got worse when someone got a message to Sri Slavkov. He was on the planet somewhere, and vanished almost immediately, perhaps expecting to be arrested himself."

"Or taken into protective custody?" Bethany pressed.

Harcrow grimaced. Pana jolted hard. Bethany smiled.

"We're on your side, Durbin," Harcrow replied after a moment, quieter now.

She ignored him and turned to Pana.

"And yet, you needed to land heavy and do something."

Pana turned to the Captain and got a nod.

"I'm an outsider here," Pana replied. "Apparently, things have gotten a little out of hand and I've been specifically removed from certain chains of command."

Bethany was glad she'd put her coffee mug down, or she might have dropped it. Armando saw it as well, because his mouth fell open.

The only reason you did that was to prevent someone from issuing orders that might be found be illegal later.

But only AFTER the damage had been done.

Like all four of them having been taken out and shot, or something.

"Is this station safe?" Bethany asked, leaping over all of the other questions that weren't nearly as important.

"As near as I can tell," Captain Harcrow replied. "At the moment, things are a little concerning because I don't know who I can trust to tell me the truth. Two of the officers that we met with when you arrived have since been detained."

Bethany was pretty sure which two, but didn't pursue it.

Didn't matter. What mattered was that she was sitting dead center on a bullseye and needed to be elsewhere before it got out of hand. Like Ilan had already noted.

Even Javier hadn't been prepared for how right he was that the rot might have gotten pretty high. Or worse, had started at the top and was reaching tendrils down into the very body of the navy.

How much had Slavkov corrupted the entire organization? Bribes probably went even farther when budgets were being decimated annually. A few investments here and there and he might *own* certain admirals.

What could he do with that sort of power?

"How do we disappear?" Bethany asked. "It is not that I do not trust the two of you, but I do not trust this situation at all. How do I leave?"

"I had hoped that the ground would be relatively safer," the man replied.

Ilan's harsh laugh cut him short, but Harcrow nodded.

"As it is, I'm not sure," he continued. "We're trying to shelter you while things get worked out in private, but I don't know if that's possible."

"I will not be collateral damage," Bethany said simply, watching her three men nod. "If you can't get your own house in order, I am leaving. What will it be?"

Pana looked like someone had sunk a knife into her leg, while challenging her to remain perfectly silent. Captain Harcrow pressed his lips together until they turned white and she could see what his face would look like as an elderly man.

Silence wrapped them all up and squeezed painfully.

"Can we borrow a frigate?" Armando asked brightly. "Maybe a cruiser?"

Thankfully, she was seated, or Bethany thought she might have fallen over.

"Why?" Harcrow managed, snapping around and nearly falling over himself.

"We need to leave," Armando nodded sagely. "*Tucana* is unarmed. If you put Pana in command of something with special orders, you can send some warship off to protect us, help the Science Officer, and start swabbing your own decks here without us distracting you. That's why we came, after all."

It was a perfectly ludicrous suggestion, and Armando's confident smile was just the absolute cherry on top.

Worse, the two officers turned to one another like they were considering it. Bethany shut up and let them have some silent conversation.

"Where would you go?" he finally asked.

Bethany shrugged.

"I have a list of coordinates for future rendezvous with Javier and Zakhar," she replied, "Or find a message buoy they've left, like a scavenger hunt."

"And what would such a ship do?"

"The Science Officer is ending piracy in this entire region," she reminded them baldly. "A corridor running from the *Concord* to *Altai*, as wide as his arms can reach. More ships means more pirates destroyed. Assuming the *Concord* is actually honest about wanting to end piracy. You'll forgive me if I do start to harbor doubts on the topic, considering my last several days."

That landed like a right cross to the jaw from the way he jolted back.

What the hell had gone wrong?

Except that she knew. Dorn had known. Had seen it first. Hadn't been able to spell it out cleanly, because he taught at *Bryce*, when embryonic officers were being shaped and sent out in the galaxy.

Before the corruption set it. At least one hoped.

Dorn had taken out his crystal ball and seen **The Concord's Fall**.

Worse, he had quietly recruited a group of reformed pirates to save the galaxy, because he had no faith in his own people—HIS OWN NAVY—to do the job.

The Rising Storm still needed fertile soil in which to take root. And she had just discovered the heart of darkness at the core of the place she had called home.

Bethany ignored Captain Harcrow and turned to Pana.

"The Science Officer is a poker player," she said, a seeming non-sequitur that held a lot of relevance. "In poker, after all the bluffing, all the bullshit, all the money on the table, players have to lay down their cards, face up or face down. Which will it be?"

Utterly rude, but Bethany felt like things were literally on the verge of getting out of hand. Even Ilan was watching the hatch behind her, his gun hand in his lap in case he needed to shoot the first person through the door.

And he'd swapped out for a heavier weapon than the stun pistol he'd apparently smuggled onto the planet originally.

A man turned deadly serious. All four of them. Five? Six?

Pana turned to Harcrow and silently pled her case. Bethany turned back to the man and studied him. Armando watched.

Vivian and Ilan were primed to shoot their way out of *Fleet Operations One*.

Insane, but that felt like where they'd arrived.

"Let me make a case to an admiral I trust is on the level," Harcrow said quietly. "I can't make any promises, but I'll try."

"That's all we ask," Bethany said.

GHOSTS

Javier studied the results. And smiled. Let that smile expand to include both Afia and Regina Slayton standing next to him.

He'd had his doubts about their spy, but the woman had laughed heartily at the idea and thrown herself and her crew in like a kid with both feet and a mud puddle.

Even Zakhar unwound some of his sourness and nodded when Javier looked over.

The former *Æthelred* had been all gussied up like a Strike Corvette named *Storm Gauntlet*. As Afia had said, add a few panels here and there. Tack on some metal and extra sensors here and there to change the physical shape to be more like the old Osiris-class boats. Scan would be all wrong, but he was willing to bet his life that nobody had a solid scan of Zakhar's old ship after this long.

That, and an Arsenal ship that could still launch everything after it had been ionized. Afia and Regina had wired a whole second control system for the missile bays. That had actually taken the most work, finessing all that just right.

And they had done it.

"Piet should be flying this boat," Zakhar offered blandly.

Politely, even, but they'd already closed the hatch and yelled at each other over the topic.

"No," Javier replied simply. "I need him doing other things. Just like I need all of you. Mary-Elizabeth is the one person I require aboard this beast."

She perked up from the end, smiling like an owl spotting a rabbit looking the wrong way. They shared a nod.

Regina shifted away from the image on the screen and looked at him directly.

"What about *Eldritch Stele*?" she asked.

Javier noted that Glen Hohstadt wasn't present. He'd supposedly turned over a new leaf, but part of that was *Excalibur* carrying him and his ship to a new system nobody knew about. They had enough supplies for now, but would eventually need to restock everything.

Regina, however, had put her heart and soul into the work, per Afia.

"Gonna have to keep hostages," Javier said. "The Dragoon and her people will handle that. Unfortunate, but still better than me stealing your ship and putting all your people ashore permanently. You and Glen can still do what you do, but you'll have to take sides and stick with it."

"After watching you work?" she laughed. "I'm just glad I talked Glen out of trying something stupid back at the beginning. Djamila would have crushed us like bugs and not even noticed."

He agreed. Had, in fact, been utterly surprised when the Dragoon had handled Regina with such delicacy. Totally out of character for the woman.

But that was the old Dragoon. If Javier was having to finally grow up, he was willing to grant that same courtesy to the others.

Or drag their asses into the future with him.

Something.

Because it was coming.

Javier drew a breath and nodded to himself.

A line drawn, right here, right now. An act so magnificently arrogant, so *Le Beau Geste*, that **nobody** was going to forget him for this one.

And quite a few of them probably wouldn't forgive him for it, either.

It was what it was.

The others felt it, falling silent and all turned inward to watch him.

"While I would love to do this to the Jarre Foundation, I figure that they're the most likely to see through it," Javier announced, aware that he'd been playing this one close to the vest for long enough. "Given that we just hit Walvisbaai, I figure that by now H & W Heavy Industries is probably coming down off of their immediate, panicked alert levels and starting to figure out how to hunt us."

"Dipshit should be fully healed," Afia said, referring to Slavkov. "Dunno about recovered, because he got a lot of psychic damage on top of the physical, but he should be out of the hospital, where he is no doubt making life hell for whatever poor peons decided that he paid well enough to put up with."

Javier grinned.

"Figure I'm fifty/fifty that he retreated someplace where he didn't think anybody could get him," he said. "*Bryce* maybe. Or *Merankorr*."

"Bethany likely to run into him?" Zakhar asked, perking up.

Javier hadn't sent her on a suicide mission, though everyone had acknowledged how dangerous it was going to be. She was a red flag waved in front of a bull in an arena, in the ancient art of bull fighting.

Distract the stupid moron from the sword hidden behind it, plunging it in as he runs by.

Or hold him facing northbound when about to be attacked from behind by a moose.

"There's a chance, but I wanted her starting to move the *Concord* off high-center," Javier replied. "Amazing mass requires a lot of force to get it into motion. Or a long head start. Meanwhile, if he did run, that should have his people distracted."

"Who are you going after?" Zakhar asked in a sideways kind of voice. Like he already knew the answer and didn't want to speak the word out loud himself.

"*Ferran*," Javier grinned at him.

Zakhar closed his eyes and nodded. Grimaced. Shook his head.

Regina went white.

"You're going after **Ferran**?" she asked. "That place is huge. And heavily guarded. That's suicide!"

"So was *Nidavellir*, Slayton," Zakhar interrupted her quietly.

Like that was all that needed to be said on the subject. And it might be.

Walvisbaai Industrial Platform Number One, previously located at *Nidavellir*, until some rat in the wainscoting had stolen a Land Leviathan and its transport ship, crashing the two into a Walvisbaai facility after an epic space battle that saw everything on that side of the equation destroyed.

And only one serious casualty on theirs, the Pixie Kodiak standing next to Regina, practically glowing right now.

Regina realized all that and fell silent, mouth kind of dangling open, though no words came out.

"It is also the main H & W Heavy Industries chop shop," Javier replied. "Like you have seen, pirates need bases to operate effectively for any length of time. With *Eldritch Stele* out of business permanently, how many small-time operators either have to submit to the big players or give up and go straight?"

"A lot of them," she said. "You've digested our repair records so you know how many and who. And those are the ones outside the system."

"Exactly," Javier smiled. "Now, I'm going to do the same thing to those inside, because I want them to understand that **nobody** is safe from my wrath. Anywhere. Anytime. Anybody. If I break them now, there is a good chance that the *Concord* and the others maybe have gotten off their asses and will keep a boot in their faces before they can recover."

"Slavkov won't back down," Regina said, almost meekly, but she'd spent a lot of time around this inner circle and gotten to know them.

And understood that she might have been exposed and executed easily enough, had Djamila not felt benevolent.

"He will if he's dead," Afia growled, catching Regina sideways. "That's how this ends. That's always how this one was going to end."

Javier shared a nod with the tiny woman.

That was always how this was going to end.

PART II

Mary-Elizabeth Suzuki had supervised all the work on the *Ghost's* weapons systems during the maintenance cycle. Knew them forward, backward, and sideways, because it was going to be her ass on the line when they got there and she wanted to utterly know that it would work.

Javier had suggested a number of names for the former *Æthelred*, but *Ghost* had stuck. Nobody even called it *Storm Gauntlet Two*.

Ghost of Christmas Past. Coming for you in the cold, dark night.

Javier would be there with her. His ass would be on the same line. Not a lot of other folks involved, because an Arsenal ship didn't need a massive crew except when it came to boarding actions or reloading the bays.

Engineers to keep things powered. Repair techs when shit broke. Strong backs to get missiles into the tubes after the *Ghost* had sown the winds.

And she got to be the Reaper.

It was enough to make a woman cackle with delight. Most of the time, she managed to keep it contained.

Javier wasn't surprised.

"You okay over there?" he asked, one eyebrow up when she looked.

"Gotta top *Nidavellir*," she replied, eyes big with joy.

Because honestly, that was it. Suvi had done most of the work there, once Mary-Elizabeth had trained that girl how to lay guns. And *Excalibur* would be trailing them in, hiding nearby in case they got into trouble and needed a hand.

But she wanted to do this once without anyone the wiser.

"Gotta survive your boss's latest stupidity," he countered.

She laughed and waved him off.

"You already stole me a ship," Mary-Elizabeth replied. "I intend to use it up entirely, like what happened to our original steed, before you found us something better. Then you can steal me another one."

Arsenal ships were shit for piracy. That was the kind of job where you snuck up on someone, ionized them, and stole their shit. Or their ship.

Ghost here was a saturation bomber. Lob a stupid number of missiles at someone, intending to overload their ability to shoot them all down. The four turrets, forward two dorsal and aft pair ventral, were just to keep everyone else honest.

As honest as pirates got.

"Let me know when you're ready," Javier said after a moment.

"How certain are you about these coordinates?" she countered.

"Suvi calculated them and transmitted the file to the Jump computers," Javier replied.

Mary-Elizabeth nodded. She'd seen what Suvi had had to do at *Drako* to save all their asses. And had listened to the woman bitch about learning new mathematical expressions of gravitational calculus to do it.

If she'd plotted them, then *Ghost* was about to drop right in the middle of a courtyard, at least mentally and emotionally. Surrounded on two sides by the main platform, with a couple of smaller warehouse stations in such a way that the aft pair of guns could ionize the shit out of them.

"You ready on ventral guns?" she asked, knowing that, like her, Javier would handle those things himself instead of delegating.

"I have a firehose and an attitude problem," he replied.

Partly, they were simply stretched too thin, even with a few folks that had taken the oath and joined *Excalibur*'s crew, freeing up the bodies that had boarded the *Ghost*.

Partly, it was his ass on the line, too.

"All systems live and green," Mary-Elizabeth announced. "As you bear."

PART III

Javier had added a rocker switch over the jump button, because *Mielikki* had had such a thing, back when he'd been flying. Not that Suvi let him use it often, but it reminded him that he was manually navigating things today.

Ship was vastly overpowered for it's needs. Hardly any guns to charge, because all the firepower was in the missile racks that hardly used any once you charged the launching circuits. As a result, he'd be able to recharge the JumpDrives in basically minimum-expected-time. While massively reinforcing the shields against incoming fire.

Might need that, if he suddenly had to haul ass. And, like other systems, he had ordered a secondary bypass installed, in case someone ionized the main computers and he had to do it mechanically.

Because this was about as bad a place to get captured as he could imagine. Especially with what he was about to do. And who he planned to do it to.

One last check on the coordinates, but he trusted Suvi. More than anybody, save possibly Behnam.

And that said it all.

A nod, and he opened the rocker, a calloused thumb finding the button underneath, then triggering it.

The stars blinked and reset, and the *Ghost of Christmas Past* arrived to speak its dire prophesy.

PART IV

Captain Enzo Hammacher had taken to spending more time on the bridge of his Guardship *Harlequin*. The alerts had tapered off, but that was enough time passing without any notes about *Excalibur* and Navarre being seen.

Maybe they'd been more badly damaged at *Drako* than anyone had understood at the time? After all, *Obsidian Hawk* had been destroyed, while *Fire Eagle* and *Ice Wyvern* had gotten away largely undamaged, save at the very end.

But a general free-for-all had erupted at that moment, with everyone suddenly turning on each other and cutting loose. A lot of old vendettas come to roost, from the bits his Board of Directors had shared with their captains.

Privately, he figured that Slavkov had screwed everything up by being present, because Enzo had been in a few Board presentations to see that the man had more money than God, but it had just empowered him to be an asshole to everyone.

Nobody had gotten out of *Drako* intact. Everyone had been running like hell, from those reports. Slavkov had recalled every ship H & W owned, and put them on defense for months, so quarterly profits were going to be nil. All operating costs, no offsets.

Good thing he only had to maintain a Guardship. And *Harlequin* was an easy job. Heavy Corsair, down a notch from the big Enforcers. Cruiser firepower, but cramped if you wanted to sail any distance, because lots of generators instead of cabins or storage.

As long as he only had to protect the anchorage at *Ferran*, they could take a shuttle or runabout over to R&R Facilities. Or have a freighter deliver fresh supplies.

Easy gig. But Slavkov was an asshole, and everyone was walking on eggshells. Random inspections that hadn't died down yet. And orders kept coming in that didn't necessarily make any sense.

Worse than usual.

So, he was on his bridge today. Doing that Captain thing. Sipping some hot tea and reading various screens at his station instead of in the privacy of his office.

Mostly, being seen, in case someone important decided to call a snap inspection, because nobody knew when Slavkov was suddenly going to drop out of Jump and be an asshole in person.

"Hey, that's weird," Daron called from his sensors station.

Enzo looked up curiously, then went a little white around the edges as his screen lit up with an alert and sirens started.

Warning – Enemy warship detected – Identification: Jarre Foundation: *Storm Gauntlet*.

But hadn't they killed Storm Gauntlet *at Svalbard…?*

Specifically, the Battle Frigate *Ajax*, operated by Walvisbaai? Who had then run into that nasty First-Rate Galleon *Hammerfield*? The one that had ended up destroying *Walvisbaai Industrial Platform Number One* at *Nidavellir*?

Was this some sort of bad joke?

And then that revenant started launching missiles.

PART V

Mary-Elizabeth had come to love how Suvi liked to sit clear out at the edge of things, patiently mapping everything that moved, before jumping in closer. Most of the time, space was so empty that you were never at risk, and could maneuver on thrusters and drives for those last few kilometers when you missed your target.

Today's error was measures in decameters. Not even kilometers. Worse—for the other guy—the Jump had dropped her exactly on the three-dimensional plane of engagement that Mary-Elizabeth had worked out, once she'd reviewed the layout of everyone home today.

And, as she'd warned Javier, she was launching every damned thing she had, because this either worked, or it didn't, and she wanted to ruin some lives today.

Might be a bit of pent up anger on top of the mad cackling. Or maybe driving it.

She pushed the one button on her console that awakened the terrible dragon of vengeance.

Forty-eight columns of missiles, eight wide. Start in position 1-1. Launch 1-1, 48-8, 24-1, and 25-5 simultaneously. Sequence the top numbers down in matched pairs and the bottom numbers up. Scanners couldn't keep locks on that many torpedoes in flight, but she didn't have to, because there were no friendlies anywhere in range.

Anything a torpedo locked itself on was fair game today, and most of them were going at the station itself.

"Javier?" she asked, mostly ignoring everything except the green lights turning black as the pattern walked slowly to completion.

Three hundred and eighty-four torpedoes. If they all worked. She figured about a one percent failure rate, so she'd eat four and be happy.

The other guy was getting indigestion.

"Hosing *Beta* and *Gamma*," Javier replied. "Think that *Harlequin* is more awake than they should be. You might want to flood them with some specific trouble, because their targeting scanners just came live."

Mary-Elizabeth checked.

Shit.

Unwelcome, but not necessarily unexpected. Especially at an H & W base, where Slavkov might be keeping them on a tighter leash.

Or she had another *Hummingbird* on her hands, that damned escort that had been so effective at *Drako*. Punk.

Still, Javier was right. Like he often was. Mary-Elizabeth locked a scanner on that ship and told the system to aim the next sixteen launches that direction.

She jumped when *Harlequin* opened fire. Pulse cannon. Ten centimeter. Comparable to hers, but he had more of them. Shields took it. Held. Second one hit.

Then he was distracted enough to leave her alone, because he had his own incoming to deal with.

"Javier, keep him off my ass," Mary-Elizabeth snarled.

"Outer edge for ion cannons, unless you plan to move?" he asked.

"No, just keep him distracted," she said. "We'll be gone soon enough."

Hopefully, that other fool didn't understand that she was only staying long enough to let loose with everything, then running for her life.

Suvi would take her time keeping watch and scoring. Maybe she flooded the zone going after the puck. Maybe she held back.

All depended on the skill with which one bitch Gunner managed to blow shit up today.

Going for broke.

Station was starting to wake up. She slewed her one ion cannon across a cluster of point defense turrets and held it in place. Shorts were as good as overloads, if the charging systems hiccuped. And they would.

The one pulse cannon her *Ghost* had was useful to poke people in the eye, so she found the control tower and locked her gun on it, opening the cooling circuits and letting it pound away like a hungry woodpecker going after a worm.

Damage. That was what Javier had demanded. Fear as a secondary effect. Financial disruption tertiary. But first and foremost damage. Crack skulls together. Blow up repair bays. Shatter offices. Shiv torpedoes into financial databases so folks got a first-hand chance to confirm that their disaster recovery systems were working.

Or weren't. Systems like that were expensive in time, personnel, and materials. Some places might cut corners, and just store everything on the same station that was getting the living shit pounded out of it by an angry, middle-aged woman.

"*Harlequin* is distracted," Javier announced.

She checked her screen and nodded. Wall of torpedoes inbound, so every weapon that could was engaging them instead of her. Every ECM trick anyone knew to spoof lock-ons was active. Wasn't going to help, because nobody had any maneuvering speed right now, so *Harlequin* couldn't get out of the way fast enough, unless they turned ninety degrees away from her and overloaded their engines.

Which took them out of the action for at least three minutes. The critical three minutes, as far as she was concerned.

Half her bays empty. Five failures, which was manageable. Station looked like a mugging victim, and she had them knocked down and was about to start kicking. *Harlequin* took a hit aft. Shield generators got most of it, but she saw overloads play across the hull, so they might be off-line for long enough.

Too damned competent for her tastes. She'd have preferred more dipshits, but Mary-Elizabeth was willing to admit that the Science Officer had certainly gotten into their minds.

Especially that punk Slavkov.

"I'm getting ships running," Javier's voice intruded. "Emergency jumps out. Some are people you targeted. Some are random."

"Panic setting in?" she asked, still focused on her launch boards.

"Feels like," he said. "Want me to bring in the cavalry early?"

"Drop her on *Harlequin*'s ass," Mary-Elizabeth replied. "I'm almost done here and nobody appears to be ready to shoot back. We might hang out ionizing things for her. Not like my one pulsar is all that useful."

"Stand by," Javier said. "Gondor calling for aid on channel six."

PART VI

Suvi hated sitting back and watching, but understood the need. Two minutes lag from what was happening over there to what she was seeing as the light-speed wave got to her.

Mary-Elizabeth had managed surprise. First wave of missiles off and tracking before anybody got shields up, followed by a swath of impacts designed for maximum chaos.

Blow up defensive systems. Guns. ECM emitters. Torpedo launchers. Shield generator arrays.

Trouble.

Regina had a scan of the system that she'd stolen from a ship in for repairs a few years ago, so Suvi knew how the platform was built and deployed. An hour in the darkness with her heavy sensors, updating everything and plotting vectors for Mary-Elizabeth and the *Ghost*.

Then they both jumped inward, her landing out a bit and hiding, where she was close enough to help if Javier got into trouble.

Or, as now, when he sent a note asking her to come in blasting because they had generally succeeded and needed to ram it home.

Harlequin had too many guns for a hull that size, but she

understood the concept of a Guardship. Never go anywhere. Sit still ready to pour fire into anyone showing up.

Assuming that they weren't as crazy as Javier and Mary-Elizabeth.

She paused to do the math, and came out above *Harlequin* and broadside to him. First-Rate Galleon versus upgunned Corsair. Not even remotely fair, but the station with all the guns was trying to keep itself from being destroyed, and not reacting fast enough to a whole new dose of trouble.

Ion cannons, point-blank. Just to shut him up. Pulsars, the newer six centimeter jobs that were far more powerful than the old twelve centimeter cannons she'd been built with.

Suvi threw a few torpedoes at other ships nearby, mostly to scare them, then sent an entire wave at the station. It was the most important thing in the system, after all. And Zakhar had showed her where the weak points were in that superstructure.

She concentrated on them.

"Hey, kid," Javier radioed. "We'll hang on for a bit with defensive fire to cover your flank. Let me know when you want me to jump clear."

"Understood," Suvi replied with one of her communication shards, a burst transmission he could decipher. "Stand by for tactical update."

Because Zakhar had had her study every battle like this that she could find, anywhere in all of her books. And that was a lot of literature, dating back a long time.

Helped, when humans tended to think in two dimensions, even when they moved in three on a battlefield like this. Naval battles between biremes, or sudden raids by Viking Longboats, looked an awful lot like what was happening here, save that the arrows were a lot heavier and a lot faster.

She assembled her battle plan for the next eight minutes and sent it over. Javier was smart enough to take that and commit jazz as things moved around, but most of their targets were static. Or extremely slow to accelerate from a dead stop.

Anyone jumping clear would be gone a while, because most of them weren't dumb enough to try to bounce back into the middle of a battle with a ship like her.

Suvi started to push her engines. And focus beams forward, because *Harlequin* was having troubles after getting punched in the head a few times. She could ignore them until they managed to reset a few systems and kill the rolling, twisting spin that an exploding torpedo had imparted.

Station was scorched. Not enough, so she located all the weapon and defensive systems and blasted them from far closer than you were supposed to be able to get.

Nobody understood *Sentient* systems, except *Concord* officers who had flown aboard them in battle. And she'd been *Neu Berne* state of the art at the time of her construction. Flagship of an entire culture of militant lunatics.

Today, she was far heavier than anything else in harbor today, in terms of firepower.

She moved clear of a lobe on the station, starting to take fire from a cluster of pulsars that had been obscured before now.

Maybe because I know how to fly in shadows? Ya ever think about that?

Suvi laughed to herself and poured an entire flank of beams into a single spot not much larger than a ground vehicle. Shields overloaded under the assault because they were designed to cover a lot of space.

Ice pick time. And then the shield generator behind them went off-line and all the shielding protecting those turrets faded.

Suvi spread her fire out and blew barrels off. She wasn't going after crews, because they'd be fairly deep behind the gun itself, but if the gun stopped working—or the cooling systems ruptured, or some crazy chick cracked your crystals—then you had nothing you could do but throw rocks back at someone.

Lot of that happening as Mary-Elizabeth started hosing down anything she could reach with her ion cannons. If your ship had to reset circuits, you might be silent for three or maybe five minutes.

Bad time to be facing that.

Suvi looked around and realized that every ship capable of Jumping had done so. It was her, *Harlequin*, and the station. And *Harlequin* was a doorstop over there for a bit yet. Couple of torpedoes might finish them off, but they were a ship so she ignored them and aimed herself at one of those soft spots Zakhar had highlighted in the last four seconds.

An old weld where someone had added a tower lobe on after the station had been assembled here at *Ferran*. Possibly because someone with money wanted a private palace. That was often why you did that.

And their shields were shit right now.

Suvi tracked everything, then surfaced onto her bridge.

"Captain, we might get a kill here," she said simply, displaying damage plots and structural stability calculations.

"Agreed," he said. "Find this spot and hammer it has hard as you can. Even a partial tear ends this place for long enough."

He touched a spot on her screen and Suvi locked all her Probe-Cutter logic onto it.

"Javier, I'll be coming to rest," she sent. "Keep *Harlequin* shut down."

Then she turned and started to close with the station.

PART VII

Javier laughed at Mary-Elizabeth's reaction.

"Is she nuts?" the woman asked, then started muttering. "Definitely your kid."

He had to agree.

As far as he knew, he had no natural offspring running around out there. And no expectation of any in the future, Behnam specifically being done and having done something about it.

But yeah, Suvi was his kid.

He called up an updated scan she sent over, adding a couple of digits of sensitivity and details to what the *Ghost* could do. Then he put extra power into the gyroscopes and let them swing his ass around where he could drive closer to *Harlequin*.

They were not a problem at the moment, but he stayed broadside so all four turrets could bear as they slid closer. And aimed the back two to hose him.

"We're out of torpedoes," Mary-Elizabeth announced. "Or I'd finish him off."

"Better to let him survive, I think," Javier countered. "His repair yard won't be doing anything for a while, so they might have to do as much repair as they can, then go find a mobile yard somewhere."

"Like *Eldritch Stele*?" she asked. "We mean enough to Trojan Horse people?"

He paused and actually wrote himself a note to ask Djamila later. How stupid could they get, if they could put Glen and Regina somewhere where they could capture ships he and Suvi had damaged?

"Maybe," he said as he typed. "Keep these folks fuzzy so Suvi can work."

"Oh, you better believe that," she replied.

He watched her lock the pulse cannon onto the ass end of the ship, zero the gyro-stabilizers, and turn it onto a slow metronome rate. Not as fast as the gun could go, but it had better range than the ion cannons and would distract while the ship got closer.

And three layers of ionization had a longer range than one, if you didn't have to maneuver to keep from getting mugged on the dance floor.

"Shields gone forward," she said as they closed. "Starting to shatter armor plates on the hull itself."

Javier nodded and ignored her, taking Suvi's latest Jump coordinates update and making sure it loaded cleanly. Drives were recharged, so he could bounce out any time he wanted, but Suvi wasn't done. And the two small stations Mary-Elizabeth had targeted where largely smoldering hunks of scrap at this point.

Like the main station.

Suvi was kicking the guy to death. Best image he could conjure. But then, she'd been as pissed as the rest of them at *Drako*, and only able to force those assholes onto the defensive, save when she'd taken out *Obsidian Hawk* or *Blackstone*.

Here, payback with interest.

He did a quick check, but anybody who could go had already jumped. Gone. That left ships with damage or failed systems, and any of those who opened fire had gotten at least a couple of missiles, so they were all tumbling and smoking, too.

Harlequin suddenly lit up. Back half of the ship turned to plasma, venting every direction as a reactor failed.

From the image on his screen, the safety defaults had worked, so it was only plasma venting off a reactor, and not the aft third of the ship detonating.

Still, they were off-line for days at a minimum.

"That's that," Mary-Elizabeth laughed, shutting down the weapon systems for now. "Anybody else need my attention?"

"Not that I can see," Javier replied.

"Can we go home now?" she asked.

"Suvi, what's our status?" he asked.

"Jump when ready," she replied. "I'll be a few minutes behind you."

Javier nodded and located his rocker switch.

And the stars changed.

PART VIII

Zakhar was in command, but understood that, like as at *Drako*, that was a strategic thing. Suvi reacted simply too fast for him to have any tactical inputs that mattered.

But she was good enough at what she did these days that he didn't worry. All she needed was the occasionally guidance from him. A nudge in the right direction, when things didn't have any clear direction and it was time for random choices.

Suvi had silenced every weapon system that could stretch far enough sideways to reach her. Every shield generator on this hemisphere. Just about anything else that looked important. Plus anything else that she could reach. After that, anything that looked halfway interesting.

At the moment, she was pounding furiously on a set of girders that had been exposed when several levels of armor plating and hull had been stripped away previously.

A doctor, having carefully cut away skin and muscle to get to the bones underneath.

Those were failing as she hit them again and again.

Correction. Had failed.

"Suvi, calculate for me the vectors involved, now that both parts are separated," he said quietly.

Took a few seconds, but that was her need to scan the two hunks of mass and determine which way they were going, now that they were no longer connected. Large portions of the station had been dark before. The rest went out now, leaving only places obviously running on battery power, but those should be sufficient for a few days.

Wasn't like she planned to shatter the place down into components no bigger than a person. Hell, the smaller of those two was still five times the size of *Excalibur*.

But it would have to be captured by a tug and pulled back into alignment to be reattached. After someone stripped back about a hundred meters of girders and installed new ones, the old having been melted, twisted, and otherwise deformed.

The screen updated, showing how the two parts would slowly drift apart over the next four days.

"Put a barrage into roughly here," he said, touching the screen.

Her guns had largely fallen silent, but erupted again, imparting energy and momentum on the smaller portion. And rotation.

Anything to make it that much harder to capture.

Everything was so high in orbital space that it would probably take a year to fall down and hit the planet. If they couldn't manage to repair it that time, she'd done far more damage than he could have ever dreamed.

"And a few shots here, aiming for spin," he added, watching her twist the cue ball around a three to hit an eleven and drop it in a corner pocket.

"Excellent," he smiled. They shared it on the screen where she was watching him. "Put me on a system-wide channel. Maximum broadcast power. No encryption. I want everyone hearing me. Remembering today."

"Push the red button when you are ready to speak," she replied.

Zakhar took a deep breath and considered his words. No

doubt, they would be recorded and transmitted on to anyone who would listen. That would include reporters somewhere.

Anywhere.

Everywhere.

His voice was as big as the galaxy today, potentially.

"This is Zakhar Sokolov," he said, drawing deep on lessons in public speaking and forty years of service in somebody's uniform as his voice got dark and serious. "You have been warned and did not listen, so it became necessary to chastise you. The Science Officer has declared an end to piracy and you did not listen, so he will be coming for you. All of you. Everywhere that his fleets of vengeance can track you down and destroy you. You will listen. It is no longer enough to reform your ways. If you wish to survive, you will vanish so entirely that even the bounty hunters he has hired cannot find you. Nothing less than that will do. Zakhar Sokolov will hunt you. Eutropio Navarre will hunt you. Most importantly, *The Science Officer* has had enough and intends to destroy you, root and branch. This will be your only warning. After this, there is only the end of the pirate clans."

He cut the line and nodded to himself. On her screen, Suvi's mouth had fallen open and her normally pale skin had gone almost white.

Zakhar winked at her.

"There's somebody out there even worse—even meaner— than Captain Navarre," he said simply.

"I've known that for years, Zakhar," she nodded. "But this is the wake up call that the rest of them needed."

"There's a storm rising, Suvi," Zakhar reminded her. "What they are feeling are the first winds kissing their cheeks. It will get worse from here. Jump as you bear. We've gotten their attention, I think."

PART IX

Enzo was amazed that he'd survived. Sure as shit, that beast could have finished *Harlequin* off if they'd wanted. Especially after he'd lost magnetic controls aft and one of the generators had blown.

Lucky for him and everybody else, they lived in a repair yard, so all of *Harlequin*'s systems were in tiptop shape every day. That had kept them all alive, because he'd served on ships where a year's sailing meant that things had torqued or aged enough that any of those venting systems might have failed to open, and white hot plasma would have gutted the entire ship.

As it was, their databanks were mostly hosed. Along with a lot of other things. Maybe six months in a repair facility, but the one that was his home base was in even sadder shape. And he could see it out of a porthole if he chose.

Hammerfield had broken the base into pieces. Big ones, but you weren't supposed to be able to do that.

Enzo looked up from his screens as Daron spoke.

"Boss, is it even worth salvage at this point?" his sensors officer asked, gesturing around. "You heard the man. They're coming for us. And one of those ships was named *Storm Gauntlet*, like it was back from the dead. How big a force are we facing next time? And what kinds of angry ghosts?"

Enzo didn't have a good answer. And anything positive he tried to share would be a lie, because he kinda felt the same way.

Worse, Avery also looked up from his gunnery station, watching close. Everybody else was busy elsewhere, repairing anything they could, but he needed the three of them on the bridge, in case trouble came back.

He was still the Guardship, even if they couldn't sail and could hardly fight.

The three of them were alone, at least for a short time.

"I don't know," Enzo admitted. "And I'm not sure of much. We can't be combat capable for weeks, I'm guessing, so if they bounced back, it wouldn't take more than a couple of shots to do to us what they did to the station."

"Where's that leave us?" Avery asked.

All three of them were speaking in quiet tones. Hushed. Conspiratorial.

Enzo considered his reply carefully.

"Fucked," he said simply, drawing nods from the two.

Then he paused and considered how long he had known these men. Not his best friends, but officers that he relied on. Men he trusted.

People maybe facing that same noose that he saw shadowed on a wall in his mind when he stopped to think about it.

Enzo went ahead and committed treason.

"What would you lose, personally, if we got life support and Jump Drives repaired, then left?" he asked them.

After all, his retirement accounts might be about half forfeit, but a dead man can't enjoy a brandy and a cigar. He found that he'd rather be alive and broke.

That had potential later.

Daron and Avery both flinched, but not as bad as he'd expected. Like, maybe, they'd been having the same thoughts?

"Where?" Daron asked.

"Someplace we could either abandon ship and vanish, or collect bounties for the hull, like happened with *Storm Gauntlet* originally, from what I remember," he offered, wondering if one of them would betray the rest and see them all hung. "I think I'd rather survive what's coming."

"They could have taken a couple of extra minutes and finished us off easy enough, there at the end," Avery replied. "Not sure if that was mercy, but really certain that we're getting any next time."

Daron nodded.

"Next time, let that ax fall on somebody else," he said.

Enzo sighed carefully. Then opened a line aft.

"Engineering," a tired, gruff male voice answered.

"This is Captain Hammacher," Enzo replied. "I'm looking at notes from Command. Mostly rumors on the shadow network, but you know how those go."

"Aye, sir."

"Rearrange all your resources to focus on life support, engines, and Jump Drives," he ordered. "Suggestions are that we might end up departing this system and hauling ass somewhere else for most of our repairs. I don't want to be left behind, or have to leave the ship for whoever comes along."

"Be nice, being somewhere else," the man mused. "I'll let the boss know."

Enzo cut the line and got shallow nods from his fellow conspirators.

"Avery, keep watch and be ready to shoot before asking permission," he ordered. "Daron, find me someplace where we can run. Preferably a transportation nexus, so the whole crew can scatter to the four winds. And keep this under your hat."

"Oh, yeah," both men agreed.

In his mind, Enzo considered that he had just rolled the dice.

Committed treason.

But he wanted to get out of this thing alive.

Instead of the alternative.

VENGEANCE

PART I

Bethany woke muzzy. The inside of her mouth tasted like a colony of slugs had laid eggs that had hatched.

Yuck.

Beeping had drawn her to the surface.

She opened sleep-crusted eyes and tried to wipe them, but couldn't move her hands.

"Ah, good, you're awake," a voice fell out of the dark heavens and buffeted her. "You have caused me a great deal of pain, young lady."

Male voice, but higher pitched. Possibly sang at the top of male tenor and gave sopranos a challenge.

Bethany blinked. Then squinted. FAR too bright in here.

Her eyes were merest slits, leaving everything black and bright yellow as she looked around.

Two figures looming over her.

She was flat on a bed. Chained to it.

More blinks.

Two men. One in the archetypal white longcoat of a doctor.

The other fat and bald. Sweaty as her focus improved and she was able to track on him.

Bethany felt the chill take hold as she realized where she knew the man.

Valko Neofit Slavkov.

Public Enemy, Number One.

That asshole, himself.

"Excellent, you recognize me," he smiled. "That will make this better, Durbin."

Bethany kept her own counsel on that subject.

"What happened?" she asked, probing at her short-term memory and coming up with fuzzy bits and sharp edges.

"Heavy stun was necessary," Slavkov preened, then scowled. "Your comrade put up a tremendous fight, but he was only one man. And nobody I cared about, so we left him behind. You've been sedated for a few days as we made our escape. Now, you will be my prisoner. My hostage against whatever the hell Navarre thinks he's going to do next."

Bethany let the man's anger wash over her and carry away the dull bits, like a blade being honed on a stone, though she had no idea where that image came from.

Fit, though. Refreshed her, because he was her enemy, just as much as Javier's. Maybe not for the same reasons. Nor the same scale.

Still the same asshole who had tried to kill her at *Drako*.

She owed him a ration of pain.

Bethany blinked at the man and stayed silent.

"I just wanted you to know," he nodded, a savage smile marring an otherwise unattractive face. "If you behave, you might even survive, because it is my understanding that you didn't come along and join my foes until much more recently. My fight is with Sokolov and Navarre. They destroyed my Leviathan. And ruined everything. They will pay."

He swept up and stormed out, missing only the opera cape flourish to make one man seem like a two-bit villain from a three-penny opera.

The doctor had remained silent. She turned her attention to the man.

"Any lingering mental issues?" he asked. "Your vital signs are all normal, save for a few thing that a woman your age could address with a good, commercial multivitamin."

The contrast between the two men whiplashed her harder than anything, but she nodded.

"Water to flush it out of my system?" she asked, hearing her voice a painful croak.

"Changed your IV to pure saline," he replied. "That got you awake. Another hour and you should be able to walk, at which point my understanding is that you will be taken to a holding cell."

Bethany looked around, but all medbays seemed to be identical. Like a props department had a single book of plans that they all shared.

"Where am I?" she asked.

"The *Golden Gazelle*," the man replied. "Slavkov's personal yacht. Were we military, I'd be Chief Medical Officer or something, but this is a private service vessel, so I'm just the doctor in charge of seeing that everyone remains healthy. He's gotten more serious about that sort of thing since he nearly got killed at *Drako*."

Bethany kept silent. Suvi had apparently come within a meter or so of killing the man when she'd raked *Obsidian Hawk* from surprise.

Pity.

The doctor handed her a cup of water and released her left wrist.

"Drink this," he said. "My instructions were to keep you healthy as a prisoner, so I'll be adding that multivitamin to your breakfasts from here in. The stun didn't have any lingering effects that I can see, and the weakness you're feeling right now will wear off in the next hour, then you'll be sent on and locked up in a cabin, where my understanding is that they have largely disabled everything but the entertainment unit."

Bethany shrugged. Tried to shrug. Still otherwise chained to the bed. But apparently not important enough to torture, which was good. Hostage for later, but if Slavkov thought that Navarre would stay his hand over something like that, the man was an even bigger fool than she'd originally expected.

And then there was Javier. A whole other layer of pissed over and above anything Navarre had ever been credited with.

It was going to get ugly before it got better, but she was a librarian. Patience was in her bones.

She'd spend however long memorizing everything she needed to know in order to add to the book that someone was going to demand she write later.

The War of the Pirate Clans, Volume Two.

Because Valko Slavkov was a dead man walking. People as lethal as Djamila Sykora were coming after him, and the Dragoon barely made the top five in that category, which frightened Bethany as much as it warmed her.

She closed her eyes and started a breathing exercise to focus all of her rage down into a single diamond she could hold right behind her belly button.

She'd need that, too.

PART II

Ilan smelled the nastiest thing he'd ever encountered and tried to lurch away from it, but someone had hold of his head and someone else his arms. Still, he thrashed as little as he was able, then opened his eyes.

Took a second to focus. Some asshole had hit him with a heavy stunner. He recognized the hangover effects.

Viv scowled.

"You okay?" the man asked.

"Where's Bethany?" Ilan asked, shaking his head now that Viv was pulling those damned smelling salts back and letting him breathe.

"No idea," Armando said, holding his head and now in the process of standing up and lifting him to his feet.

Nobody ever appreciated how strong the big guy was, mostly because he was a teddy bear, not a Kodiak. The Kodiak was back on the ship.

"What happened?" Ilan asked.

"You tell us," Viv said. "We were supposed to go grab dinner, but you didn't answer the comm or the landline, so we knocked. Got no answer, so I picked the lock and found you out cold on the deck, bed mussed, blood in a few places, and the boss gone."

Ilan felt his nose and eyes, but nothing seemed to be bleeding.

"Looks like it came from someone else," Viv nodded. "You put up a fight and they stunned you."

Ilan blinked. Sucked a breath deep and growled at the crap coating the inside of his brain, shoving it aside.

"Door opened," he remembered. "Surprise. Mob rushed in. Got one, I think, then they dogpiled me. Fists, elbows, knees. Maybe she screamed. Dunno. Then darkness, so I'm assuming somebody caught a clue and hosed everybody with a stunner, then sorted out bodies. Surprised they left me behind. Or alive."

"Same, bubba," Viv nodded. "Must have mistaken you for someone a lot nicer, because I can already see from the look in your eyes how ugly things are likely to get."

"I will remind both of you that we are in the middle of a major *Concord* naval base," Armando said, sliding back into those Kibwe radio tones.

"We already knew they were bent," Ilan said, looking around.

Still in his and Bethany's cabin. She'd been on the bed. He'd been in a chair reading. Chair was back in the corner. Nothing else seemed to have been messed.

The other two followed him to Bethany's messenger bag. Watched him pull Suvi out and open her up. Connected her to a wired line and let her talk to the station.

"Status?" he asked.

"As you described it to Vivian and Armando," she replied, sounding more like a sailor answering an officer, but he supposed that he was in charge until Bethany got back. "They grabbed bodies and fled without saying anything useful or incriminating beyond being here and kidnapping her."

"Locate Commander Ioannidi and ask her to join us here, without any details beyond that," Ilan ordered, becoming the officer the situation needed. The Combat Engineer. What Afia demanded even more than the Dragoon. "Keep watch for anything out of the ordinary, whatever might qualify, and see if they took her off the station and where. I understand that security here will be a lot tighter than *Sovereign Nakhimov*, but at the same time, it might not be, so exercise caution but not cowardice."

"Aye, sir," she replied. "Pana is already headed this way, for an expected late dinner and planning session. Undertaking a security sweep now, as a prelude to attempting to access certain systems."

Ilan nodded and put her down for now. Suvi had broken into a casino, so he was pretty certain that a mere naval base wasn't going to be any harder.

He needed to figure out how to get Bethany back.

And who he needed to kill in the process.

PART III

Ilan had his gun pointed at Ioannidi when he opened the hatch, but she was alone and entered when he waved her in. Corridor empty as well, but they had been put in an out of the way section for visitors.

"Where's Bethany?" Ioannidi asked as she came to rest.

And maybe realized that she was in the middle of three angry men.

"Somebody took her," Suvi spoke up from her clamshell. "Knocked Ilan out. Vivian and Armando found him eleven minutes later. I doubt that whoever did it has had time to get her off the station, but have not been able to locate her as yet."

Ilan let his scowl speak volumes. Might have etched hull metal with it, from the way his cheeks hurt.

"Somebody kidnapped her?" Ioannidi barked, voice all angry, surprised, and protective.

"Right out of the middle of your biggest base," Ilan agreed. "Who do you trust around here?"

It was like throwing cold water in her face, but it worked. She blinked and reset, suddenly an officer again.

"Captain Harcrow is probably it among senior people," she said quietly. "I've been kept off to one side."

Ilan nodded.

"I need you to convince him to give you a ship," Ilan said simply. "An armed ship. Preferably a corvette or a frigate that either you are in command of or the commanding officer has been specifically put under your command for the duration of this emergency."

"Why?"

"Because I sure as hell wouldn't want to stay on this station, or even this planet, if I'd just done something that egregiously stupid to someone as angry as Javier," Ilan replied. "Zakhar and Djamila might be bad news, but Javier's coming for the soul of whoever did this."

"And me," Suvi added.

"I love you, Suvi, but Javier scares me more," Ilan replied.

"Same, Ilan," Suvi said, so she understood that things were going to get OUT OF HAND.

And he was going to help.

"So, someone kidnaps Bethany and runs like hell for deep space?" Ioannidi asked.

"Hostage for later," Ilan nodded. "The three of us guys are nobodies, or he'd have grabbed us, too. I'm presuming either the big dipshit himself, or one of his top lieutenants did this. They'll run. Either they have access to a *Concord* warship, or it's a civilian ship, but they'll run. If the Admiralty is that completely corrupt, they might hold her here, but that just paints a bigger bullseye on the side of the hull than Walvisbaai had at *Nidavellir*. They thought they were invulnerable, too, Commander."

She'd gone white, listening to him, but so had Viv and Armando.

"That's a declaration of war on the *Concord*, Yu," she whispered.

"No," Ilan growled back at her sharply. "Javier already declared war on the pirate clans. If your people did this, then they've chosen to side with the pirates. Chosen Javier Aritza as their mortal enemy. Because The Science Officer is coming for them, whoever **they** are. Pretty uniforms and a bunch of warships aren't going to stop my people from destroying a bunch of pirate scum."

A part of him shrugged in amazement at the words coming out of his mouth, but he was back at *Ugen*, which was still a better place in his mind than *Nidavellir*, because Afia had nearly been killed that day.

At *Ugen*, he was the guy who rode to the rescue.

Here, he merely presaged the arrival of the entire Mongol Horde, coming for your fucking soul.

Ilan was good with either outcome.

Ioannidi shook herself once, then nodded.

"Do we tell anybody?" she asked.

"No," Ilan said simply. "You talk to him and see what he can do to help, without telling him why you are in a hurry, because someone, somewhere is listening. I don't want them knowing what we're up to until it's too late to stop us."

"I'll need to talk to him directly, then," she replied.

"Go," Ilan ordered. "We'll use this as a command post for now, but don't bring anybody we don't know with you. Or send any strangers."

Her face got inscrutable, then understanding dawned.

Folks would be looking at his barrel when the door opened. And anybody giving him any reason got taken down hard with a stunner, tied up, and MAYBE got an apology later.

She left. Ilan looked at his three helpers.

"Suvi, how long ago?" he asked.

"Eighty-six minutes," she replied instantly.

"Long enough to be off-station," Ilan grimaced. "Can you tap a public line or something and get arrivals and departures? I don't need anything but a name and hull classification."

"Doing that now, but nothing has jumped out at me," Suvi said. "However, this is a major base and ships are constantly coming and going, so I might miss something."

"Long as you watch and keep notes," Ilan told her. "The

Concord chooses sides. Today. Now. Either they help us, or we have to sneak out of here, steal a ship if he have to, and tell Javier what happened."

"We likely to come back and blow shit up?" Armando asked.

"You were at *Nidavellir*," Ilan told him. "If we have to top that, we will. Someone is going down hard for this. That much I promise. All I need at this point is an address."

"In that case, let me start wandering stupidly and aimlessly around the flight decks, like a lost civilian," Viv said. "Maybe I'll see something, but more importantly, maybe I'll see something we can steal if we assume that they don't throw our asses back on *Tucana* and ship us out."

"I already assume that they have confiscated it and towed it somewhere," Ilan replied. "Up and until the moment we sail out of here on her. Go do your thing and see if you can let Suvi know as you go. Armando, what do you need?"

"Had been planning a public relations campaign," the big guy said. "Think I need to up my game and aim one at the admirals on this station and another at the civilian population below us. They probably don't know what's being done in their names, either of them, and could use a good deal of sunlight."

"You and Suvi," he said, waving the man off.

Ilan found the chair he had knocked over and set it up where someone coming in wouldn't immediately see him.

Next asshole coming through without knocking was going back out with a smoking hole THROUGH their chest.

PART IV

Vivian had initially resented having to take classes in acting, but Spider had made it a requirement. Said that even a good thief screwed up occasionally and got discovered or arrested.

The key in both cases was being able to sell someone a tale of woe and bullshit entirely fabricated on the spot. Confusion was usually enough to get them looking the wrong way so you could make a break for it.

Here, he was in the middle of the biggest naval base in space. Even the Khatum's main one wasn't this big, but she merely controlled one world and got hired to provide security to a small sector of space.

The *Concord* still had delusions of hegemony.

At the same time, he'd spent enough time around his crew of folks to understand that those dreams were fading. Lots of weapons, but not enough money to have everything they wanted, so starting to lean into *Sentience* as a solution again, after a century of moving away from such things, watching *Neu Berne*'s final failure over the exact ship he was sailing on these days.

Station was big, but not as crowded as he'd been expecting, so Vivian was able to wander a bit. A few times, he'd even run into someone and merely nodded as he kept going, looking like a man on a mission.

Folks had fallen for it and ignored him passing.

He found himself on a mezzanine level. Or something. Hard to classify it, save that one big hallway had transteel windows on both sides, inclined so you could see down into the big bays below. Flight bays. Lots of them, but all civilian ships, so he supposed that he was in the right section of the base for scouting.

Cargo ships. And a couple of couriers, but he was mostly focused on cargo. Easier to slip aboard a ship like that if they were loading big crates. Either just walk aboard or find the right box to ride in, but he never trusted that sort of thing.

Still, it gave him several ideas, so Vivian walked the entire length of the corridor. And found that it went on a ways, eventually ending up at an area with larger bays that docked to external ships, with crews busy moving boxes out to an airlock.

At one point, he came around a corner and nearly ran into a group of folks watching some bay. Nobody was paying attention, but they seemed intent, so he slipped around the far side of the group and peeked.

Nicer bay. Somebody important was doing things, because there were a lot of bodies in uniforms moving around. And seemed intent, over and above these folks watching. Vivian had a feeling, so he slipped away and found stairs down.

Main deck. The hatch he wanted had two alert guards with tablets, checking boxes and faces, so Vivian turned away and headed after an empty flatbed hauler, maintaining a safe distance as the machine beeped. Stumbled into a break area and saw several folks trying to ignore one another. Better, all of them were civilians, with badges on their hips where they could access secured areas.

The bay he wanted wouldn't work. Too secure, but Vivian wandered over to a machine and bought himself a bottle of juice, moving to a ratty couch and collapsing into it in a pretty good example of a guy that had just pulled a double and needed a nap.

Couple of folks like that around here. He fit right in.

A woman on the far side of the couch smiled wanly at him, like she was considering hitting him up, but too exhausted to get anywhere with it. He matched her smile.

"Bad day?" he asked in a quiet voice.

"Crash load," she replied. "Got pulled off a freighter to put a bunch of boxes on a yacht for some rich punk. Got him gone, then back to the first job. Just now getting a break after six hours."

"Yacht?" Vivian asked. "Like for an admiral or something?"

Stupid. Always play stupid.

"Civilian," she shook her head. "Somebody with a lot of friends, though, because they had him loaded from the same deck as the admirals use."

"I am obviously in the wrong line of work," he grinned.

She matched it, still pale and sweaty.

"Same. Hey, where's your badge?"

So, she'd been looking for his name.

Vivian looked down like it should be right there on his hip. Then went to his other hip. Then looked on the couch.

"Shit," he muttered. "Don't tell me I broke the hook again."

She nodded sagely.

"Happens to me a lot, too," she said. "Hopefully it didn't just leave on whatever ship you finished loading. Security will give you shit about getting a new one."

"They do," he nodded. "Gonna have to backtrack now and see if somebody found it. See you around."

And exit, stage left, as if pursued by a bear, in case she comes and asks for a comm number he didn't have. Or decided to turn him over to security and get him arrested, because Vivian was pretty sure he wasn't supposed to be in this part of the station without a badge, but nobody had stopped him yet.

Walking back the way he'd came, he found an alcove with a workstation, both currently dark. A basic terminal lounge sort of place, if you had important people who were waiting for something. Maybe drive them up on a cart, then park them here with booze and entertainment, while they waited for the ship to open for loading.

He'd seen enough folks like that in his time, though Javier and the others were far better.

Vivian looked both ways, but nobody seemed to be anywhere in sight, so he slipped behind the desk and hunched in. It was a trick Spider had taught him. How to make yourself invisible socially.

He turned his attention to the keyboard, hoping that it wasn't all that secured.

Powered up, he got to a basic menu and asked for departure schedules from a cargo standpoint instead of people. That sort of thing shouldn't be top secret or anything. And it wasn't.

He sent the information to a printer, then nearly peed his pants when the screen flickered once and a message appeared.

Hi, Viv. It's Suvi. Watching you on a monitor.

Right, she'd done this to *Sovereign Nakhimov*, but nobody had needed a cat burglar at the time, so he'd stayed on the ship instead of getting station time. Probably just as well, considering how all that went down.

"Looking for our friend to have left in the last two hours, probably from this deck," he typed back, letting her work and realizing how much access she must have to talk to him here.

And how much trouble he could get into.

"Can you have the system create badges, in case?" he typed as she worked.

"Yes on two," she typed back. "Think I found our friend on one, so you won't be here long. Anna loaded his ship."

Anna?

He must have said something. Or mouthed it.

"The woman in the lounge," Suvi typed. "Tracked her backwards in footage and found the ship. *Golden Gazelle*, but ownership records and the like are set behind a security wall that's frankly a little scary. Plus, sudden priority cargo load and departure overrides that should have raised a stink."

"Make a note to tell Ioannidi," he replied with his fingers. "For Harcrow's investigation. Might be more evidence of malfeasance."

Because he'd seen enough of it since entering the *Concord*, though he hadn't mentioned things to Bethany. Not his job, especially not if they were asking for help.

Still, helpful to locate the bad guys. If they could be neutralized.

"FOUND HIM!" Suvi's message appeared. "Social page in a local newspaper, hosting a party on his new yacht *Golden Gazelle*. It's our buddy."

"Timing makes presumptions," Vivian typed. "Route all this to Ilan and Ioannidi. I'm headed that direction now."

"Stand by," she said, and the printer beside him suddenly started hissing and whirring.

A moment later, a badge emerged with a reasonable picture of him on the front and his traveling name. Not the one he'd been born with, but Vivian Aafjes, which was who he was these days.

"This will get you home fastest," she typed. "Just don't try to access that one spot on Bay Nine you were looking at. They might know about our friend and have decided to run like hell after helping him."

"Gotcha. Outbound."

He rose as the screen went dark, new tag hanging and jauntily headed the way he'd come. And avoiding Anna, just in case.

Bethany was far more important.

PART V

Pana had kept it cryptic, getting into see Captain Harcrow. Ilan seemed pretty intent on just stepping in and taking command to hunt down whoever had captured Bethany, and she'd seen the white hot rage in the back of that man's eyes.

Dumb idea to get crossways with Ilan Yu.

She closed the hatch and sat across from Captain Harcrow without either of them speaking. He raised one eyebrow at her, but they were both Intelligence people.

Sometimes, that job involved coloring outside the lines.

"Please activate any jammers you might have handy," she said quietly.

His eyes got big, because they were in his office. Should be secured already.

From whom?

Still, he reached under his side of the desk and she heard a faint click before he nodded.

"What happened?" he asked.

"About two hours ago, someone apparently broke into the cabin where Bethany and Ilan were staying," she said, voice still pitched low. "Stunned him. Kidnapped her. Ilan is organizing a mission to find and rescue Bethany, and assumes that she has already been removed from the station. He asks you to assign his mission a warship, under my command one way or the other, so he can go in pursuit."

Captain Marc Harcrow had gone surprise white. Then rage red. Finally focused white again, his jaw muscles standing out where he was grinding his teeth. Probably to minimize the profanities.

Pana understood that feeling. At least Ilan trusted her. About as far as he might anybody right now.

"I'd ask how, but we're already past that," Mark replied. "And have triggered the sorts of investigations that I don't think can be swept under the rug later to hide them. Yu is certain that they have left this base?"

"I got the impression that they expect your next efforts to roil the waters, sir," she said. "That anything off-center is likely to draw unwanted attention, so bad guys—their words—would rather go to ground than attempt to bluff it out. Especially as we are dealing with a rich and powerful civilian who might be able to bend the rules far more than most people. At least as long as there are no lights shined on the situation."

She watched Harcrow turn inward, racing through reports and meetings as he reviewed things. Having a near perfect memory for such details was almost a requirement in this job, so she understood.

His eyes came back to the present and watched her closely.

"How good are your line command credentials?" he asked obliquely.

"Sufficient, sir," she replied, chin coming up. "At *Purton*, we occasionally got to add ships to the museum, so I have taken temporary command for intelligence purposes and disposal afterwards."

He nodded. Considered.

"We have a ship," Harcrow continued. "*Concord Warship Trinity*. A corvette configured for long missions and covert surveillance, so somewhat stripped down crew and a good deal of automation, plus space to add a dozen long-term passengers who might be intelligence operatives. More importantly, the vessel does not appear to be a warship externally, but a standard freighter, possibly the next category up from the vessel that Durbin and her crew arrived in."

"What do we do with *Tucana*, sir?" she asked.

"Take it into custody and impound it for now, I think," he said sharply. "It is unarmed, which is why I presume they are asking for a warship."

"They are going after a particular person with singular attention, Captain Harcrow," Pana offered delicately.

"And you will not repeat this, even to them," he said, waiting for her to nod, "but I am not convinced that they were wrong to do so. I have been granted compartmentalized information about the subject in the last twelve hours that has me wondering why nobody ever did anything about him before this."

"Ilan is convinced that the admiralty staff, at least at *Merankorr*, is totally bent," she countered. "Again, his words."

Harcrow nodded but didn't speak, so Pana drew her own conclusions.

"I think everyone has grown too comfortable," he said. "Let's use that as our euphemism, Ioannidi."

Silence fell for a moment.

"You pack," he ordered. "I'll have details for you in an hour, though I'm not certain the state of the vessel without asking. Orders will arrive for you, then you will descend into radio silence and presumably deep cover, as we cannot be certain which flag officers might not be working in the best interests of the *Concord*."

"All of them would say they are, sir," she offered, rising.

"Perhaps," he said. "But many of them would be wrong, and it appears to be our job to separate the heroes from the villains."

She saluted and departed, unwilling to offer any wry commentary on that observation.

She wasn't sure there were any heroes out there.

No, that was wrong. This Science Officer appeared to be one. And had brought his entire team to bear on the *Concord* itself.

Worse, she wondered if she'd been on the wrong side all this time.

At least the wrong side of history.

How did she fix that problem?

P VI

Bethany hadn't gotten to the complete bottom of the entertainment options available, but that was mostly because Slavkov had a sadistic streak that he liked to indulge in. A lot of slasher vids in his library. And a lot of pornographic stuff that had only a thin veneer of vanilla at the top before descending into...

Best not to go there. She was a librarian. Organizing information systems was in her blood and bones, but Bethany found that she was happier not knowing the details of things that Valko Slavkov apparently needed to enjoy himself.

It was one thing to have two or more consenting adults consenting at each other. His collection verged heavily over into power games of various flavors, where rape wasn't a sex thing, but an element of control. Usually exercised via fear and/or pain.

She'd gone deep enough to start drawing certain conclusions, but those merely reinforced her previous understandings of the punk.

To keep boredom at bay when she couldn't take notes, Bethany had started watching a show called Starlight Aion, starring the same guy that had been in Suvi's favorite, Paragon Grieving that she had used on *Sovereign Nakhimov* and later stolen to watch.

He was a good actor. And she wondered if Slavkov had some intellectual friends who came aboard occasionally, or if this was part of some standard entertainment package, tucked in a corner a man like him might never know existed.

It filled the hours, and provided her with a focus point upon which to meditate as she organized and memorized her notes to date. She would be getting out of this. And would need to update Javier and the others with all she had learned, pitifully slim though it was.

Posterity would also want to know, if nothing else, and she was Ship's Historian.

Eternity was her job.

A knock and the hatch opened. Pause. Head appeared, because they were smart enough to assume she might attack someone. Hadn't, but reserved the right later.

"Let's go," a man said.

One of a small mob of interchangeable goons. Bethany was tall and lean. Stayed lean because Emma St. Kitts had demanded everyone up their exercise routine. The two men at the hatch both outweighed her by about double. And had the scarred ears and broken noses of men used to getting into the scrum for the puck.

She paused the show and rose. Wasn't time for food, and they usually delivered that anyway. She presumed Slavkov had questions. Or wanted to taunt her.

Something.

So far, none of this had gone beyond intellectual torture. Confinement.

She wondered how soon he might move on to physical abuse.

Whatever form it might take.

Bethany screwed her emotions down tight and emerged from the cabin, walking between the two towering men as they went forward and up two levels, her room being on the lowest deck.

Slavkov had a suite. Probably close to two hundred and fifty square meters, which was impressive on a ship this small. But it was his yacht. She'd gleaned that from the doctor, who was a talkative type, as long as none of your questions got too sharp.

Mostly, she had learned to ask open-ended things and let him ramble.

Today, it looked like Slavkov wanted to pour equal parts derision and triumph over her.

Like usual.

First goon took her to a chair and sat her down with a heavy hand on her shoulder.

Like usual.

Slavkov rose from behind his desk and began to pace back and forth, well out of her reach.

Like usual.

"I want to talk about the Land Leviathan," he said, sounding more intellectual and less homicidal today, which was a change she welcomed.

Bethany adjusted her face to show a receptive attitude.

"They managed to steal it while it was boarding for transport?" he asked.

"That is my understanding, having interviewed several people involved," she replied in her Librarian voice, reminding him that she'd come along much later. And thus, was not one of the people who'd done such an insulting thing to him. "Javier recruited assistance from the Khatum of *Altai*, including certain personnel. They were able to sneak aboard the transport ship after it had landed and the Land Leviathan was in the process of loading. The crew were captured and later released, having been merely employees unable to stop an assault by a highly-trained commando unit."

The Gun Bunnies. And all the help Djamila had found necessary, including some especially frightening people, given the observations about Spider that she had dutifully recorded.

"And *Nidavellir*?"

"Again, my understanding is that they felt the need for a shield they could use while attacking the station, so used your transport and the Leviathan," she said, keeping all emotion out of her voice. "Two birds, one stone, as I believe Captain Sokolov has described it, but I'd have to check my notes for attribution."

It was weird, pretending to be merely an employee who wasn't on very personal terms with the senior players. Like she'd been when she first boarded *Excalibur*.

So much water under so many bridges. Today, she was Javier's Ambassador to *Merankorr*.

And a prisoner of a rich punk who didn't like being told no.

"Can they be bought off?" he asked, pausing his pacing to turn and look directly at her, thinking himself safe even, with a desk and five meters between them.

Bethany pretended to consider her answer, understanding that more than one of her friends had described the end goal as heads on stakes as a warning to future generations. Starting with Valko Slavkov.

"I can't say for certain," she replied primly. Librarian with no emotional attachments.

About as far from the truth as you could get.

His grimace was telling.

"I'm told that every man has a price," she offered as a deflection before he got too far down that path. "Perhaps you need to locate Aritza and ask him what his is?"

Heads. Stakes. But we don't say that. Not yet.

"Where would I look?" he demanded.

"I had a list," Bethany replied carefully. "On my computer, but I have not seen it, so I am not sure it was captured when I was. Without that, I have a few fallbacks memorized, but those are specifically for use if someone got separated from the others and had to make their way alone."

"Like now," he nodded, pretending like he wasn't holding a metaphorical leash around her neck.

Power games. That was his thing.

"Like now," she offered, playing along.

"What do you suppose his price is?" Slavkov mused, eyes off over her shoulder.

Bethany shrugged with the shoulder not being held down.

"Before *Drako*, he was on his way back to *Altai*, where I understand he intends to retire and teach," she said, leaving off all the details that anybody who knew The Science Officer would be able to fill in.

Like how stopping moving might actually be impossible for the man.

The only question she really had was the future scale of his so-called puttering.

Gardens or worlds? Dorn Hetzel's Rising Storm was probably less than a generation out. Under twenty years. She'd be middle-aged when it started. Javier close to retirement. Zakhar done.

And a galaxy in need of rescuing.

"I just need to find his price, then," Slavkov mused.

He nodded to himself, and gestured to the goons. She got pulled upright and escorted out, back to her episode and whatever other shows she could find to entertain herself while waiting to be tortured or rescued.

Because if Valko Slavkov thought he could buy off Javier at this point, the man was the galaxy's biggest fool.

Still, some men never learn.

LE BEAU GESTE

PART I

Djamila had made a list. Checked it regularly. Filtered it through a dozen of the most dangerous—most competent—killers she knew, most of whom she had found as polished diamonds and turned into warmakers.

She considered that list as she rapped on Javier's hatch, then entered a moment later when it opened. Wasn't like he would be surprised, since Suvi had watched her approach.

Still, the look on his face was more pensive than usual.

Except that such expectations were for an older version of their relationship. The old rivalry, carved into stone with rules but no less deadly than the need to make victory look like an accident rather than an assassination.

The Arms Race, they had called it privately.

Djamila swept in and sat. He had a workbench rather than a desk, though he still sat behind it. Instead of papers, he had a single tablet and a lot of tools at hand where he could use to tinker or weld, because at the end of the day the Science Officer was a technical nerd. He needed Zakhar to actually exercise command, never having learned those skills and entirely uninterested in them today.

Especially as they were unnecessary.

"What's up?" he asked, looking up from what appeared to be a new version of Suvi's combat drone. Like she'd first met on *Svalbard*, when the two women had taken on all the pirates to rescue Javier.

Did he already understand where the situation was going? He might.

"Reviewing recruiting needs," she replied, watching him move, hands doing something with muscle memory that didn't require eyes looking down.

Like her, shooting backwards at a scene she had memorized on entering a room.

"Do we have time to recruit individually?" he asked her, eyes locking on. "Or are we hiring someone's private mercenary company?"

She paused and parsed her words.

"Are we going to be at this long enough to send Behnam a note and request she send a troop transport?" Djamila asked.

He stopped working and pursed his lips.

"I'm hoping not," he replied. "Mostly because that might be six months sail either direction from here, presumably with however long it takes in the middle to pack a ship. And I fear that the *Concord* might decide that we're serious about being an invading army and all that shit if we go down that path. I reserve the right to change my mind, though."

Djamila nodded. About the same conclusions she had reached, where giving her foe too long to dig in meant that it was harder to dig them out later. If she could force him to ground, that would be one thing, as she could send in focused assassination missions at that point, but she had no way to embargo an entire planet, even after she found that punk.

"I think we need to move to a shorter-term solution," she offered. "One perhaps two steps on this side of *Altai* sending troops, but only two."

His eyes narrowed.

She'd say Navarre was looking out, but Djamila probably

knew Javier Aritza as a person better than anyone else alive, save only Mina's instinctive understanding of the man.

Behnam was the other half of his soul, but the better half. Suvi, the daughter he never had.

If warfare grew intimate enough to qualify, she'd been his lover for over a decade, described in that way.

They didn't necessarily need words to communicate. Instead, he was reading her soul, in ways that even Zakhar and Farouz didn't. Couldn't.

Shallow nod at whatever he saw.

"Where in the galaxy," he began in a laconic tone, "could I possibly find an army of elite killers good enough for you to hire them on short notice and turn them loose like a wave of ancient Viking berserkers to pillage and ravage, when everybody still thinks that the Europeans of that age were the more sophisticated culture because they later erased most of the records suggesting how primitive they were socially?"

Djamila felt a chill hand drag delicate fingers across the nape of her neck at his words.

Lovers in warfare, an intimacy even closer than the flesh.

"There is a place," she suggested lightly, playing this like a form of puppet theater because his words had already turned it into a morality play of sorts.

But didn't that describe this entire situation?

"Do tell?"

"A land of Vikings, if you will," she nodded.

"Can they subordinate themselves to a *mere woman*?" he asked sharply. "A child of enlisted parents, born and raised on the wrong side of the starport and never granted the ability to shine, because she lacked the proper family connections? Can they stand second behind a woman who should have been promoted to top command because she was better than they were, in all the ways that mattered?"

No smiles between them. Romance to the Death, perhaps,

but that had passed, leaving only respect and admiration, expressed in most obscure ways.

"I believe so," Djamila replied. "They will need someone to give a speech. A presentation. The Rising Storm, in all of its implications. A recruiter, if you will. And an outsider, because while I might command the troops, they will need to be fired with the righteous fury of someone intending to make the galaxy a better place, regardless of the opinions of those folks benefiting from the current and unstable state of things."

"And Zakhar can't do that?" he pressed, words low and compact, like delicate whispers on her flesh.

"He could," she agreed. "Navarre might do an even better job, but for all the wrong reasons and thus give them all the incorrect assumptions about their purpose in this endeavor. It will need The Science Officer. He will have to stand before them and sound the clarion call that rouses nations to march forth."

"And that's not worse than just letting everything catch fire and burn to the ground?" his anger caressed her with gossamer wings. "That's not handing someone the match and pointing them?"

"It will be about honor, Aritza," she countered simply. "About rising above yourself and doing what civilization itself requires of you, regardless of the personal cost. These men and women are among the few I know who could answer that honestly."

"Because history has painted them as among the worst—most evil—folks to ever set foot on a starship's decks," he offered.

"That was one hundred and twenty-eight years ago," she countered. "They have lived in peace for the last eighty. Poor and impoverished of body, but not of spirit. There are those who still believe the old ways were better, but they are fewer with each generation."

"Because folks there are growing soft?" he challenged.

"Because the *Concord* was right," she admitted. "And the *Union of Man*. And *Balustrade*. And all the rest. Conquest by arms doesn't do anything but hurt people. If your culture is advanced enough—*better*—then people will naturally gravitate to your side. And if they start fleeing your ideals, that should be the moment when you stop and wonder if you have gone astray."

"And have you gone astray?" he asked.

Djamila bit back her response and studied his eyes. Here was an officer of the *Concord*. One of those men and women who saw themselves as the good guys, rising to hegemonic power when everyone else had fallen in the aftermath of the Great War, exhausted and broken in spirit.

However, that had been four generations ago. And rot and corruption had set in, because the watchers had stopped measuring themselves against that ledger. Had grown fat and lazy.

Had assumed the superiority of their civilization, when it was finally obvious to her eyes that they had gone as sour as her own ancestors had. Possibly for the same reasons.

Certainly, the same overwhelming arrogance.

"There was a dream," she offered, taking him back. "There at the very beginning, long before galactic war became the outcome. Even then, it was unnecessary, but you cannot always convince folks of that, save in retrospect. That dream was of the protector. It got perverted later. Transformed into the Invader. The Occupier. The Overseer. But in the beginning it was still pure. And, I think, still lives underneath any veneer that might be in place today. It will require your efforts to draw it to the surface."

"And they will not listen to you?" he pushed.

"They must." Djamila felt her chin come up. "But it will not be sufficient. I can lead them, but I cannot inspire them. I cannot fire them with that righteousness of saving the galaxy from itself. That will be your task. You are equal to it, however, or I wouldn't be here."

He rocked back and considered her, like a good lover pausing midway to make sure of himself and his partner before continuing. War and romance—rage and intimacy—were but sides of one coin, after all.

"How big of an army did you envision, if we raised this flag?" he asked.

Djamila nodded. That was question, wasn't it?

Too few, and it greatly limited her strategic and even tactical options. Too many and it threatened a jihad—a crusade itself—upon the galaxy, which was exactly what the current situation did not need.

But it is utterly impossible to conquer and hold an inhabited world without first either bombing it into submission, or flooding it with perhaps as many as four percent of the overall population in troops. For any major worlds, that would require millions. Far more than this needed.

And, she smiled to herself, they were not conquering. They were liberating. Removing villains. Excising evil like a cancer, then letting the patient recover at their own pace, with the hope that it would take them less than the time Hetzel had given them for the spark that would create conflagration.

"For now, a full cohort," she said, speaking her evil aloud to her lover, that it might become a thing cast in flesh and bone.

A challenge to the gods themselves, given that she was asking this of two *Concord* officers and the Khatum of *Altai*.

Awakening the dragon itself from its slumbers.

Threatening the very galaxy's future.

Again.

"Did you have one in mind?" he asked, tones turning tender and triumphant finally. "And will they go for it?"

"I will make them," she challenged him. "After you convince them that this is the thing that the future itself **requires**."

He considered her more. Watched her eyes, her hands, even her hair, coming in gray now finally.

Even Ballerinas of Death age. Slow down.

They must become even more deadly when the body begins to fail them, that their enemies do not rejoice.

This thing, they could do. And do it with righteous indignation at a galaxy that had fallen far short of its own, outspoken ideals.

"Who?" Javier finally asked her.

"The Dragon Watch," she said, touching the spot on her left shoulder where she had once worn their unit patch.

When she had been of them. A trooper, limited by her birth and nothing more, so she had set out and carved herself a place in the galaxy that didn't care.

But today, the rest of them must rise above themselves as well.

And she would need The Science Officer to achieve that. Nobody else could manage the task. Even he might not, but in that case, nobody could and they were on a fool's errand.

Righteous, still, but doomed to failure.

Javier nodded and rose, holding out a hand that she took. It was more powerful than a lover's kiss, because it sealed them into history itself.

"Suvi," he said simply, waiting as she turned to see the woman appear on the screen.

Djamila gasped when she saw it.

Normally, Suvi wore the green uniform of a *Concord* Yeoman. The same color as Zakhar had worn for so long, neither of them adding any badges, because the color and the cut was enough.

More recently, she had taken to wearing a variety of costumes, ranging the entire rainbow of colors and fashions as designed by people like Adrian Ahmad.

Today, Suvi had gone formal.

Djamila had grown up in the slate-blue verging onto gray, but that was the infantry. Suvi wore the uniform of a *Neu Berne* naval officer. Probably what the *Sentience-In-Residence* would have projected when he commanded this vessel.

Scarlet, long sleeve shirt. Not cotton, but something stretchy if still a little loose, with refractive elements in it that looked like glitter. Black trim around pockets and seams, to show things off. Standing collar in black, with the correct badges for rank and assignment, exactly where they should be

Djamila blinked back tears.

"Sir?" Suvi asked, eyes on Javier.

"Calculate a course to *Neu Berne* itself from our next resupply rendezvous," Javier ordered in a tone that had taken on a resonance that even Zakhar only rarely possessed. "We'll be moving the entire force that way and establishing a new base in a different hinterland."

"Aye, sir," she said, and blinked back out.

Djamila turned watery eyes on Javier's hard smile.

"Zakhar used a phrase at *Ferran*," he said. "I find that it makes things even better, if we go and recruit your crazy kinfolk to do this thing. He referred to them as my *fleets of vengeance*. Plural. Many such forces that I can send out to crush my enemies."

"We are not unleashing *Neu Berne*," she said sharply.

"No," he agreed. "We're recruiting them to the side of justice, which is even better. Or worse, depending on who you are."

Djamila felt the shiver possess her entire soul for a moment. The rest of the galaxy might not see it that way.

They would be wrong.

PART II

Piet had taken command of *Storm Gauntlet* after Javier had done his thing. And taken Mary-Elizabeth with him back to *Excalibur*.

Piet was handling both command and gunnery duties for now. Kova Bychova was aft with her engines. Mikhail Dominguez was his Pilot, and Tobias Gibney his Science Officer.

Suvi didn't need the help, but Piet had made the case to start splitting up the command crew anyway, so they could be on multiple vessels at once, doing things.

And, as he liked to tease Zakhar, the man should have already retired, at which point Piet would have ascended to command of the old *Storm Gauntlet*.

Different ship today. Same outcome.

Same silliness.

WAY more firepower, as long as you were careful about how you used it. And had reloaded all four hundred missile bays before you set out.

Deep space surrounded them, but Piet was fine with that. Suvi could get anywhere faster than someone who had to land and plot each jump as slow as a human did it. She'd gone ahead of them, leaving him to meet up with *Flying Maiden* and *Eldritch Stele* as their little convoy sailed along behind her.

Zakhar's Fleet of Vengeance, though he'd blamed Javier for everything.

As one did, when you knew what was really happening behind the curtains.

"Are we really going to turn a bunch of *Neu Berne* killers loose on an unsuspecting galaxy?" Mikhail asked as Piet let the nav computers zero down where he thought he was against a dozen major stars that let him parallax his coordinates tightly.

Lots of down time when you had a long voyage, but this was a new ship to this crew, and he was the sheepdog keeping the others safe so he had to pay closer attention. Do it right.

"Only unsuspecting if nobody stops to ask just how pissed Javier is," Tobias offered. "Not like they don't got it coming, after all."

Piet had to agree with that sentiment.

"Dude, they're recruiting berserkers," Mikhail laughed.

"No," Piet corrected him, waiting for both men to turn before dropping the other shoe on them. "They're recruiting an entire battalion of people like the Dragoon."

Which, honestly, was worse, but he didn't figure that these two had really read deep into what had happened on the ground at *Ophiuchi*. And all the things Djamila and her people had done when badly outnumbered and trapped without help on a planetary surface.

"So what do we do with five hundred *Neu Berne* Assault Marines?" Mikhail asked.

"Storm a station instead of blowing it up," Tobias offered. "Or land on the surface in a couple of specially configured freighters and hit somebody's palace from all sides when you want to take prisoners instead of just bombing the place and hoping you got your target."

"Right on both counts," Piet said. "It also lets *Neu Berne* say that they did a thing, when a lot of other folks still sneer at them, in spite of hardly anybody still being alive that fought in that war. Some old prejudices die hard."

"So we're rehabilitating them, on top of everything else?" Tobias asked.

"*The Rising Storm*," Piet reminded them. "You've hopefully read at least the executive summary by now, but I would suggest you spend a week and dive deep into the details and footnotes. Javier is asking all of the major players in the galaxy to come together, here and now, in order to do something about the epidemic of piracy that seems to start as soon as any of those folks turn their backs. Not just smuggling, but all the bad shit we used to do."

"Before Mina," Mikhail nodded.

Piet was a little surprised. He'd expected the man to say *before Javier*, but there was a distinct gap between those two moments.

Javier had fast-talked his way onto the crew first. And into an officer's slot. But anyone who spent any time around the man would know how smart he was. And how sneaky.

But yeah, it was Wilhelmina Teague who had changed everything. Piet only had to go back and compare symphonies he'd written before knowing her to things since to see that. Even having Suvi as an occasional composing partner or assistant in delinquency hadn't made that big of a change.

The Shepherd of the Way, though...

"We ever hear from her?" Tobias asked.

"No, but I got the impression from Zakhar that the Khatum has her off doing her thing elsewhere," Piet replied. "Likely, any reports she files go that direction, so we'll read them when we get home."

"Should we track her down and draw her in here?" Mikhail asked.

Piet started to say something salty and caught himself short.

What could she do?

Hell, what *couldn't* that woman do? Look what she'd done to the crew of the old private service strike corvette *Storm Gauntlet*, currently reincarnated in an arsenal frigate.

"Piet?" Tobias asked as the silence stretched.

"I have no idea how to find her," he said. "But your idea has legs. Next time I see Javier or Zakhar I'll mention it to them."

"Kinda facing the twilight of the gods here," Mikhail nodded, "Feel like we could use all the help we could get. And hey, that's Mina."

Yes. It was Mina. Current galactic holder of the record for time in a cryogenic chamber while surviving mostly unscathed. Four hundred and eighty-eight years, trapped in that mine field, waiting for her prince charming to come along and wake her with a kiss.

And now out reminding the modern era of the ancient words of Rama Treadwell.

Piet had read up on the man. Vanished prophet, like all the good ones tended to do, adding that level of mystique to things when they didn't simply grow old and died.

Too easy to turn into the asshole you railed against if you lived long enough to come full circle.

Rama Treadwell hadn't.

Had simply disappeared en route one day. Never arrived at his destination, with no clues or wreckage ever found.

So one of his Shepherds had gone looking, and managed to survive into the present day.

What would Mina make of the Dragon Watch? *Neu Berne*'s most elite special forces formation of infantry, where even Djamila Sykora had only made it as far as Leader 3, an enlisted punk who knew she was better than any of her officers.

Because *Neu Berne* was stuck in its own history of aristocratic privilege.

And the future was coming.

Worse, Piet was young enough that he'd still be here when it arrived.

If it hadn't already.

He locked eyes on Tobias and let the man squirm for a bit.

"Did deep into the logs you captured with this ship," he ordered. "Find any reference to Mina Teague in the present tense.

Ask Suvi when you see her to do the same. Worse come to worst, we post a Missed Connections message on a variety of comm boards, everyplace we go, and hopefully she finds it and decides to come save our sorry asses."

Tobias nodded, utterly serious now. He started typing and Piet noted that the nav computers had finished.

"All hands, stand by for our next jump," he announced on the intercom.

The future would be here too soon.

PART III

Javier looked out a porthole at the monstrous station where he'd parked, last time *Excalibur* visited *Neu Berne* itself. Big enough to park several First-Rate Galleons inside, though he knew that it was mostly empty and abandoned these days. Whole sections shut down to save on life support and maintenance costs, because *Neu Berne* didn't have a lot of trade with the rest of the galaxy, and all of their former colonies had been forcibly detached, occupied, and social reingineered to integrate them back into the wider galaxy.

And, looking inside himself, Javier found all of those old prejudices that had been stamped into him at *Bryce* in his Academy days. The good guys, facing down the militant lunatics intent on conquering...something.

Growing up was a bitch, and more recently he'd had a chance to read histories written by folks in *Balustrade* and the *Union of Man*. Had come to understand how much those two had colluded, way back in the days before the Great War, to keep *Neu Berne* at a lower level of strength.

To keep a challenger from rising, when the galaxy was big enough to have accommodated them.

If you were willing.

He'd grown a lot less fond of the *Union of Man* over the last few years as a result. Not enough to welcome *Neu Berne* as a rising military power again, but enough to understand that they'd been pushed into a corner the first time, then ground down and crushed because the *Concord* had been willing to sell ships and guns to anyone with cash, knowing that *Neu Berne* had been too proud at the time to take them up on it.

Leaving only the *Union of Man* and *Balustrade* with state of the art fleets instead.

He nodded to himself and kept his grumbles private. What he was about to do might go down in history on a scale that put him in the pantheon with folks like Benedict Arnold, Vidkun Quisling, Heriberto Rodriguez, and a few others.

Depending on who won when it was all done.

Javier ignored that platform and turned back to the rest of the bridge. Smiled grimly at Zakhar on his throne. At Mary-Elizabeth, poised to unleash havoc as needed.

At Djamila.

Her new uniform made him blink, every time he saw it, but Javier wore the same one himself. Adrian had come up with it, when tasked with rising above mere fashion and challenging the galaxy itself with something new.

Gold. Mostly a slightly-faded mustard color. Pullover shirt with white trim and a wide collar, over a black undershirt. Black pants that tucked into calf-high boots in a manner similar to what *Neu Berne* had done, but that was because the machines aboard were already configured to turn out such pants and boots in job lots, and nobody had ever bothered reprogramming them.

Mustard gold, as far as Javier knew, was unique as a military uniform. *Neu Berne* wore red. *Concord* had a richer green than the *Union of Man,* and *Balustrade* kept bouncing back and forth between green and blue-gray on a random basis.

Javier needed to stand out. Needed Djamila to stand out. Adrian had adapted the cut of the uniform from *Altai,* but changed colors to make certain. And it was Adrian, so it all looked utterly amazing on both of them, even as he watched Djamila was watching him have final last thoughts before shit went and got extra weird.

Javier had refused a sidearm. And the sword that came with the dress version of this uniform. He was about to be surrounded by people who made the Gun Bunnies look like weekend warriors by comparison. At least visually.

He'd stack Tom and Iqbal up against anybody with a gun on a range.

Afia entered the bridge and completed the bookends look, a head shorter while Djamila was a head taller. Golden trio, ready for the revolution.

"We doing this?" she asked him, sliding to a halt next to the Dragoon.

He turned to Zakhar.

"Do not dock until they sign a contract," he reminded the man. "I figure they are honorable, but that gets squishy if they think they can take possession of my warship."

"Of MY warship," Suvi said. "I'm still unlocked on guns if those idiots decide to send landing shuttles and swarm me."

He nodded. She'd get ugly, but sometimes, that was what you needed in order to make a point with someone.

"I'll burn their palace down and salt the ruins if I have to," Zakhar assured him.

Mary-Elizabeth just cackled like a malevolent witch, but she did that.

"Let Del know we're inbound," Javier announced.

He had a date with destiny.

PART IV

Javier appreciated that they'd landed Del's shuttle in a smaller bay, rather than opening the one that still had *Hammerfield* inscribed on the hull plates.

That time was done.

Captain Ulrich Mayer had seen *Hammerfield* destroyed, then repaired the ship itself and set it to orbiting forever. Or at least until the need had arisen for its return.

Like Arthur striding out of the swamps, *Excalibur* in one hand. That image warmed him as they walked through corridors designed for humans Djamila's size instead of his.

The three of them were being escorted by a team of hardasses in pretty uniforms, but Javier had expected that. He was something of a cultural hero to these people for returning the last crew of the last flagship from the last war.

At the same time, he was something of an asshole for not giving them back a First-Rate Galleon that had been upgraded to what Suvi considered to be the single most deadly warship in service.

Anywhere.

Tough. Deal with it.

They walked, and let him set the pace with shorter legs,

because everyone here was taller than him save Afia. While she was probably still meaner.

A hatch opened as the squad lead got there, and Javier followed the group into a conference room done in late militant steel. Gray everywhere. Hammered nickel finish, except where it was chromed to a shiny polish that was probably a bitch to keep clean.

Most of the people in here were second-tier, as far as Javier was concerned. Only one would make the important decisions. Only one mattered.

Star Admiral Bashar Zupanu.

Man wasn't as tall as Djamila. Maybe one hundred and ninety-seven centimeters. Heavy build, though. Muscles from using heavy iron weights regularly, instead of lean and flexible from yoga and running, like Javier had done.

Militant child of a militant culture, iron gray hair in a flattop and a face like someone had spalled it out of granite with a blunt chisel and a sledgehammer. Like Djamila, emerald green eyes that didn't miss anything. Scarlet uniform with almost no badges or medals on it, because he didn't need them to impress someone.

Senior-most flag officer in *Neu Berne*. Even the civilian government on the planet below were merely technocrats who were in charge on paper.

Zupanu was in command.

He sat on one side of the big table. Javier sat directly across from him, with Djamila on his right and Afia on his left. Zupanu had a pair of mere Vice Admirals flanking him, but they reminded Javier of guard kittens in front of a lion, not that he would insult them by saying that.

Unless they really provoked him. Hopefully, it wouldn't come to that, because Suvi was correct that she could take every other ship and station in orbit if anyone opened fire. Between *Drako* and Zakhar's lessons in assault tactics on an anchorage, she'd gotten a little scary.

Good thing he'd programmed her right the first time.

Zupanu glanced at Djamila, then dismissed her as a flunky without so much as a word. Or recognized her and wasn't going to acknowledge anything. Afia got a slightly longer look, but again, not anyone Zupanu was interested in dealing with.

Javier felt the weight of those bright green eyes. He didn't bristle. Didn't speak. Didn't react.

He wasn't here hat in hand asking a favor, though they might fool themselves into believing that. Javier Aritza was Prince Consort of *Altai*, as far as his crew was concerned. Ambassador to a major power in the east who could challenge the *Concord*, save that they were so far apart that they hardly ever spoke. And commander of a First-Rate Galleon that had impressed the shit out of folks when they'd arrived to see it.

"The uniform is new," Zupanu noted dryly, starting the conversation in the middle like they were old comrades.

Weren't, but still a useful opening. Things had been militantly bureaucratic before, when he'd brought the old crew home. Celebrations, but formal affairs. Not drinking quietly with your buddies.

Of course, *Excalibur* had just done a thing that had made the galactic news in those days. Even *Neu Berne* had heard about it.

"Lot of new things," Javier replied quietly, apparently skipping over twenty minutes of small talk and bullshit, interlaced with threats, blackmail, innuendo, and whatever else.

"Never thought I'd see her in a uniform again," Zupanu said, nodding to Djamila. In gold instead of blue. "Nor that she would actually return. Your proposal was so utterly outrageous that we actually had to stop and listen, rather than merely discounting it out of hand. At the same time, our spies have reported some interesting and perhaps surprising results from other places."

"I'll transmit the full after-action report of *Drako III*, as compiled by the *Sentience* that fought it," Javier replied, then nodded to Djamila. "And the woman in command of ground forces when eleven of us took on and defeated an entire battalion of infantry."

Blink. Maybe a moment of pucker. Man had to know how good Djamila had been when she'd been young. If she was older and slower, she was also better than she had been then, according to her own admission on both parts.

Eleven defeat four hundred? Sound like a fair fight to you?

Javier's smile was cruelty itself, distilled and embodied.

"Have you dug two graves?" Zupanu asked.

Javier's smile warmed some. It was the ancient maxim. Before setting out for a revenge quest, you should always dig two. One for them. One for yourself.

But that assumed that you didn't have a damned good reason to come back and try to rebuild your life when you were successful. Too many samurai movies ended in ritual sepuku to keep honor intact.

Javier preferred those weird westerns instead, where the hero got the girl and lived happily ever after. Wasn't sure it would happen here, but he had a woman back home that put Afia or Hajna to shame, which was about the highest possible bar Javier could imagine.

"I have," Javier assured him. "But this is bigger. This is everyone, coming together for the purposes of doing something nobody can handle alone."

"Ending organized piracy," Zupanu nodded. "I'd say it was impossible and you were a fool, but you've already proved me wrong several times. That's also why we're talking today."

It was good. They'd passed a test with the Star Admiral. Impressed him, even, which was a hard thing to do with an entire culture of militant lunatics.

Here, that craziness worked in Javier's favor, because they were a sword he could hold in one hand.

"The four clans will be destroyed before I'm satisfied," Javier said, then nodded to Afia. "Before she's satisfied."

Zupanu turned to the Pixie Kodiak and studied her closer.

Last time, she was still recovering from the belly wound that had nearly killed her. Hadn't spoken much or engaged in a lot of hijinks.

Time had passed, but not her rage.

"The one who nearly died at *Nidavellir*," the admiral noted.

"Nearly," Afia agreed. "Should have buried me ten meters deep if they were serious."

Because she really had clawed her way back from hell in order to be here. He'd seen the medical records. But he also knew what kind of woman Afia Burakgazi was.

"How will the galaxy react, if we do this thing?" Star Admiral Zupanu asked, a shallow glance at his two silent sidekicks, but they were window dressing and nothing more. "If the *Union* or *Balustrade* wakes up to *Neu Berne* on the hunt? Or the *Concord*?"

"I've sent notes home," Javier replied. "And to the *Union*, because I have a contact there as well. Personally, their help will make it easier, but their refusal merely slows me down. It doesn't stop me from what I'm going to do."

"Another raid like *Ferran*?" he asked.

"Taking the time to salt the earth next time, yes," Javier agreed. "No two bricks stacked atop one another. That sort of thing. History books kind of lessons."

"*Neu Berne* lacks a naval force sufficient to challenge the clans," he replied, pain etched even deeper in his face at having to admit to any sort of shortcoming to an outsider.

"Even a corvette flying my flag indicates that you're serious," Javier offered. "Committed. A handful of assault shuttles to go with the one I have lets me increase my flexibility. Intelligence that you have accumulated. Any and all further my mission, but there's still the key point. The reason I came here."

"The Dragon Watch," he acknowledged. "Sykora's note suggested that merely ordering them into action would not be enough."

"They'll fight, sure," Javier agreed. "Be better at it than probably any equivalent unit I could field. But they'll do it for the wrong reasons."

"Wrong?"

"They'll do it for duty," Javier said, flashing back to images of samurai top-knots slowly tumbling forward after the hero had made the requisite two cuts to silently disembowel himself, before a friend decapitates him with a perfect horizontal slice.

Pretty in movies. Required in that sort of culture.

Inappropriate here.

"Duty," Zupanu agreed.

"I demand something bigger," Javier said, catching the look of disbelief in the man's eyes, that there might be something bigger than duty.

"Bigger?" he asked.

Almost gasped, but caught himself short.

Javier nodded and let the moment hang pregnant for a long heartbeat.

"Your troops will be serving justice, Admiral," Javier said. "They will transcend duty and protect civilization itself from the toxic and decaying forces of piracy. They will be protecting the many worlds currently subject to such depredations as piracy inflicts, as well as every future child born, because your people will be making the galaxy a better place. Better than the *Concord* has managed. Or *Balustrade*. Or the *Union of Man*."

The two sidekicks had gone white. Zupanu's mouth fell open a shade before he managed to slam it shut again.

Javier felt the women on both sides of him nod, however shallow. Like they'd known. But they probably knew him the best anyway.

Behnam was merely the woman he was madly in love with.

Afia Burakgazi and Djamila Sykora had been with him in the worst of times. And the best.

"And when you are done?" Zupanu finally managed. "When you have annihilated organized piracy?"

"I will take off my badge and ride off into the sunset, Admiral," Javier said. "Return to *Altai* and call it good. The Khatum is accepting immigrants willing to swear a new fealty. The *Concord* might rise up and remember who they were when I was a pup. The *Union* might stop sneering down their noses at you. *Balustrade* might turn polite. But you will have the moral advantage. All of you. The ethical high-ground, because you will have been first to take a stand and commit—as a civilization—to doing this thing."

Honestly, Javier wondered if standing up and punching the man in the mouth might produce less of a shock, from the way his mouth did fall open now. The way the sidekicks looked like they were on the verge of medical or religious events, depending on their particular bent.

But Javier knew these people. He'd only had to watch Sykora for all these years to know who they dreamed of being in the small, dark, quiet spots inside.

Zupanu turned to Djamila, like a man wanting to confront a ghost. Her smile was superior when Javier looked, because they hadn't been willing to promote a mere enlisted trooper to a rank of command, lacking, as she had, the family name and wealth that a man like Bashar Zupanu must have had to sit here today.

And a lot of Sheriff Javier's future deputies would return home and ask why not when they took off their badges, so Javier could see *Neu Berne* undergoing perhaps a generation of change before the storm found them.

If he was lucky. And successful.

There was always a strong chance that he started Dorn's war himself in the course of trying to stop it, but Javier had always been a gambler. And the odds favored him today.

Zupanu took Afia's measure next. Deadly calm certainty, compacted into a woman barely three-quarters his size. But he was only three-quarters her toughness. Maybe.

Green eyes locked back on Javier. Pause. Certainty that was stumbling in the man's mind.

"You'll convince them?" Zupanu asked simply.

"I will," Javier promised.

Because that was what it would take.

PART V

Djamila hated to admit that she wasn't home. That this place was
no longer anything but the land of her birth. It did not hold her
soul.

As soldiers filed into the auditorium, she watched them from
the side of the stage. Most would still be shorter than her, but not
by nearly as much as other places. And there was almost perfect
silence, broken only by the occasional shuffle of a foot or the
squeak of a chair as someone sat. None of the whispering or
giggling that you might have elsewhere.

Even another *Neu Berne* unit would probably make noise, but
these soldiers had been instructed to be silent and observant. That
they were already on the clock and their prospective employer and
commanding officer were both watching and looking for reasons
to *disqualify* them, so that some other unit could take their place
instead.

Any other unit be given pride of precedence.

Looking out, Djamila saw all the game faces looking back, but
it did not warm her. This was no longer her home. That would be
on *Altai* when she returned. When she and Zakhar and Farouk
could work out more fully what it meant that they no longer had
to go out and save the galaxy.

When tomorrow arrived, because once upon a time, she and Javier had discussed all possible tomorrows, never imagining this one.

Never imagining this one.

Silence. Attention. Focus. Five hundred-odd men and women in the blue-gray of the Assault Marine infantry.

Poised.

Waiting.

Djamila glanced over as Javier stepped up next to her and scanned the crowd for something.

What, she had no idea, but he found it, because the man nodded once, then walked out to the center of the stage and took his place behind the lectern.

She had asked if he wanted company out there, her and Afia joining him, even if only to sit behind him where they might share the load of expectations, but he had demurred.

"I'll handle it," he had said.

Nothing more. Nothing needed.

This, then, was The Science Officer legend itself, extending another rung into the future.

Djamila Sykora expected no less.

The room made no noise, but five hundred breaths being drawn at the same time imparted a physical impact she felt. Javier stood there and scanned the crowd slowly, as though looking for familiar faces he might greet, but all were strangers.

At least to him. Djamila saw one face she recognized, standing at ease along the back wall at the top of the hall, arms crossed behind him in a uniform that still fit, in spite of him retiring a few years ago.

How had her brother Ziya arranged an invitation to this thing? Or had he been summoned when she returned, that he might somehow convince her to convince Javier to do something?

It was good to see him again. Like her, gray and older, approaching fifty in his case. Still taller than her and muscular as all of her brothers were, no doubt his children in service somewhere, though she didn't think any of them were Dragon Watch today.

At least none of the younger faces out there reminded her of anyone she knew.

Ziya stood next to Admiral Zupanu, so it might be anything that drew him. She wondered if her brother was here to volunteer to serve aboard *Excalibur*, where he could be measured by one of her lovers. And against.

Javier drew a breath and the room settled.

"I used to be a pirate," he announced to the group, causing an unconscious spasm to ripple through the crowd as he paused. "Before that, I was an explorer. Before that, I was a *Concord* naval officer. I was your enemy, in all the ways that mattered."

He paused again and let that settle in. Faces scowled, but discipline held. As they both knew it would.

"I have done many stupid and criminal things in my time," Javier continued. "Sometimes, they were even my idea, but for a chunk of that, I was also a Janissary-slave aboard a pirate ship. And we did crime."

Again, the pause. That moment of hanging tension.

"I got over myself," Javier told them. "Grew up. Looked at the galaxy differently. I stopped being a pirate and went back to being an explorer. That was fine, but my past decided that it didn't want to be my past anymore, and the old pirate clans that had become my new enemies decided to assassinate me at *Drako III*."

Here, the pause was longer. Scowling at the men and women scowling back.

"They failed," he said simply. "They brought an entire fleet of pirate warships and lost three of their four flagships, broken and eventually dismantled in place. They dropped an entire cohort of troops on me on the surface and eleven of us defeated them. Eleven. You want to know why?"

Djamila wondered if anybody else had pins being stuck into their voodoo dolls as she stood there.

Javier held out a hand. A fist. A finger pointing.

Five hundred faces rotated to stare at her, most not recognizing her in gold. With gray hair.

But they stared. She stared back.

"Because the Ship's Dragoon never has a bad day," Javier thundered at them now. Or it was her ears pounding with emotion. Something. "Because she trained her killers to a level most of you hope to achieve on the best days of your lives. Most of you will fail. Will fall short of what she considers the dead minimum to be allowed to even serve on her team."

Rude. Probably not wrong. But rude to rub their faces in it, except that she understood what he was doing.

Challenging them. Challenging the Dragon Watch itself to admit that someone could be better. Could set a standard higher than they could.

The scowls got ugly. Nobody spoke, but five hundred quiet growls had a tone like a bandsaw hitting mahogany.

Javier let them have their moment.

Silence fell like nightfall.

"I am here, because the pirates have decided that nobody can touch them," he called, overriding that growl purely with his unamplified voice. "That no law can bind them. That no jail will last long enough to matter. They are wrong."

Djamila had never sailed on water, but she felt the winds begin to turn behind the boat Javier was commanding. Felt the sails shift and tighten.

It was probably a good thing the Science Officer had never gone into politics, because she could see five hundred hardened killers in the palm of his hand, breathless.

"I have sent an Ambassador to the *Concord*, asking for ships to assist my mission," he said, voice suddenly dropping low and *demanding* that the audience fall silent to hear him. "Similarly, messages have gone to the *Union of Man*. They both have better ships. They do not have better people."

She felt her own head come up. Her jaw jut. The Dragon Watch matched it without exception.

"I am here because I need an army," Javier pronounced. "And you are the best there is. I need a sword that will smash down the pirates while protecting the innocent. Will bring law and order to a galaxy sorely lacking. Will understand how to withhold the blade and return to barracks when the task is done, to revel in the glory accumulated without falling into the trap that consumed your ancestors, when they decided that they had to conquer the galaxy. That is unnecessary today."

Listening to him speak, Djamila wondered if anybody else had just been gut-punched, or if it was just her. Except that faces down there showed similar emotions.

How well had Javier Aritza been studying her all these years, that he could faultlessly play these men and women like an antique cello?

Not even Zakhar knew her this intimately.

Lovers in warfare. It had impacted them both. Transformed them.

Rebirthed them, like so many others.

"The Dragon Watch will go forth into a place where the pirates think they can operate unmolested," Javier called. "You will challenge them, in the names of all the innocents who cannot stand up for themselves. Some will see you as the lesser evil to be tolerated, but they are wrong. You will be the greater good. Never lose sight of that, nor let any fool challenge you, because you alone will be acting with honor, at least until others rally to *your* standard and demand the right to stand *beside you*, resisting the darkness and the rising storm that will engulf us all if you cannot succeed."

Afia leaned into her abruptly and Djamila found herself drawing strength from the shorter woman.

Not smaller. Merely shorter. Same amount of power in a much tinier frame.

All the rage at the galaxy that had shaped them.

There was an ancient word. *Jihad.* The *Crusade of the Righteous* to reshape the world. Or the galaxy. Without Javier, she could see something like this spiraling out of control and triggering Hetzel's war, so it would be necessary to prevent that from happening.

It would be necessary to drag on the leash hard when their natural exuberance overtook them.

When they wanted to go *too far*.

"I will rely on you to hold the sword," Javier said, again so quiet that the room fell to life support blowers and nothing else. "It is as simple as that. You will help me defeat evil. Can you do that?"

Silence. Shock. Djamila felt it.

Then the roar built, coming first from a single voice, somewhere in the back, possibly her own brother, like the sudden whistling harbinger of the greater storm. Others joined it. Roared.

Rattled the entire room.

Djamila found her own mouth open and answering that sound with her own. Her, who should know better.

But she had demanded that Javier come here. Turn his charm on these people.

Offer *Neu Berne* a place in the wider galaxy that nobody else would, because they saw only the sword, and not the warrior holding it.

The greater good.

And the storm was coming.

PART VI

Afia felt like the Pixie Kodiak Javier teased her with, surrounded by freaking storm giants, but nothing was going to intimidate her. She'd known the Dragoon for more than a decade, and none of these putzes were Djamila's equal.

"Combat Engineer?" the woman in front of her confirmed.

Task Force Leader Haniyya Jehad Al-Amin.

Commander, Dragon Watch.

"Combat Engineer," Afia agreed. "What your culture calls a Sapper. The ones who have to go in to fix it, build it, or dismantle it. While under fire, if that's what it takes."

"And you will command the engineering detachment?" Al-Amin pressed.

Because neither Javier nor Djamila were fooling around. Al-Amin would answer to the Dragoon. The Sappers would answer to her. And Ilan, when that boy made it home, because *Excalibur* only had two qualified Combat Engineers.

Qualified to levels the Dragoon considered acceptable.

Afia nodded and studied the rest of the storm giants around her.

Al-Amin was a meter-ninety tall. Close enough to two heads

higher than Afia. And still shorter than the three men with her. Big men. Section leaders. Hers. Sappers with a lot of muscles. Hopefully, some between their ears, too.

Harper Avignon. Zamir Nagi. Raid Ahmad. Last one's first name was two syllables, but looked like it should have been one.

All three impressive on paper. Most of the Dragon Watch was.

Paper didn't stop beams.

Afia slung her bag back around her back so she had free hands. Could pull up both her shirts to show off the scar from a hunk of metal that had somehow only scratched ribs and hipbones in passing, without shattering either.

Still nearly killed her. But for Ilan.

Ten meters deep, if they were serious.

"They tried to kill me at *Nidavellir*," she told these storm giants. "Opened fire on our lifepod. Scored a hit. My other combat engineer saved my life. People that did it decided to come back for a second try at *Drako*. We're going to kill them. If you don't have the steel to walk into that fire with me right now, ask for a transfer somewhere safer, because Combat Engineer is usually second in line, behind either the Dragoon herself, or one of her Pathfinders. Rest of the army comes up behind us later."

Scowls, but someone had briefed these people, because they kept their mouths shut. Djamila also had the rank to send some dumbass home if she had any reason. And would listen to her Kodiak.

Avignon studied her. Senior of the three by age. All of them Leader-4 by rank because *Neu Berne* didn't consider Sapper to be a job requiring an officer.

Dumbasses.

"We leaving any survivors?" he asked her simply.

"If they can outrun us," she growled. "Science Officer gave them a chance to walk away last time. And has put the galaxy on notice that he's coming for them. Anyone that doesn't run now doesn't survive what I intend to do to them. Which is annihilation, plain and simple."

Nagi stirred.

"Ethical high-ground," he offered in a firm, quiet voice, showing her that at least they taught their non-comms how to think about those sorts of things.

"You want to take them prisoner and haul them back here to imprison them, that's on you, buttercup," she rumbled. "*Concord* might offer rewards. *Union*, as well. Don't care. Planning to blow shit up and breech hulls to get in where our people can take a station or a ship in hand-to-hand operations. People are going to die. People who have it coming."

"We all have it coming," Ahmad noted dryly.

Afia nodded. Man wasn't wrong.

She looked back to Al-Amin. Woman was a bit uncertain about the whole thing, but she was an officer, in a land where officers went to pretty academies and got to wear fancy uniforms. Didn't get down in the muck and mire and grease to get the job done when shit went wrong and beam fire was incoming. Sent these other three off, with orders to die in the process.

Infantry might expect to be led by an officer, but these were Sappers. Her people.

They'd be keeping up with her. If they could.

"Do we know who's first on Aritza's list?" Al-Amin asked.

"Fourth," Afia corrected her. "Fifth, if you want to count what we did to *Obsidian Hawk*, *Blackstone*, and *Kymni Gauntlet*. You people are coming in somewhere in the middle, after we already took *Eldritch Stele*, then *Æthelred*. After we went and blew the shit out of *Ferran*. Bad guys have had nearly a year to rethink their career choices, so I have no pity for them now. None at all. Personally, hoping Javier saves Walvisbaai's main headquarters for last, but that's because I have unfinished business with a few people."

Even storm giants could know disquiet, but they were newbies here. She'd lived with that seething rage for years, unable to rip somebody's throat out, though she had a list of names.

And now, looking at these folks, a team.

Al-Amin nodded. The three men did as well.

It was going to get ugly, but that was the job of a Sapper. Of a Combat Engineer.

They got shit done when shit got ugly.

And she would.

THE FOUNDATION

PART I

Javier was in the library today, because he felt like changing things up and had spent too much damned time in conference rooms lately. Planning. Planning some more. Reviewing plans. Making more plans.

He wanted to stand in Bethany's Library and stare out that wide transsteel porthole at the sun rising over *Neu Berne* itself. Remember the first time he'd seen it. Lights of Zurich below. Pretty view. And honestly not one he'd ever expected to see again.

But change is the nature of living.

Hatch opened and bodies started arriving to bother him. And most of them were even people he liked.

Just getting a little crusty at having to deal with people right now.

Javier was looking forward to sailing back into the darkness.

To going home.

Wasn't there yet.

Still, he ignored everyone for a time and watched the view. Let them settle in. Didn't turn around until Suvi appeared in a nearby screen.

His smile was for her, and gone when he finished turning around.

Zakhar, commanding *Excalibur*.

Piet, commanding the *Ghost*.

Djamila and Haniyya, commanding ground troops.

Captain Hayfa Alfarsi, commanding the newest ship in his fleet of vengeance. *Relentless* was called a destroyer by those folks, but that meant gunboat destroyer. It wasn't even as big as *Storm Gauntlet*—the original Strike Corvette and not the newer Frigate—had been.

Still, as typically overgunned as he would expect from Djamila's people. Reasonable sailing qualities. Good enough for what he had in mind, because he had the Dragon Watch, too.

Afia and her three team leaders rounded out the meeting he'd called, not counting the woman surrounding all of them because she was the ship.

"I feel like the detective about to announce whodunit," Javier said, moving to a comfortable chair and grinning.

The newcomers were starting to understand that they could roll their eyes at their commanding officer, but it had taken a week for them to unbend. And Afia razzing him publicly on more than one occasion.

"So why have you summoned us together," Djamila asked, voice lurid in ways that still surprised him. "Did you have a confession to make?"

Javier couldn't help but laugh. Alfarsi looked like she wanted to die at this behavior, but he couldn't blame the woman.

A week ago, she'd been one of their senior naval captains, in spite of commanding a tiny ship. *Neu Berne* simply didn't have any sort of star nation that required them to maintain a big fleet. Not like the *Concord*. Or *Altai*.

Javier focused on Captain Alfarsi and nodded.

"We run, as you have discovered, a bit looser than you are used to," he reminded her. "Because folks know when to relax, and when to cinch it up an extra notch and get ugly. I wanted everyone settling in some. Getting used to names, faces, and procedures, because I have something rude in mind."

"You?" Afia asked in a tone of sarcastic disbelief that didn't fool anybody.

He smiled at her. Then let it fade. Harden.

Hers went with it.

Navarre and the Pixie Kodiak.

Cold as the space between stars. Maybe between galaxies.

"Next target," he announced, looking around. "Want to hit someone from surprise. And take advantage of the fact that we went and recruited some serious help to do it. But we have to move fast. And quiet, because we will piss off a raft of folks when we do this. That means that we'll have to get in, get done, and get gone in the shortest possible time frame."

They all watched him warily. Even the ones that knew him best. Especially the ones that knew him best.

"Who?" Zakhar asked.

"The last place anybody in the galaxy should be expecting us to hit," he replied, pausing to look around the group. "*Zygeerish*."

Half of his team jumped in surprise. The other half were lost.

Javier nodded to Zakhar. Watched the man draw himself inward, then shrug.

"Had to happen eventually," Zakhar agreed. "And yeah, nobody will see this coming."

"If I may?" Al-Amin asked. "Who?"

"A place a little less seedy and corrupt than *Nidavellir*," Zakhar replied. "Not by much, but perhaps enough. Better run, anyway. It is the home offices of the Jarre Foundation. Our old bosses when we were pirates."

Afia's eyes were glittering.

"Going after Audol University?" she asked, practically licking her lips.

"They have a university?" one of the Sappers asked in shock.

"Training facility," Zakhar replied. "Place where new sailors can get the equivalent of ground school, before heading out on a ship. It also trains engineers, gunners, troopers, and command officers. University makes a good cover, when you need bodies coming in, especially if you want to upgrade them over time. Place also offers degrees in accounting and business for that side of things."

"Because money is power," Javier agreed. "At *Nidavellir*, we destroyed their main platform base, but gave everyone time to abandon station and get to safety. After blowing all their hull to shit."

"How do we top that at *Zygeerish*?" Afia asked.

"Board and storm," Javier replied. "Pull another *Ferran*, but do it backwards this time."

"Because you have the troops to take the station this time," Djamila said. "I do."

"Figure we drop *Flying Maiden* on them, like we did *Æthelred*," Javier nodded. "Except that we don't need to sell them with dance hall girls this time. You lead a force that kicks in the door. Rest of us drop out hard and close, hitting them with all the assault shuttles at once. Take the place. Then mine it and blow it to hell. Don't really care if we drop it on the planet in big pieces this time, because everybody involved has pretty much chosen this way of life."

"No," one of the Sappers snapped sharply, though still quietly.

Avignon. Spoke the most. Not the most opinionated of the three, but the most willing to get up in your face when he thought he was right.

When he thought you were wrong.

"No?" Javier asked.

"You asked for the sword to protect the innocent," he replied in a hard voice. "I have no doubts that there are a lot of people living on the surface of that world with no choice about it. No opportunities to go elsewhere, save piracy, because they are too poor to pack up and leave."

Javier bit back his response. He'd been born middle class. Raised by his grandparents because both parents had been serving with the fleet.

Lots of folks enlisted to escape bad situations. Javier could see where *Neu Berne* Assault Marines probably had an *exquisitely sharp* understanding of that kind of poverty. The *Union of Man* and *Balustrade* had made it a point to shatter their economy three generations ago, in order to keep them from ever rising again.

And Javier had recruited them for that incredible stubbornness.

They matched wills now, but it wasn't a contest.

The man was right.

Javier nodded to him to accede.

"We'll shatter it, the same as we did *Nidavellir*," Javier said. "Then blow the pieces to pieces, so nobody below has to worry about some asshole dropping a burning platform on their homestead."

Avignon nodded back. Point made. Honor served.

Javier made a note to remember that he was dealing with folks who wouldn't cut corners on this one, because he had challenged them to put their own honor on the line first, and bombing a *Concord* world would be unacceptable.

As it should be, even if they were pirates.

PART II

Zakhar had finally pulled rank on everybody, after only threatening it for the longest time. After all, Javier was the only person who technically outranked him.

It had become necessary here, but that was because, looking deep, he found that he had a small soul and an evil streak a kilometer wide.

Flying Maiden. Hadn't been the name when it had showed up with a load of supplies for Glen and Regina at *Eldritch Stele*, but it had been changed after they'd discovered that surrender was a better alternative than being hunted down and annihilated.

Suvi had been having a particularly grumpy day, as she'd explained afterwards.

Today, they had a ship. One hardly known to anyone, and likely a complete cipher at *Zygeerish*, which was the entire point.

And Zakhar hadn't planned on asking for volunteers to serve on the ship, expecting Javier to pull the same stunt as last time.

Nobody had been prepared when Collette Plamondon demanded the job of captain for this charade. Woman couldn't fly a ship, but didn't need to. Suvi could fly *Excalibur*. Zakhar was mostly an advisor these days anyway.

But he still knew how to fly a junky old freighter that had seen better days.

So he'd pulled rank on everyone else and accepted the job as First Officer under Collette, which had surprised the shit out of her and everyone else.

It was good to pull a fast one on people occasionally. Kept you young.

He'd even demanded that she sit in the big chair, while he was handling things from the pilot's station. Mostly a matter of him sitting on the right instead of the left, but mindset mattered.

He looked over at the woman and recognized her nerves.

"You'll do fine," he said.

"I am standing in the airlock on *Æthelred*," she replied firmly. "With a pistol in hand, volunteering to board the ship alone and scout for Afia and the others. I do not believe anything has frightened me as much since my first kiss when I was thirteen."

He smiled.

"Turned out pretty well," he reminded her. "And you've got everyone aft today to handle things for you. All you have to do is look official."

"No, I must look slinky and seduce them with my words and my charm," she corrected him in a haughty tone that worked perfectly.

Adrian had outdone himself for this mission. Collette wore a top that plunged down to what little cleavage Collette had, in a dark blue that made the ruby on a platinum pendant at her neck stand out like a sunrise.

Her hair was up and held with chopsticks. Starting to gray a little underneath, but she was playing the role of the Madame today, not one of her working girls.

An entire brothel on stardrives, which was honestly a gambit Zakhar couldn't remember anywhere. And word would get around eventually, but he doubted that Walvisbaai and Jarre were on intimate terms right the moment.

That might change later, when they started feeling the walls closing in.

For now, they would try their luck once again with misdirection, which was honestly Javier's signature move, when you got right down to it.

Zakhar nodded at the galaxy in general, then opened an intercom.

"All hands, stand by for jump," he told them, knowing that his disappearance would trigger a countdown that saw the rest of this thing called *Vengeance* arrive, guns blazing.

He just had to work a fast one, first.

Collette grinned.

"Pilot, take us in," she ordered.

"Aye, sir," Zakhar laughed, pressing the button.

PART III

Collette drew a breath and considered how she was, yet again, tempting fate. At the same time, she felt more alive today than she could remember.

Much as she loved working for Burdine and Chay, this was something larger. And a job she could do that would free up someone else. Someone better with guns.

All she had to do was hold minds, and every waitress worth her salt learned that task early.

The *Flying Maiden* dropped into real space at a spot marked as Entry Port on their maps, most of the crew having been quite familiar with *Zygeerish* from their former lives.

Her former life had been at Zhang Xiu, as a waitress in a failing bistro in Barrowclough. Not that Chay and Burdine had made bad choices. Merely that circumstances made most restaurants fail.

And his would have, but for a cousin with an impossible dream.

She had been saved by Afia. Collette had adopted the woman as kin for that and intended to pay her back for all the things she had done for the small family that had come together to run a dying bistro.

Collette opened the radio line and focused her will on the massive orbital platform ahead of them, cognizant of the many guns and missiles that could be unleashed on them without warning.

"Jakro Hall, this is the starship *Flying Maiden*," she sent. "Requesting landing assignment and transmitting cargo manifest now."

She looked over as Captain Sokolov pushed a button that produced a quiet beep.

Collette focused on her breathing. On her arrogant superiority to whoever might be answering the comm. Another thing waitresses learn, when dealing with *prima donnas* in fancy suits.

"*Flying Maiden*, this is Jakro Hall," a man's voice came back, light with confusion and shades of disbelief.

Like a man who had just been told that Chay was going to make his favorite dish from scratch as a birthday present. As had happened a few times, for especially valued customers.

"Go ahead," she said, letting triumph and superiority color her tones.

"You're a brothel ship?" he asked, still lost.

Still confused.

She had asked, and apparently nobody did that in a ship, instead placing such establishments on stations or planets. Where they might fail, if the economy dipped at the wrong moment.

Like restaurants, you had a high rate of fixed expenses on a daily basis, and no guarantee that you would break even. And it wasn't a factory, where you could lay off half or more of your workforce in slack times and hire them back later.

Service industry jobs that went away took forever to fill again with quality people later, and she couldn't imagine trying to staff a bordello with random strangers walking in off the street.

Unless everyone else was desperate. More desperate than even she'd ever gotten.

"*Oui*," she replied, dropping back into her native tongue

automatically. "Ninety percent female. Ten percent male. And flexible as needed. We have orders to report to Jakro Hall and handle your needs first, before moving on to other departments. Is there a problem with the sequence?"

Long pause.

Assume success, plan for victory. It had been something she had heard early and only later come to understand. They would clear her to land. The Dragoon would go to work. Simple as that.

Beside her, Captain Sokolov appeared poised to jump them to safety at the first hint of trouble, which was why Collette could concentrate on seducing a total stranger over the radio, instead of that one that had walked up and lusted after her at *Ferran*.

Collette still smiled at the memory.

Nobody had ever *lusted* after her. Not like him.

She'd even considered giving the man a gift of herself as a present, once he was a prisoner, but rules had been strictly enforced.

And they had gone on to destroy that system.

Today, she was liberated to seduce more men. Or women. Whoever might *lust* after her.

Power.

She had discovered that it was an intoxicating aphrodisiac.

Today, silly pirate men would be arguing with one another about looking gift horses in the mouth. Djamila Sykora, of all people, had reminded Collette how sexist the modern age had gotten, after being so much more egalitarian in earlier times and other civilizations.

It gave Collette hope that they could change back later, but for now, the thought of having a bordello suddenly arrive would no doubt froth these men as nothing else might.

Her job was to confuse them. To wind up all that energy, then send it off randomly when someone slapped them across the face instead.

"*Flying Maiden*, you are cleared to dock," the man finally

replied. "Medical records have been transmitted to our doctors for review. A team will meet you when you arrive."

"It is good," Collette replied, then cut the line and confirmed that it was off before activating the intercom.

"All hands, stand by."

PART IV

Djamila had gold on under her combat armor.

Not that you could see it, but it framed her mindset, just as the pistol on each hip did. Beside her, Afia was practically vibrating with energy, as was Avignon, the only one of the Sapper team leaders directly accompanying this ship.

Al-Amin and the rest were aboard *Excalibur*. Del and five other assault shuttles, about to be put to use delivering combat troops under fire.

Today, they were aft on *Flying Maiden*, in the same bay where all the dance hall girls had been arrayed the first time, but everyone here was armed and armored for an assault, because they were moving as soon as the hatch opened. Scans would show a mass of bodies, but that was about it.

And exactly what was expected, because you couldn't do much more than count heads unless you were in the room.

By then, it would be too late to stop her.

Afia turned to Harper Avignon.

"You sure about this?" she asked.

"I can't exactly hide behind you, ya know," Avignon replied with a laugh. "You, however, can vanish into my shadow as we move. Plus, you're more important alive than I am, when all is said and done."

Djamila understood the logic. Death before dishonor, but more importantly, protecting senior officers sometimes meant using your life to do it. She'd made that same calculation in her youth.

Harper would be second through, behind only her. Even the first platoon of Dragon Watch was going to be third, pouring in like water rupturing a dyke with Afia leading them.

But Harper Avignon was leading the Dragon Watch into battle. They would see it that way, because she wasn't one of them anymore. Had been, once.

Before.

Not today.

Djamila nodded as those two rearranged. Glanced at the Leader-4 who would be leading everyone else. Got a calm nod back. And a bit of a growl on the team line, but that was one hundred people making a quiet noise under their breaths, multiplied into a sound.

The hull rattled. Thumped. Hissed as airlocks started to equalize pressure. Beeps as the hatch began to open.

"Landing bay, I have visuals on the far side," her love said simply, obviously watching on a camera from the bridge. "No change."

Even someone listening in would not be able to parse that message and come up with anything approximating the right answer.

Two people on the far side. Waiting. Bureaucrats with clipboards, as the old saying went, all set to fill out the correct forms, stamp them with the right chops, then file them appropriately.

The airlock opened. The hatch itself came to rest.

"Djamila, you're on," Zakhar said simply.

She moved.

From calm stillness to the whirlwind of destruction that had once been nicknamed the Ballerina of Death, in the blink of an eye, she *moved*.

Long legs drove her forward, sprinting by the third stride. Already most of the way through the airlock and seeing shadows on the far side.

Two of them. Standing side by side but not touching. Probably male, but hard to tell because she only saw them as obstacles in her line of movement.

Djamila split the difference between then, slamming elbows into jaws and hips into ribs as though a bull charging with horns.

Both were unprepared for violence. That would probably help them later, because both appeared unconscious before she was past them, with a long second to actually collapse bonelessly to the deck, where a later team would be tasked with getting them out of the way of being stepped on then taking them into custody.

Bureaucrats. Not warriors. Not worth the challenge, and no honor to be accumulated in combat.

Djamila moved.

PART V

Leader-4 Harper Avignon had demanded place. Rank, seniority, and occupation had favored him, so he was second through the airlock in the wake of the Dragoon.

Sykora had been one of them in her time. Seven years with the Watch. Seventeen years retired.

Harper had watched the woman train for this mission.

Even the Dragon Watch lacked the vocabulary to describe what Djamila Sykora had become as a civilian, but he had also met the troopers known affectionately as The Gun Bunnies. Any of those men could step lateral into a senior position with the Watch. Both of the Pathfinder women were better than anybody in the entire unit.

The Dragoon...

She was simply on a plateau Harper had only ever heard rumors about. Never seen. Not even in the elite of the elite.

Goddess of Death, perhaps, incarnated today for vengeance, someone had whispered, either in awe or fear.

No other way to describe her.

Harper knew the plan. Knew the timing. Exploded into motion immediately on her heels, because they had trained that.

If he tripped right now, First of the First of the First would simply run over him, an obstacle on the deck to be trampled.

He was not allowed to fail. Would not allow himself to make a mistake. At the very least, his friends would NEVER let him hear the end of it.

He chased death in her wake.

First two victims went down exactly as it had been on paper and in training. The Dragoon hardly slowed as she took both out. Harper stayed right on her ass because that was the job.

Far side of the room had an open hatch. The Dragoon went through it at a dead run. Harper only slowed enough to slap the hull next to it.

"Afia, first target!" he yelled, then kept going.

She would either blow the controls or order someone to shoot them. Probably the latter, but everything from here in was on a decision tree that had been pruned as much as possible, leaving only basic options.

Move, shoot, stop.

Sykora went straight. Harper followed, still marveling that he was barely able to keep up with a woman more than decade older than him.

Goddess of Death. No, Ballerina. Someone had called her that. Ballerina of Death.

He hadn't understood.

Then.

Realization flowed through his being like a religious epiphany.

Even the Dragon Watch itself was only second best. Or third.

Somewhere far behind this woman, because she was competing with the single most deadly being in the universe.

Herself. Yesterday.

Movement.

Harper had a rear-facing camera on his display.

Afia, leading First in their wake, but letting space develop because someone would eventually be dumb enough to step out and try to shoot him in the back.

Several more platoons would be pouring in behind First, tasked with anchoring important points and keeping the inevitable counter attack from gaining any momentum.

Until the rest of the Dragon Watch arrived.

Harper watched forward again.

Dragoon, whirlwinding destruction ahead of him. She'd finally drawn a stun pistol and used it, not losing a step. Worse, she had one in each hand, firing down side corridors as she crossed.

He'd say that she didn't even look, but she probably did. Absorbed both sides peripherally, placed targets, dropped them.

Harper simply had to keep up with her. If he could.

First alarm finally sounded. Amateur hour, because they'd penetrated nearly one hundred meters inward and up two decks when the sirens started up and bulkheads slammed shut.

Theoretically, they were trapped until the defenders could gather up their strength and rush whatever chamber or zone the invaders had been isolated in.

Harper was alone with the Dragoon, Afia's team having been cut off.

Exactly like they'd trained it.

Sykora slowed finally. Walked halfway up the wall, compressing long legs to absorb momentum. Harper sidestepped and slid into place by the hatch, already on his knees studying the controls.

Helped that Afia had examples of the security and control systems this station used. A *Concord* standard, for all the obvious reasons, so not one he was all that familiar with. Would have previously taken him as long as ten seconds to even figure out how to override it.

Took him five to kill it instead.

Laser cutter out and drill the screws holding the faceplate in place. Toss the plate to one side and draw wirecutters left-handed. Laser here, here, and here. Cut there. Bridge these two with the wirecutters themselves.

The door clicked, jolted, and slid right back into the wall.

Later, he would compare times with Afia, but he'd seen her work and understood that she had probably just done it in four, wherever she was.

Sykora was in motion, already shooting. Harper was after her as fast as he could rise and run.

On paper, it was insane to launch a full frontal assault without backup. Two people, challenging an entire armed platform?

But audacity and misdirection were the keys here. The Jarre Foundation would wake up to what was happening, but not fast enough to stop Sykora. Not if Harper could keep punching open doors for her.

Corridor. Bodies, but all on the deck unconscious already. She had a ten meter lead on him, and would probably maintain that until the next barrier was thrown up.

At least long enough for him to knock it down.

PART VI

Javier was in Zakhar's big seat, with him off playing hero. Not that Javier was jealous or anything. This was Zakhar getting even with him for *Ferran*.

Still, he got to play big, bad commanding admiral badass today.

Or something. At least look good in all the after action reports, because he'd showered and had his beard and hair trimmed carefully, like a man about to catwalk the red carpet, where it was all a poledance for reporters and cameras.

"Countdown status?" he asked.

"I'm green," Suvi replied. "Piet and Hayfa report readiness for action. No updates from Zakhar. Expecting the first note from him in nineteen seconds, indicating that they have docked. Nothing appears out of the ordinary with the feed."

Javier grinned. Zakhar, aiming a comm laser into the darkness so everyone out here could follow along, with a four minute light-speed delay because his fleet was sitting out a ways. Not invisible, but really hard to see if you weren't looking.

They'd be found and challenged eventually, but that would probably be measured in hours, if they continued to sit here quietly.

He didn't need that long.

"And docking achieved," Suvi said. "There goes Djamila and the tall Sapper."

"Harper," Javier replied. "Good kid. Might offer him a job later. Like the way he operates."

"All three of the Sappers under Afia meet my criteria," Suvi replied. "Okay, Piet and Hayfa have turned over control to me. Jumping now."

Javier was watching on his screen, with all the physical shields up in here. One moment, darkness with a bright light in the distance. The next, a wall of metal that happened to be a station in orbit of *Zygeerish*. Biggest one around here. Only one that mattered, because all the pirate economy flowed into it, then went down to the surface.

The Jarre Foundation might be unto gods, as far as the locals were concerned. Or Mafia bosses, exacting tribute and inflicting punishments without any sort of legal system containing them.

Kinda like *Nidavellir*.

The *Concord* should have done something about this place a long time ago, but he understood that they were on the downhill arc of history at this moment. Just as the others were starting to rise.

Gonna get ugly, unless somebody did something about it.

Audol University. Javier had only been ashore here twice, still something of an outsider at the time, for all he'd been a Centurion under Zakhar. Honest-to-freaking goodness orbital university, quietly corrupted, then acquired out of bankruptcy court and turned into a front. A cover.

A place for an entire supposed nonprofit organization to train people.

Wanna buy a bridge? Got one cheap.

Javier watched Suvi open fire. Torpedoes to keep defenders busy. Ion cannon to neutralize defensive nodes. Pulsars to blow shit up.

Shields weren't even up. Merely running at navigational level to deal with random orbital debris. Not all that hard to knock right back down, then watch as the generators got blown to scrap because Zakhar had the full technical specifications of this station and had handed them to Suvi.

Maximum carnage ensuring, but only on military systems for now.

Not people.

First inbound torpedoes as the station finally started to get their shit together. *Relentless* was earning her name as he watched, hunting down every single one of them and blowing them apart, then pouring spare turret fire into any section of station nearby that looked hostile.

And then Piet began his latest symphony.

Or should have. Javier was sad that he didn't have synchronized music playing as he watched a hose of torpedoes erupt from the *Ghost*.

Arsenal ship. Expensive, because you have to buy a bunch of reloads after any major engagement. Or steal them from someone, like he'd done.

At the same time, there was nothing in the galaxy that could suppress them except another arsenal ship. Or a squadron of escorts all dedicated to swatting hornets coming to sting you to death.

Audol didn't have that, because some mean punk had just put a hundred elite killing machines ashore in the middle of their command node.

Jakro Hall. Even infantry combat training might not have been prepared, but the folks in charge of weapon systems sure as hell weren't ready to face Djamila and her new friends, shooting everything that moved.

"Javier, first defensive forces are finally waking up," Suvi said. "Want me to turn and go after that Guardship?"

"Nope," he replied. "Tell Hayfa to handle them, then have Piet route a salvo in over her shoulder when she has their attention. I want you blowing shit up."

"Roger that," she replied, then looked back down at her screens and went to work.

Hopefully, he wasn't making a mistake, but *Relentless* was supposed to punch well above their weight.

Time to find out.

PART VII

"Order acknowledged," Hayfa replied. "Engaging now."

She paused and studied the readout for a moment, adjusting her entire mindset to the new battle she had not been expecting just yet.

Relentless was overgunned for a small hull. *Barbary Coast* was likewise overgunned and bigger. Light cruiser for firepower, perhaps. Not enough to take on *Excalibur*, but the station was supposed to handle that.

The *Sentience* had assigned *Relentless* the task of protection, then added offense.

"Defensive Systems, engage enemy warship," she ordered.

"Standing by," Bashir replied, fingers already moving as *Barbary Coast* began accelerating towards them, several torpedoes in space closing.

"Gunner, to work," Hayfa continued.

"Engaging now," Monika answered.

Monika Sykora. Supposedly a third cousin of *Excalibur*'s Dragoon, though that was only a rumor Hayfa had heard.

"Pilot, rotate around the engagement sphere until enemy vessel commits," Hayfa ordered. "Then pivot and close. Alert

Storm Gauntlet to engage at that moment so we can ride in behind their attack."

"Aye," Hanane said.

Hayfa settled and watched.

Barbary Coast wasn't madly charging, but wasn't hanging back, either. Looked like they were trying to find a middle zone where they could shoot at *Relentless* without being too close to *Excalibur*.

Probably expected her to hang back close to the Galleon. That would be the surprise, then, when he had committed to closing and was not in a position to easily back away.

Relentless was built to engage pirate ships. Not vessels as large or powerful as *Barbary Coast*, but certainly criminals come raiding.

Her vessel was small. Compact. Cramped, even. At the same time, it had been built extra sturdy, even by modern warship standards, so she was confident that she could take more damage than they could.

"Opening fire with Pulse Cannons," Monika called. "Ranging initially, but target has minimal deflection at present."

Behind them, *Excalibur* was ranging with Pulsars. Smaller weapons at the bore, where they gained range and hitting power over the older Pulse Cannons *Neu Berne* was still using, unable to afford bleeding edge technology.

Relentless, if nothing else, was earning even more foreign currency than the Dragon Watch. High Command could hopefully use that to build or acquire better warships for what the Science Officer was convinced was coming.

It had become time to stockpile against winter.

"Defense, how are you holding?" Hayfa asked.

"They are primarily guns, Captain," Bashir replied. "Torpedoes are being intercepted. Shields on forward facing are stable, but that will change when we close."

"Prepare to reinforce starboard shields when we approach," she announced. "Hanane, take them down our starboard side when you move. I want to cross their flight path and pinch their minds."

"Acknowledged, Captain."

More fire, both directions. Medium range for now, so not all that effective. About now, a pirate would probably flee, since they were usually attacking.

He was defending his base today, while it was under attack by a battleship that had several unfair advantages, not the least was the arsenal ship pouring an overwhelming rate of fire into various sections as ground troops neutralized system from the inside.

Hayfa doubted that *Barbary Coast* would simply shear off and seek greener pastures, though they could be induced to run.

It required only the right inspiration.

And it would come down to will, she decided. *Neu Berne Fleet Operations* against a pirate. Even a committed one.

How badly did he wish to fight?

Relentless was in the process of attacking a pirate stronghold. Granted, a *Concord*-affiliated world, but a criminal one nonetheless.

Neu Berne was taking a stand. Drawing a line in the sand.

Drawing their sword and strapping on their shield in the name of the future.

"Pilot, come about and accelerate," she finally ordered. "Have *Storm Gauntlet* engage. Let the *Sentience* know your path and let her redirect you to maintain her own firing corridors. Gunner, go for overload."

Let us see if you have the will.

PART VIII

Djamila was still outrunning her support force, but that was a calculated risk. And Harper had done the impossible, both in keeping up with her and in keeping the corridor open in front of her that Djamila could outrun any attempts to stop her, because she was already past the spot on the map where a security barracks was marked.

And Third Platoon was assigned to neutralize them.

How far could she get before she had to call for help?

Djamila decided to challenge the gods themselves today and see.

Another door jerked open as Harper defeated the electronics that wanted to keep it closed.

At some point, someone might finally open a corridor to space and think that vacuum might force her to slow down. She could just as easily slip outside the station at that point. Let Harper blow an airlock or even hull section apart and depressurize part of the station, since both of them had armor and air.

How far could she get?

Something about the day told her that the gods were favoring her foolishness, so she pushed.

"Up here," she pointed at a hatch indicating stairs to the next level.

The one where she could find the command node for Jakro Hall itself.

Could she take it out?

If nothing else, she and Harper could badly derail all the defenders that way.

He got the hatch opened and she took stairs three at a time upwards, eyes locked on the landing and both pistols centered. Stunners only, but set to something heavy enough that someone would be out for fifteen or twenty minutes.

Longer than she needed, one way or the other.

At the top, he took out the next hatch so quickly that it was almost like pushing the open button. But then, the Jarre Foundation had never anticipated someone launching a physical assault. Or getting this deep.

Even a *Concord* raid would be telegraphed well ahead of time, allowing folks the leisure to hide all the incriminating evidence.

Or disappear into the hills.

Djamila exploded out of the doorway, firing both ways at shadows that thought she would peek first.

Three targets down and neutralized. Someone was finally tracking her movement and vectoring forces in to stop her. It would turn into a firefight quickly enough.

She checked. All three had armor, but not sealed.

"Next section, you will close bulkheads and blow a wall out," she ordered Harper, waving him into motion as she started running again.

As long as they were concentrating on her, they weren't paying attention to Afia.

Or Suvi.

PART IX

Javier figured that his job was watching. Color commentary occasionally, but only because. Zakhar was the technical expert at fighting a warship.

Luckily, Javier's daughter had gotten pretty damned good at it over the last few years. Definitely since *Nidavellir*, which had been a lot closer than today.

Excalibur had also been upgraded significantly since then, too.

And he had the *Ghost* and *Relentless* covering his ass today, instead of throwing a mangled transport at them like a rock.

Speaking of…

"How's Hayfa doing?" he asked.

Screens showed details, but those were dry, technical facts. He wanted emotions.

"Piet ruined their tee time," she replied, apparently making a golf joke. Because she was almost as big a dork as him. "Hayfa is currently in the process of routing them, because they had to decide if they wanted to get punched in the mouth or stabbed in the stomach and chose the lesser death."

"Might be a reason we did it that way," he reminded her.

Sure, lots of red on *Barbary Coast*'s readout. More than

Relentless, but that was a warship as envisioned by the same culture that had produced Djamila Sykora, so it was supposed to be tougher than you were.

"They're trying to get away from her now," Suvi said. "Stand by for a couple of parting shots."

Javier understood that her Pulsars were state of the art. He'd asked Behnam to install them for that reason. Better range. Better hitting power.

More boom for the drachma.

And Suvi had apparently been sandbagging, because she suddenly tattooed *Barbary Coast*'s hull with her flank turrets that didn't have anything else to shoot at. Couple of solid booms in there, watching more things go red.

Whoopsie.

Then *Barbary Coast* vanished.

Smart move on his part. Emergency jump. If nothing else, he was out of action for five to eight minutes, but Javier was pretty sure that captain would be taking their time coming back.

If they did.

That much damage, they might be waiting for *Excalibur* to leave, not understanding that this wasn't merely a raid.

He wondered if they would decide to throw themselves on their swords at that point, or get while the getting was good.

Barbary Coast was a month in drydock before they were ready for combat again. And he was about to smash the only dock handing for that level of repairs.

"Hey, station just stopped firing," Suvi announced.

Javier couldn't tell if she was put out or surprised.

He dialed a few scan screens in closer, then started laughing.

Took his daughter a moment to catch on.

"Is that...?"

"The Dragoon, and her sidekick, standing on the outer hull, pointing guns at someone inside the command node?" he asked. "Looks like."

"I'm scanning a bomb on the hull," Suvi said. "So apparently she's holding them hostage by threatening to vent their bridge to space. Pretty sure anyone not surrendering at this point gets a beat-down by all the others. Looks like nobody is in armor, so at best they might grab emergency suits or something."

"How's the rest of the battle?" he asked.

"Couple of ships just now finally winding up to do something, but nobody in position to threaten me," she replied. "Oh, hey, I know that hull!"

Javier watched a screen flip to a new image.

Not a ship he knew, until she attached text to it.

"Seriously?" he asked.

"Yup," she laughed. "*Kymni Gauntlet*. Last of the fuckers who got away from me at *Drako*. Want me to smash it?"

"Hell no," he replied. "Scan it for repair status. That's a Jarre Enforcer."

"Confused," Suvi informed him petulantly.

Javier nodded. There was crazy, then there was **CRAZY**.

"Gonna steal it, kid."

PART X

Hayfa contained her sigh. Zakhar had warned her that the Science Officer occasionally had flashes of inspiration that might look like madness to most people.

Zakhar had specifically told her to listen to the man when he went off the rails like this, and do so with an open mind.

"You are certain that it can be done?" she asked Aritza when he finished his explanation.

"I am certain that we can get it far enough away that we can finish the job," he replied. "*Eldritch Stele* is two jumps from here. At that point, we're running like hell anyway, and circling back around to recruit. I can get people from *Neu Berne* just as easily as anywhere else, and I'm way more willing to trust you folks than a bunch of retired sailors who walked in off the street."

"I am assigned command of *Relentless*," she attempted to deflect him, but Aritza wasn't having it.

"And I am your superior officer in *Altai* service, which you are," he countered. At least he was still smiling. "You will turn over command to your first officer and take command of *Kymni Gauntlet* as Commanding Officer, Captain Alfarsi. You folks work out how much you can thin your crew down for now. Something more than a skeleton will transfer, unless we can somehow recruit some locals, in which case you'll have a bunch of Dragon Watch aboard as a security crew enforcing my will."

Worst? She could see it working out that way.

Flashes. Genius? Madness?

Could you get a shim between the two?

"Understood, Admiral," she replied, implying that he held such a rank.

Nobody would understand *Science Officer* as supreme commander, anyway. Not unless they were here, now.

Hayfa cut the line and turned to Monika.

"You heard the man," Hayfa said, watching her Gunner swallow a bit nervously. "We have a couple of hours. You take my station and get ready to settle in. I'm headed aft to talk to Engineering and see who they can spare."

"Would he really recruit pirates?" Bashir asked.

"They used to be Jarre Foundation," Hayfa replied. "Supposedly, the least worst of the four big clans, though I doubt that there was much difference. If nothing else, they would have better records of the personnel available. And he is deadly serious about putting the Dragon Watch aboard to keep watch against troublemakers. I have no doubts about Al-Amin's people. Nor should you."

Nods.

Deep breath.

Contained sigh.

Hayfa rose and nodded Monika into her new command, while she got ready to send a prize crew aboard *Kymni Gauntlet*.

Was the Science Officer serious about impressing it into *Neu Berne* service?

P XI

Katya Velichkov understood that any movement probably got her shot, right this moment, so she stayed perfectly still.

Most of her.

Her face was alive with scowls that never found voice.

Even when Sokolov and Aritza entered her bridge, at the head of yet another mob of armed giants. Seriously, none of them was less than a whole head taller than her, plus combat armor indicating service with *Neu Berne.*

Then Katya's brain finally processed the patch on the left arm, and she went perfectly cold.

The Dragon Watch? What the fuck was going on here?

"Hiya," Aritza said, looking around.

Katya focused her rage on the man. Better than Sokolov. *Kymni Gauntlet* was only now just ready to sail again, after everything that one had done to them at *Drako.* Mostly supplies and a final shakedown, things moving slowly because everyone had pulled back extra hard after Sokolov had started hitting various pirate targets, like Walvisbaai and *Ferran.*

And they had just smashed Audol University into the ground. With an army of *Neu Berne* killers.

Katya nodded when Aritza walked right up and smiled at her.

"Zakhar says you're among the best that Jarre has," the man announced.

She studied him closely, having only ever seen fuzzy images in the past.

Perhaps a decade younger than her, though the beard was fully white and his hair was coming in gray. Hers was fully white, but she was fifty-five and had been in this business longer than most of her current crew had been alive.

"Perhaps," she answered to fill the silence.

"Audol is done," Aritza continued. "I've chased off everybody who could challenge me. Disabled enough systems that even the university can't defend itself. And I still have three-quarters of an arsenal ship available to finish you off. Or anyone else giving me any reason whatsoever."

"Why are you on my deck?" Katya asked, officer to officer instead of plaintive prisoner.

"My deck," he growled back. "After I kill the station, I'm stealing your vessel, Velichkov. Zakhar speaks highly of you as a generally honorable person, so I'll offer you a deal. One time. No second chances. Cross me and I'll have you killed without a moment of hesitation. We clear?"

The scowl was back. Nothing she could do about that.

"What do you want?" she managed to ask without getting herself shot.

"This is *Neu Berne* Captain Hayfa Alfarsi," he said, turning to the only short person in the group, and still Aritza's height. "She's taking command of his vessel. You can stay on as her First Officer and escape what I'm about to do to the Jarre Foundation. You can refuse and I'll put you ashore right now in an escape pod aimed at the surface to save you the extra trip. *Kymni Gauntlet* is leaving with me. I'll see about recruiting your crew, but I'm only taking sailors. Ground troops get left behind."

"They were all transferred ashore when we came into dock," Katya replied. "Most of them are out on other ships today. And about half of my crew are on leave."

"Can you sail with what you have?" he asked.

Katya did the math. Studied the man. Studied the woman.

Considered her fate.

Turned to Sokolov.

"How did you manage it?" she asked him, ignoring everyone else.

"*Excalibur* has a *Sentience*," he replied.

"I'm aware of that," she snapped. "They aren't that good."

"He upgraded her," Sokolov said, nodding to a suddenly smiling Science Officer. "Since then, I've assigned her a lot of homework on historical combat. She's even better today than when she fought you, to say nothing of when she did in *Nidavellir.*"

Upgraded? A *Sentience*? Could you do that?

Obviously, from the way both men were smiling. As were the killers outnumbering and vastly outmassing her overwhelmed command staff.

"What's my fate?" she asked the two men.

"If you want to go straight, I could use the help," Aritza said. "Suvi talks highly of what you and a ship named *Hummingbird* did at Draco. I'm recruiting the forces that will destroy the four clans for good. Then returning to *Altai* when I'm certain that Slavkov isn't coming after me again."

"*Altai*?" she asked.

"Or you could apply for asylum at *Neu Berne*," he smiled cruelly. "They're going to be building up forces to make sure folks like you don't return. Same with the *Concord*, the *Union*, and *Balustrade*. But understand, the decision you make right now binds you for the rest of your life, whether that's measured in minutes or decades. Do not cross me and expect to live long."

And he was serious. That much was obvious from the way he stood, as if willing to challenge her and her people all by himself.

A part of her wanted to scoff as his delusions, but she'd just watched this Science Officer dismantle the port defenses of

Audol, while she'd been stuck in her dock trying to get things powered up from cold reactors.

And they had heard rumors about *Ferran*. Accurate ones, it seemed.

Katya also understood that she was only getting this chance because Sokolov had spoken up for her, based on whatever past dealings they had had, however many years ago.

Must have been positive, but she honestly couldn't remember.

Still, in roughly six months, these two had smashed half of the pirate clans by destroying their biggest bases. How long until the law decided to get serious about finishing the job? Or riding in afterwards with guns drawn to arrest everyone involved.

"Does *Altai* offer amnesty?" she asked quietly, ignoring the gasps and squawks from Antoniy and Mihail behind her.

"I'm a citizen these days," Aritza replied, eyes as hard as diamonds. "And technically Prince Consort, but that's a completely different conversation. You play it straight with us, and we'll match you step for step."

And they were going to kill Slavkov. Of that, Katya had no doubts whatsoever.

After spending time with the man at *Drako*, she found herself agreeing that the galaxy would be a better place with that son of a bitch no longer in it.

What did that say about anything?

"How will it go down?" she asked Sokolov instead of anyone else.

He'd been one of them. Once. For a long time, too.

"Prize crew if you submit willingly," he said tersely. "Marines keeping everyone honest. Rearrange crews when we get everyone to our mobile base for repairs from this action, mostly to break things down and keep any of your troublemakers separated off, if you had some names that you wanted gone now, and were maybe concerned that they'd work themselves up to something stupid later."

Katya could see it, but they spoke the same language in ways that the others wouldn't.

Pirates had their own cant that way.

"I can get you three or four to maybe just put ashore right now," she nodded, turning to Aritza. "Couple I think are spies for the Board. One does the minimum amount of work necessary to keep from getting in trouble. Might as well sweep the decks."

"Hayfa, your new First Officer, Yekaterina Velichkov," Aritza said. "I'm told commonly called Katya, but you'll have to get there yourselves. Velichkov, Captain Alfarsi, your new CO. What do you need to undock and jump to a set of coordinates about eight light-years away?"

"Supplies," she said. "Crew recall got me most of the people I need. We can take on the remainder quickly enough. Do you want any random crew that offer to join, since I'm pretty sure you're about to blow the station in place?"

"Tentatively, yes," he said. "We'll put strangers on *Excalibur* or *Relentless* for now and let them work off a ransom. Suvi's working with Sykora to steal as much of the station's data banks as they can in the time before we need to flee, so we might have the names of double agents that need to be killed."

Katya nearly threw herself on the deck when Antoniy Kovachev suddenly stood up.

"Put me ashore," he said, voice going up half an octave as there were a LOT of guns pointed at him.

"Antoniy?" she asked.

His face grew hangdog and he shrugged.

"My name would come up, Kat," he said, gesturing carefully to the Science Officer. "Board of Directors put me aboard your ship as a double agent to watch you. Figure they'll find that and shoot me out of hand. Rather run right now."

She was aghast, having had no idea. Still, she turned to the man deciding their fates.

"Fair," Aritza said. "I'll leave a note in your file that you might be worth talking to if we see you again later, but you can go with this man and pack."

She watched Antoniy and a couple of giants depart without a word.

Everything had just changed. Worse, she didn't think the changes were done.

Worst, Katya was pretty sure she had just changed sides. And joined the winners.

What did that say?

She turned to the stranger.

"Captain Alfarsi, what are your orders?"

TRINITY

PART I

Ilan studied the bridge.

Just because, he had taken an Engineering station off to one side, while Ioannidi had taken a spot nearby and issued orders that the actual commanding officer was handling.

Lieutenant Commander Vaughn Yueh, Commanding Officer, *Concord* Warship *Trinity*.

Watching her, the woman made him think of a curious cat, bright blue eyes like an unhooded hawk that didn't miss anything on her bridge. Luxurious red hair, medium-length and worn in a pony tail. Woman had a wide-hipped build and narrow shoulders, with freckles, everywhere he could see, which was mostly face and hands. She had a crooked nose that added to her hawklike visage.

The ship was generally pretending to be civilian, so she wasn't in uniform. Instead, her wardrobe was off-beat and worn tight, with a violet and gray color scheme today.

Both Yueh and Commander Ioannidi turned to him now. He scowled back at Ioannidi.

"We pretty sure that's the right one?" he asked.

"Registered to Slavkov," she replied. "Left in a major hurry less than an hour after you got jumped. Not even circumstantial evidence at this point, but I figure I have enough to justify intercepting them and boarding.”

“Are we pirates, or do you have a warrant?” he asked, glancing at Yueh mostly to include her.

How the hell had he ended in in charge here? Except that he was the Combat Engineer, and that meant something. Plus, they’d taken Bethany and he was going to kill someone for that.

Probably a lot of someones.

Pana Ioannidi was a stranger who had become something of a friend. Vaughn Yueh was under orders, but had been pretty casual about things, getting them aboard without questions or complaints.

But Ilan was making command decisions.

And had the first one in front of him. Did they chase down a yacht that was running, or let them get away? How devious was this Slavkov punk? Had he sent the ship ahead so everyone would go after it and he could disappear, or was he trying to get as many light-years between him and *Merankorr* as possible, knowing that someone like Ilan Yu was coming for his ass?

The two women glanced at each other. Ilan had spent enough time around Javier to understand whole conversations that he was being excluded from, but that was fine. Bethany had said that Pana was a straight-up spy.

He was pretty sure that *Trinity* was a spy ship, so Vaughn Yueh was also a spy.

Probably the sort of folks that had hunted folks like him, back when they’d been criminals.

Gauntlet was on the other fist today. One he intended to use.

“We have a document that will stand up in court,” Yueh said quietly. “It allows us to board that vessel, looking for suspected contraband. It also covers us if we have to use force in the process, though this is Valko Slavkov we’re talking about. Anybody getting crossways with him is generally looking at getting their career through down the shitter.”

“Understand me, Lt. Commander,” Ilan said slowly, waiting

for the woman to lock those cobalt eyes on him like turrets. "I intend to kill Slavkov before this is over. Whether he is aboard that yacht or hiding somewhere else that he thinks will protect him from me. There's a list. Get me a little drunk sometime and I'll even tell you some stories about places like *Svalbard, Nidavellir, Ugen,* and *Drako.* Slavkov can try to run. He cannot escape me. Ever. Even hell will not be far enough. Am I clear?"

Woman had the decency to pause and study him before saying anything. And got a lot more serious as she did.

"You are," she replied.

Ilan rolled the dice, knowing that he only got one chance at this, and willing to trust his gut on this one. Slavkov was a coward. Build everything from that.

"Then take us out," Ilan told her. "And set whatever course you need to chase down the *Golden Gazelle.*"

"We're not fast," she reminded him. "Probably won't get to him until he lands where he'd going."

"You have the direction?" he countered. "A guess where he lands next?"

"Vector suggests Alkonost," she replied.

Ilan nodded. Smiled.

"What?"

"It started there," he said simply. "Fitting for it to end there."

That was where Javier had first been hired by Slavkov, when everyone thought he was Navarre.

And the place they'd stolen a Land Leviathan.

History might not repeat itself, but it sure felt like it rhymed.

To be concluded in Guardians of Tomorrow

READ MORE

To read more of my fiction, sign up for my newsletter. You'll also get a free book!

http://www.blazeward.com/newsletter/

ABOUT THE AUTHOR

Blaze Ward is a prolific Indie writer and publisher who works mostly in Science Fiction and Light Thriller, with occasional forays into lots of other genres like superheroic fantasy.

You can find more of his titles at www.blazeward.com/books, www.KnottedRoadPress.com and wherever else you buy your books.

He also edits Boundary Shock Quarterly, an SF magazine he founded in 2018, and Thrill Ride Magazine.

ABOUT KNOTTED ROAD PRESS

Knotted Road Press publishes dynamic fiction set in exotic locations. Our authors cover a wide range of genres including science fiction, fantasy, mystery, literary, and poetry. We also have unique non-fiction voices in genres such as autobiography, business, cookbooks, and how-tos. We offer both DRM-free ebooks and print books for a global readership.

www.KnottedRoadPress.com